REMEMBER, I LOVE YOU

CLAUDIA CARROLL

Boldwood

First published in Great Britain in 2025 by Boldwood Books Ltd.

Cover Design by Alice Moore Design

Cover Images: Shutterstock

A CIP catalogue record for this book is available from the British Library.

Paperback ISBN 978-1-83533-462-1

Large Print ISBN 978-1-83533-458-4

Hardback ISBN 978-1-83533-457-7

Ebook ISBN 978-1-83533-455-3

Kindle ISBN 978-1-83533-456-0

Audio CD ISBN 978-1-83533-463-8

MP3 CD ISBN 978-1-83533-460-7

Digital audio download ISBN 978-1-83533-454-6

This book is printed on certified sustainable paper. Boldwood Books is dedicated to putting sustainability at the heart of our business. For more information please visit https://www.boldwoodbooks.com/about-us/sustainability/

Boldwood Books Ltd, 23 Bowerdean Street, London, SW6 3TN

www.boldwoodbooks.com

This is for all the hopeless romantics out there...

PROLOGUE

'It's your worst nightmare, isn't it? You always think it'll happen to someone else, but never, ever you.'

'Mum? What are you talking about?'

'I can't believe it.'

'You can't believe what?'

'I came away without my diarrhoea tablets.'

'*What* did you just say?'

'Here I am, God knows where, miles from home. Suppose I get caught short? I'm in bits, Connie. And my IBS is playing up like you wouldn't believe. Suppose I have a little accident? What then? Did anyone think about that, before you all abandoned me in this horrible place?'

Connie stood in the corner of the cafe, a banjaxed mobile phone the approximate size of a car battery clamped to her ear, with every single eye in the place focused on her and her alone, riveted.

Look at them, she thought. *Look at their hopeful little faces. They think I'm being imparted with the meaning of life, death and the universe. They're hoping they'll be next in line for a mind-blowingly deep call from the other side. Little do they know all my mother can talk about is her IBS.*

'Are you still there, Connie, love?'

'Of course I am, Mum.' *You're speaking to me from beyond the grave. I'm hardly likely to hang up on you, now, am I?*

'Well, then, you'll have to come and get me, there's a good girl. I can't stand it here one more day. There's no telly, there's no one to talk to, there's nothing to do and the whole place smells like cabbage—'

Connie paused, but then there really was no easy way to tell your mother that she'd been dead for the past two months. That this phone call was a complete mystery. That none of it made any sense. That now she was worried she was losing her mind.

The mobile phone she was on was decades old; the battery life was brutal and, sure enough, her mum's voice started wafting in and out of coverage as it quickly ran out of charge.

Connie began to panic.

'Mum, I love you so much and I miss you every day,' she shouted down the phone, terrified that this was it, that she'd never get to hear her mother's voice again. There were more than a few understanding nods from the regulars at the cafe, who were all avidly tuning in.

'Mum?' Connie yelled uselessly to silence from the other end of the phone. 'Are you still there?'

Then nothing at all.

Just silence.

1

CONNIE

It had been eight long weeks since Connie had lost her beloved mum and grief had flattened her. In one fell swoop she'd lost not just her best friend and confidante, but the person she loved most in the whole world. People kept saying, 'Sorry for your trouble,' but this wasn't trouble. This was gut-wrenching, heart-ripping pain and a deep, debilitating sadness such as she'd never known before.

She and her mum had lived together for years, ever since her dad had passed away, and over that time had grown as close as two peas in a pod. 'Sure, why would you throw money away renting a place of your own,' as her mum used to say, 'when there's plenty of room for you here?'

So that was what Connie had done: moved lock, stock and barrel back into her old bedroom, with Eminem and Coldplay posters from the nineties staring down at her, as if absolutely no time had passed since she'd moved out. At first, her living back in the family home had seemed like the perfect solution, even just temporarily, till her mum got used to living as a widow. But the pair of them had got on so famously that the years had whizzed by and somehow, in spite of repeated slagging from her friends about being in her thirties and still living at home with her mammy, nothing had changed. The only difference was that Connie's teenage posters were long since banished, and now in their place were framed production stills and programmes from some of the shows she'd appeared in down through the years. Her mum used to say the two of them had the perfect living arrangement: she had company round the clock, and as Connie was an actor 'resting between jobs' the money she saved on rent made this a complete no-brainer.

It was all so different now though. Now Connie found it unbearable living in that lonely, empty house. None of the laughs they used to have, no more long, gossipy chats about the latest audition she'd done, or the latest eejit she'd met on Tinder, or the nights out she'd had with her gang of pals. No one to pick over the news of the day with. Just that horrible, awful silence.

And Donald. *Jesus save me,* she thought. Donald.

Donald was her older brother. There were only the two of them in the family and, now that Mum was gone, they found themselves jointly making all the decisions about what to do with her estate, with the family home being top of the list.

Donald was married and living in Paris with two kids of his own, and, as he never failed to remind Connie, 'I *really* wish I could drop everything and come over there to help you, but you have to understand I can't just leave Francine and the kids, plus I have all the pressures of my job. It's OK for you, Connie, you're an out-of-work actor, it's not like you're doing much else, now, are you? You're living in the house anyway, so it's far easier for you to clear the place out and get it ready for sale. Sooner we get rid of it, the better.'

Sell, sell, sell, that was all Donald wanted. A nice cash payout for himself, with the bare minimum disruption to his life. But for

Connie, this was huge, this was life-altering. This was her home, a happy home, and she literally had nowhere else to go. Her mum and dad had lived there for almost forty years; they'd first moved into this dotie, red-brick terraced house when Donald was a baby; years before Connie herself was even thought of.

But the house had to be sold whether she liked it or not. What alternative was there? Buying out Donald's share of the place just wasn't a runner for her, given that she'd sod all in her bank account to start with. In the last twelve months, the only work she'd picked up were a walk-on part in a soap opera, a line in a movie where she played a Viking in a wig like a Brillo pad, and in which her one and only line was cut, and a TV commercial for JAZZ! washing up liquid, where she had to do 'jazz hands' at the camera and for which she'd been paid a pittance. Whenever she was on a bus now, or walking down the streets near the house, you could be guaranteed some smart-arse would shout at her, 'It's you off the ad, isn't it? G'wan, love, do jazz hands! You're gas, so you are!'

Kate, Connie's best friend, had been nothing but encouraging and positive. 'At least when the house is sold, you'll get a few quid out of it,' she'd said. 'You might be able to buy somewhere else that would be yours and yours alone.'

'Yeah, but where to buy?' Connie had shrugged. 'That's the problem. The way property prices have gone now, I'll be doing well to afford a little shoebox in the back arse of nowhere, a good two-hour drive away. That's if I'm very, very lucky. My life is here in Dublin and all the work is here. Moving away doesn't make any sense.'

'Well...' Kate had said kindly, 'you're always welcome to stay with us, you know that.'

Connie had smiled fondly and silently blessed Kate for being that kind of pal. The kind who'd let you crash on her sofa for as long as you liked. But then Kate was a happily married woman with three little boys all under the age of ten, and, much as Connie doted on each of them, her fear was that having an out-of-work actor crashing on your sofa indefinitely would wear thin very quickly.

Like it or not, the family home was going to be sold. And in the space of a few short months, she'd have lost everything. The roof over her head, the house that she'd such happy memories of and, most of all, her fabulous, feisty, irreplaceable mum, the best friend she'd ever had or ever would have.

Her actor pals had been great, calling and texting at all hours of the day and night to ask her to join them whenever and wherever they were going. 'We need to get you back out there again,' they'd all clamour. 'We need to put the smile back on your face.'

Sure enough, this particular evening they were at it again. Well-intentioned calls and messages had been pouring in for Connie all day, asking her to meet up with the gang in Doherty's bar, 'For a few drinks and then to see where the night takes us!'

Time was when Connie would have shoehorned herself into a tight pair of jeans and a dressy top and been straight out the door to meet them in ten seconds flat. She'd have been right there in the thick of it with her pals, giggling at nothing, bitching about how few acting jobs there were, gossiping, drinking, maybe even going out dancing, then wearily crawling home at dawn the next morning with a very, very sore head, but a very, very happy heart.

Not now, though. Now, she hadn't the strength or energy to go out and smile at the world and pretend everything was OK when it so clearly wasn't. The thoughts of having to act upbeat and positive were too much for her. The main thing she was fast learning about grief was how bloody exhausting it was. How nihilistic. How her factory default setting these days was, 'just leave me alone, I don't care'.

Now she wanted nothing more than to crash out on the sofa in front of the telly, doing absolutely nothing and talking to absolutely no one.

She wanted peace. She wanted solitude.

Most of all though, she just wanted her mum.

2

LUKE

'I hate you! And I don't want to go to school today!'

'Come on, sweetheart, you say that every day and once you get there, you always have a great time.'

'I'm not going and you can't make me.'

'Amy, please, you're going to make us both late.'

'I'm sick! I can't go if I'm sick!'

Quickly, Luke felt her forehead. All normal, thankfully.

'You're not a bit sick, pet. You ate a giant pizza last night – you couldn't do that if you were sick, now, could you?'

He looked down at his six-year-old daughter, frowning and petulant with her bottom lip stuck out and her arms folded, clearly trying to rack her brains for an excuse that might actually work this time.

'You did my tights wrong,' she grumbled. 'I'm not going to school with the wrong tights.'

'What's wrong with them?'

'Mummy always left them on the radiator for me, so they'd be nice and warm on my legs. You didn't! You're stupid!'

Luke sighed deeply, glancing down at his watch. Almost 8 a.m. and he had a huge project meeting at the office in exactly half an hour. He so did not have time for this. But then he remembered what one of a string of child psychologists had counselled him.

'You have to remember that Amy is only six years old. She's just been through one of the most traumatic experiences that any human being can possibly go through. This would fell a grown adult, never mind a little girl. This is all new for her, it's raw and she's trying to process it as best she can. From time to time, she may take it out on you and, even though you're grieving too, the best thing you can do is react with love and compassion, reassuring her that everything she feels is normal.'

Then the clincher. The very thing that made Luke want to leave and find some other bloody child psychologist. 'But, of course, in all this you have to look after you.'

Yeah, but look after myself when? he'd wanted to snap back, pent-up frustration getting the better of him. What kind of a useless platitude was that? *I'm desperately trying to keep the show on the road here. I work a twelve-hour day in a high-pressure environment. I'm barely hanging on to my job by my teeth. I'm trying to juggle after-school childcare for Amy. I get home exhausted beyond words and then, somehow, I have to try and be the best parent I can to her. Time for me?* he fumed silently. *What planet are you living on?*

When Luke eventually managed to steer Amy into the kitchen that morning, there were even more rows and temper tantrums.

'Nooo!!' she screamed at him, thumping the table with her little fists for all she was worth.

'What now, love?' said Luke, frantically trying to get her to eat a bowl of porridge, while simultaneously putting on the tie and jacket of his good suit, and calling the office to say he was running late and that they'd have to start the meeting without him. The biggest pitch meeting the architectural firm where he worked had seen in months. The one that could potentially turn things around for them. The one that would hopefully copper-fasten his own job and secure his future. He should be there now, up in the conference room, glad-handing clients and mentally prepping for such a monumentally big moment.

Jesus, he thought, barely recognising his life. *What would Helen say if she saw me now?* Mornings used to be so easy when she was around. Mornings were effortless. Mornings were happy. Mornings and late evenings when Amy was fast asleep and when he'd get home after work. The two of them would have dinner together and maybe even crack open a bottle of wine. But then, pretty much any time of the day was great whenever Helen was around.

'You didn't make the porridge the way Mummy used to!' Amy was yelling at him, her poor little face raw red from screaming. 'You did it in the microwave and Mummy never, ever did that! Now it's all lumpy and disgusting!'

'Please, love! We're already dead late and you can't go anywhere till you eat breakfast!' But just then, Luke's call was answered, so he immediately had to switch tone. 'Hi there, Dave? Yeah, it's me. Look, bit of an issue this end and I'm running late...'

'I'm not eating this!' Amy screeched in the background, as if she were being tortured. 'You can't make me! It's yeukky, it's disgusting!'

'Shh, honey,' Luke hissed, covering the phone with his hand. 'Daddy's on the phone to work—' Then straight back into his work voice. 'Dave? Yeah, hi. Sorry about this—'

But then Amy really started letting rip. Loud, unmanageable

screams as the tears streamed down her little face. Followed by the words that never failed to cut straight to Luke's heart.

'I want my Mummy! I want my Mummy!'

'Luke?' came Dave's voice from the other side of the phone call. 'Everything OK? Things don't sound too good your end.'

'No, not at all!' Luke fake-laughed, as he tried to shush Amy and soothe her down with his free hand. 'I'll be with you just as fast as I can. We're a tiny bit delayed, but we're on the way,' he lied.

'Luke,' said Dave worriedly. 'I understand what you're going through, we all do. But the thing is, the clients are here waiting on you, asking where you are. We can't really have this pitch meeting without you. You're the project manager.'

'I'll be there in twenty minutes,' Luke said reassuringly, trying to guide Amy up and out of the kitchen to even more screams and sobs. If they left right now, he figured, and if he really aced it at the meeting, then hopefully this blip would quickly be overlooked. Maybe the clients would understand, maybe they'd be OK about it. Maybe.

'Come on, Amy,' he said, grabbing her school coat from the back of the kitchen chair and trying to shoehorn her into it. 'I'll grab a banana and a yoghurt and you can eat in the car. How does that sound?'

'No yoghurt – yeukky!' she yelled, clinging to the edges of the kitchen table as though her life depended on it. 'And no banana either – I hate bananas! I hate them nearly as much as I hate you!'

Luke knelt down so he was face-to-face with her.

'Sweetheart, listen to me.' Hating that he had to be firm, but knowing he had no choice. 'You need to stop this right now. Daddy has to go to work and you have to go to school. You know this. And you know we can't be late.'

But Amy had the last word. In one fell swoop, she deliberately knocked over her bowl of porridge so it landed all over Luke's head, over his shirt, jacket, tie, over his trousers, all over everything.

3

LUCASTA

'Turn on the radio, love.'

'I most certainly will not. I'm trying to finish a chapter and I'm way behind schedule as it is, thank you very much.'

'Quick! Now! Radio 1!'

'Johnnie, I already said no! Now will you kindly bugger off and leave me in peace? There's a good man.'

But the radio on the bookcase beside her came on anyway, without her even touching it. It was Rod Stewart, singing an oldie, 'Da Ya Think I'm Sexy?'

Lucasta took off her reading glasses, looked up from her typewriter and sighed.

'I suppose you find that amusing, do you?' she said to thin air.

'Ahh, now, my darling girl. Just because I'm not with you doesn't mean I don't wish I were up in the bed beside you, for one of our early morning quickies. I could never start the day without a good squeeze of you, love.'

'That's quite enough of that,' Lucasta said, briskly getting up from her desk and striding over to the bookcase where her old-fashioned Roberts radio sat, before snapping off Rod Stewart's gravelly voice. 'Now off you go and find some way of amusing yourself for the rest of the day. I'm working here and I need a bit of peace.'

'Till later, then, my lovely. When you're in bed tonight, I might just pay you a little call, then. Wear the black nightie with all the lacy bits on it, just like you used to.'

'Johnnie! That's quite enough from you! These days, that's known as sexual harassment and you can be cancelled for it, you know.'

'Even though we're married?'

'Goodbye, Johnnie,' Lucasta said firmly, before staring at Johnnie's ashes for a bit, then hauling her eighty-something bones back to her desk by the window and plonking herself down again. But thanks to bloody Johnnie and all his sex pestering, she'd completely lost her train of thought. She was now staring at a blank page on the typewriter in front of her – her idea of hell. Sighing, she took a sip from a cold cup of coffee – served from her 'lucky' mug, the one her publishers had gifted her when her very first book had sold over a million copies – and stared out of the window.

She was sitting in her garden shed, now converted into an extremely practical home office, lavishly laid out with shelf after shelf of her beloved books stacked floor to ceiling. Her own publications featured there too, naturally – all seventy-two of them. And the many, many foreign translations of her books. And the volumes of short stories she'd written. And the framed letter from the president, congratulating her on reaching the milestone of her eightieth birthday, then hailing her as a 'national treasure'. And the photos of her surrounded by various Hollywood glitterati at premieres of her books that had made it to the silver screen. And her wedding photo with Johnnie, taken over fifty years ago now, along with a tiny jar of his ashes in front of it, so she could be close to him all day long. And discreetly dotted here and there along the shelves were the many, many awards she'd picked up along the way.

Mind you, Lucasta was the first to downplay her stunning success and would humbly tell people that, while awards were all well and good, the only practical use for the bloody things was to biff a burglar over the head if her house was ever broken into. 'Otherwise, they're just dust gatherers, you know. Given half the chance, I'd flog them off on eBay.'

Her eye drifted back to her typewriter, which was an ancient, battered old Smith Corona that she'd written every single one of her books on, and which she'd fondly nicknamed Daphne. 'Laptops and computers be damned,' she'd say to her publisher. 'Daphne is the only thing I'd ever trust my work with.' But the blank page was still there waiting for her. Lucasta, however, was no believer in writer's block and was quick to inform guests at the many writers' events she spoke at that it was a complete myth. 'Keep on writing,' she'd happily enthuse. 'Better to bash out your ABC than to sit there staring uselessly into space.'

'Come on, Sausage, bring me inspiration,' she said to her faithful little corgi, who sat in his basket at her feet, before diving straight back into her story. It was the latest instalment in a wildly popular adventure series she'd created, centring around a plucky Victorian heroine called Mercy, who constantly found herself in the eye of the storm. So far, Mercy had served as a housemaid to the young Queen Alexandra when she was still Princess of Wales and dealing with a lying cheater of an absent husband, the future Edward VII. Mercy had subsequently volunteered as a nurse during the Great War, where she'd met husband, who'd then tragically died; she'd been an 'IT' girl during the roaring twenties, became a spy for the allies during the Second World War and now this latest, non-chronological volume was called *Mercy on the Titanic*.

Lucasta was just about to launch into a fresh paragraph when, out of nowhere, Sausage's ears pricked up and he began to growl, low and threatening.

'What's the matter with you?' Lucasta said impatiently. 'Mummy's trying to work here, do be quiet.'

But now the growling had turned to barking, getting louder and more insistent as the hairs on Sausage's fur stood sharply upwards.

'What's the matter, darling?' Lucasta said, bending down to pet and soothe him. 'Smell a fox outside you want to chase?'

The barking didn't stop though. Then, out of nowhere, Lucasta heard a brand-new voice begin to speak to her, loud and clear. A fresh, youthful voice – most definitely no one who'd ever been in contact with her before. *Well, well, well,* Lucasta thought. *This is getting interesting.*

'Hello?' Lucasta said, into thin air. 'Anyone there? Who is it this time? Who are you?'

'Can you hear me?' came the reply. A woman's voice, light and floaty. More of a gentle whisper really.

'Who's that?' Lucasta probed. 'Who's there? Princess Diana? Is that you again? Oh, for goodness' sake, I've told you umpteen times before, both your boys are happily married with families of their own and both seem to be doing terribly well.'

She heard a snort of derision.

'It's definitely not Princess Diana here...'

'Who are you, then?' Lucasta asked gently, staying glued to her chair, afraid to move a muscle in case she scared whoever this was away. 'Hello? Are you still with me? You sound so light and breathy – Marilyn Monroe again perhaps?'

There was a silence before the voice spoke again.

'I'm so sorry to trouble you...'

'Oh, don't worry a bit about that at all, dear,' said Lucasta, with a dismissive flick of her wrist. 'I have spirits speaking to me day and night. Round the clock, you know. And as long as they don't pester me for sex all the time like my late husband, Johnnie, I'm always delighted to help.'

'The thing is... I don't know where else to turn...'

Now, though, whoever was there – a lady, this was most definitely a lady – began to get distressed and Lucasta had to really strain to hear that feathery, light-as-air voice.

'Hello?' she asked worriedly. 'Are you still with me?'

Silence, just the background noise of a clock on her desk ticking.

Bugger it, Lucasta thought crossly. *Just my bloody luck.* To have had a brand-new spirit reach out to her only to lose that precious connection.

She sat statue-still in her office, straining her ears for all she was worth, but no, absolutely nothing doing. She waited a moment barely taking breath and was just about to give up when she could have sworn she caught something or someone coming back into focus again.

Yes! she thought jubilantly.

'Hello there?' she said softly, anxious not to terrify the poor soul away. 'I'm here and I'm listening.'

There it was, that voice again, but far fainter this time, tuning in and out.

Ahh. That generally indicates a young spirit. Lucasta knew of old. Someone who'd only passed over quite recently. Whoever this was, though, Lucasta sensed the poor lost soul definitely had some important message she needed to get across. Quite badly too.

Just then, with appalling timing, there was a loud, insistent hammering on her shed door.

'Lucasta, it's me. Your book proofs have just arrived and they need your urgent attention.'

'Oh, for goodness' sake, not now,' Lucasta grumbled under her breath. Next thing the garden shed door clattered open and in stepped her private secretary, Phoebe, tall, grey, lean, unsmiling, neat as a pin and, as ever, dressed head to toe in black. The two had worked together for decades; Phoebe had begun 'taking care of correspondence there simply isn't time to manage' for Lucasta on a temporary basis way back in the dim, distant eighties, and all these years later had never left. She was the perfect assistant and never put a foot wrong, but right now, Lucasta was ready to throttle her.

'I heard voices,' said Phoebe, sniffing the air disdainfully as she stepped inside. 'Were you speaking to yourself again?' Pointless asking Lucasta if she was on the phone; she simply didn't allow any modern-day technology into her sacred writing space.

'I was most certainly not speaking to myself,' Lucasta replied primly. 'There was someone here... a new one. Someone who'd never come to me before. And then you had to go and scare them away, didn't you?'

Cynical about all matters 'otherworldly', Phoebe rolled her eyes, then carefully placed the copy-edited draft on the desk. 'Your US editor needs these back in exactly ten days' time. So I strongly suggest you get cracking. Now, please.'

It was as if Lucasta never even heard her.

'Something's up, Phoebe, dear,' she said. 'Mark my words. I don't know what, but something is most definitely up.'

'Did you hear what I just said?'

But Lucasta interrupted her, sitting bolt upright as Sausage started barking furiously again.

'Shhhh! Quiet, both of you, please!' she said. 'Whoever this spirit is, she's trying to come back to me.'

'Is she now,' said Phoebe flatly.

'Yes? Hello? I'm still here and I'm listening,' Lucasta said to thin air.

'Did you hear what I just said about the deadline?' insisted Phoebe, folding her arms impatiently.

'Oh, dearie me...' Lucasta trailed off, completely tuned into another world. 'Well, of course I'll help you however I can... but... really? Is that what you want me to do? And would you please mind telling me... what the hell is a Bereavement Cafe?'

4

CONNIE

One dismal, damp Friday evening, Connie found herself up in the attic of her mum and dad's house surrounded by stacks of boxes and bin liners, tackling the godawful job of having to pack up a whole lifetime of memories. Not exactly the easiest task when both parents had been lifelong hoarders, who didn't believe in throwing out as much as a single bus ticket from the eighties in case it might come in handy again.

'You have to sift through "the treasure from the trash",' as her pal Kate kept at her. 'You never know what gems could be buried up in that attic that might turn out to be worth a fortune. I watch *Cash in the Attic*. I know what I'm talking about.'

Connie had made three distinct piles, one to keep, one for the charity shop and one for a skip outside her front door that was already stuffed full to overflowing. So far, after weeks of this, the pile marked 'keep' was niggardly, consisting of a few of her old homework copies with gold stars on them and photos from school plays she'd been in, just for a bit of sentimentality. The pile for the charity shop was equally modest, mostly old M&S sweaters belonging to her mum, plus her prized Agatha Christie book collection, which made Connie well up when she looked at it now. There were also a few posters of her mum's favourite movies in there too, among them *Casablanca*, *Double Indemnity* and another old classic, *All About Eve*. Her mum had a lifelong thing about film noir and knew so much about it, she could nearly have gone on *Mastermind* taking it as her specialist subject.

The bad news was that the pile earmarked for dumping was now towering over the edge of the skip outside, threatening to spill all over the pavement. And that was only a fraction, Connie thought, of the shitty, shitty shite up in the attic she still had to somehow plod her way through.

It was one of those days in May when it was more like winter than spring; rain was lashing down and, from high up in the attic where Connie was hard at work, she could hear it battering off the roof, as if there was a violent storm brewing.

Just then her phone beeped from her jeans pocket and she instantly went to check it, in case it was the estate agents pressuring her yet again with one of their passive-aggressive texts, wanting to know exactly when the house would be ready to go on the market. But it turned out to be Donald, blithely posting pictures of him and his kids all having a ball at Disneyland Paris.

Having fun on the roller coaster!

The arsehole had shared a giddy-looking photo of himself with Francine and the kids wedged into one of those little train cars, all roaring with laughter and looking as though they hadn't a single care in the world.

Hashtag, vomit, Connie wanted to ping back, but restrained herself. With a deep sigh, she rubbed her eyes and promised herself that she'd just work her way through one last storage box, then call it a day. She'd been at this decluttering lark since early that morning and after all, there were only so many manky Christmas decorations and ancient kitchen utensils you could face in one day.

Then a strange thing happened. As she hauled down yet another cardboard box from high up in the eaves, she was struck by how much lighter this one was than the rest.

Weird.

'SPARES' was written in black felt marker across it, in her mum's scrawly, spidery handwriting. And sure enough, when Connie opened up the box, out tumbled a load of spare plug adaptors, spare batteries and spare extension cables, the kind you were always looking for but could never find when you needed them. *Well, at least some of these might come in handy,* she thought, delving into the box and dumping a load of adaptors into her paltry little 'keep' pile.

Then, out of nowhere, she heard what sounded like a phone ringing.

It was very, very quiet and very, very faint, but it was most definitely a phone. A mobile phone. Not her own phone though – the ringtone was completely different. This one sounded weak and watery, kind of like a bat squawking. *Sounds too close to be coming from the neighbours,* Connie figured. She followed the noise, then spotted a dim-looking light flashing from the very bottom of the box she'd just opened. Something electrical that still had a bit of charge in it maybe? she wondered.

Fumbling around the best she could through the spaghetti junction of wires and cables, she eventually yanked out an ancient, knackered mobile phone, one of the really early first-generation ones, thick and unwieldy, roughly about four times the size of any smartphone now, and with a mad-looking black rubbery ariel stuck to the side of it. Probably from the early nineties, Connie guessed, back in the days when no one had mobiles, except show-off gits and drug dealers. And her brother, Donald, of course.

Then a distinct, almost pin-sharp memory came back to her. This had been Donald's phone and, of course, everyone had slagged him far and wide for even having it in the first place. It hadn't been long till he'd upgraded it though and Connie suddenly had a vivid memory of him pompously handing this one over to Mum. 'So I can call you directly from my next business-class flight to the States,' he'd bragged at the time. Astonishing that it was still such a lucid memory for her. Word for bloody word.

She scooped it out of the box and stared at it as it kept on ringing. *How can this still be working?* she wondered, completely baffled. *How the feck can it even have any battery life left?* The thing looked as if it hadn't been charged in twenty years. And still, somehow, the phone kept ringing. And ringing. And ringing. Feeling like an eejit for even trying something so pointless, she put it to her ear and pressed a surprisingly heavy-looking green-coloured button to answer.

As she expected, there was nothing, no sound at all. Rolling her eyes at her own stupidity, she was just about to toss the phone and the sheer bloody weight of it into the 'junk' pile, when all of a sudden she thought she heard something down the other end of the phone – wind maybe? It was like a whooshing sound, the exact same as when she used to hold a seashell to her ear on the beach as a kid.

And then, a voice.

An unmistakable voice.

'Connie? Connie, love... can you hear me?'

'I'm sorry?' Connie said hesitatingly.

'It's me.'

'Who?'

'Me, you eejit! Who else did you think it was?'

Jesus Christ.

Connie froze on the spot. This couldn't be happening.

There was no way, no possible way. Her mother? The voice was faint and crackly, but it sure as hell sounded like her.

'Connie? Are you still there, love?'

'Mum?' she said disbelievingly. '*Mum?* This can't be you. Is this really you?'

'Of course, love,' came the reply, sounding every bit as chatty and warm and normal as her mum always did. 'Now, you haven't forgotten this is bin day, have you? But what I really want to know is what's happening in *Coronation Street*. I'm completely lost without my telly here. Oh... and who's on *Graham Norton* tonight? And while I think of it, is there anything decent on Netflix? You have to fill me in properly, love. If you don't, I'll come back there and haunt you!'

I'm hallucinating, Connie thought. *This isn't real, this can't be happening.*

But as hallucinations went, it was so bloody realistic, it was freaky.

5

LUKE

'So. Talk to me. How are you doing, bro?'

Bro? Had Dave really just called him 'bro?' Jesus. This was much, much worse than Luke had originally thought.

'Thanks for asking, Dave,' he replied with what he hoped was a professional smile. An *I've got this* smile. A smile that said, *I'm on top of it.* 'Sure, things at home haven't been easy lately. My daughter and I are still very much adjusting. But all you need to know is that we are getting there.'

'About six months now, is that right? Since the funeral?' Dave sat back in his black leather office chair and swivelled, playing with his goatee beard and looking thoughtful.

Five months, three weeks and two days, Luke wanted to answer.

'That's right, yeah.'

'And your daughter is, what, nine or ten?'

'She's six.' That was the thing about working in a young firm like this, Luke had to remind himself. No one else had kids, so they basically hadn't a clue. Dave, the boss, was in his early thirties, a good ten years younger than himself, as were the rest of his colleagues. Like Dave, they were all young, cut-throat professionals – Luke hadn't a clue if any of them were in relationships or not, all he knew was they certainly seemed to live the lives of unattached people. These guys regularly put in fourteen-hour days from the office – and made bloody sure they were seen to do so too – then went out on the batter all together as a gang every chance they got.

'Amy, isn't that your kid's name?' Dave asked.

'That's right.' He remembered. Nice touch. 'And once again,' Luke added, doing the very thing he'd vowed not to, which was bring his personal life into work, 'thanks for being so understanding about this morning. It was a blip and it won't happen again.'

Although it wasn't a blip. This was happening all the time lately and, for the life of him, Luke could see no way out of it. He had to work and, much as it broke his heart to leave Amy for any length of time, the kid had to go to school. She needed her pals, her teachers, her little routine. So what else was he supposed to do?

'Course, we all feel for what you're going through,' Dave said, still swivelling in his chair and combing his beard with his fingers in a most annoying manner.

'Yes, but as I've already explained—'

'It's hell for you, I appreciate that.'

'Thanks, Dave. Your understanding means a lot.'

'I lost my grandmother not so long ago, so I do know what you're going through. Grief is tough. I get it.'

Yeah, right, Luke had to restrain himself from saying. *Because losing your granny is the exact same as losing your beloved wife, soulmate and mother of your child.* He said nothing and just nodded though. This, he knew, was Dave's ham-fisted attempt at being sympathetic.

'But we're still left with a bit of a problem here, aren't we?'

Dave went on. 'Unfortunately, that was a huge meeting this morning and it was more or less over by the time you got here.'

'I know and I'm sorry,' Luke said, hating that he had to apologise for trying to cope with work, when he was drowning and trying so hard just to keep his head above water. *I'm sorry that my wife got stage four cancer. I do hope her death in no way inconvenienced you.*

'Thankfully, Nick was here to take over from you,' Dave said, picking up a biro and clicking at it non-stop. 'We all owe him a big thank you.'

'I'm very grateful to him for stepping in,' Luke replied through gritted teeth. Nick was a young, freshly qualified hotshot architect, married to the job and so ambitious it was terrifying. *Just like I used to be, back in the day,* he thought. Before he'd met and fallen deeply in love with Helen. Before she'd changed his whole life for the better with a flick of those long, elegant piano fingers of hers.

'Of course, the last thing I'd ever want to do is give you a hard time over it, far from it,' Dave said, sitting forward now. 'But it just seems like you and me are having more and more of these chats lately. I hate having to remind you, but you're late on the McKinsey project and you haven't even submitted drawings for the Reynolds' extension yet, even though it's long overdue. We're a team here, man. But no team can function unless everyone is pulling equal weight. And you're struggling. Which is perfectly understandable, under the circumstances,' he added hastily.

'Yes, but I can assure you...'

'So if you need to take some more time out...?' Dave suggested. 'Then that's cool. Take six months, get your head together, focus on your kid... do whatever it takes. Then come back to work ready to hit the ground running. How about that?'

Luke looked at him warily, and this time the silence in the room started to grow uncomfortable.

'And would this be paid time out?' he eventually asked. He had to.

But at that, Dave shook his head.

'No can do, I'm afraid,' he said. 'Compassionate leave just isn't part of the deal here unfortunately, for any of us.'

'No,' Luke sighed. 'I thought not.'

'When I lost my grandmother, I was back at my desk two days later. So I'm not asking you to do anything I didn't do myself.'

He's young, Luke reminded himself. *This is him trying to be nice.* It was just so fucking annoying to have to listen to and, frankly, he'd had enough. Unable to stomach much more, he stood up.

'Look, I'm on it,' he said firmly. 'All of it. I'm a damn good architect, Dave, and you know it. My record speaks for itself. So no more lateness and no more excuses. Those projects will be completed on time and on budget – you have my word.'

A lie though, and they both knew it.

* * *

Later that afternoon, Luke was at his desk working furiously, madly catching up with every single project deadline he was behind on, when his phone rang.

The school.

His heart sank as he heard the principal's voice on the other end of the line.

'Mr Wright? Stella Mackey here from St Teresa's. I'm afraid it's Amy. She won't settle today and I think you need to collect her. I know you're at work, but the child is distressed. You really need to take her home.'

'Leave it with me,' Luke told her, trying his best to sound calm, while beads of sweat were starting to prick at his shirt. *Christ, how am I going to deal with this? I'll ring Clare,* he thought. His sister, who had been so unbelievably good about collecting Amy from school, taking her home and then feeding her, minding her and watching over her till Luke could pick her up after work.

'And, Mr Wright?' Stella added, just before he hung up. 'I think it's a good idea if you and I have a private conversation as soon as possible.'

'No problem,' said Luke. 'I'll make an appointment.'

'After school today, please,' Stella said firmly. 'My office, 4 p.m.'

* * *

That afternoon, Luke had to leave the office early – yet again – faithfully promising that he'd work on the McKinsey project at home for the rest of the day. But at 4 p.m., there he was, gently rapping on Stella Mackey's office door at the school.

She made him wait. Even from the other side of the door, he could hear her crisply enunciated tones on the phone. So he resigned himself to hanging around, glancing at his watch and wondering how long this would take, and how much work he could cram in for the few precious hours before he had to get to Clare's house to collect Amy.

Why does the principal even want to see me in person? he wondered, pacing up and down the empty, silent hallway, now that school was over for the day. *Couldn't this have been done over the phone?* It wasn't as if the school didn't know what he was dealing with. Stella Mackey herself, as well as Amy's teacher and most of the other parents, had all been at the funeral, for fuck's sake. They all *knew*.

The corridor where he was waiting was bright and sun-drenched and lined with a neat row of coloured plastic high-backed chairs that were doll-sized, which immediately made Luke feel like Gulliver in Lilliput. The walls were decorated with literally dozens of mad, crazy, colourful pictures that the kids from each class had drawn. He wandered over to take a look at them and was instantly surprised at how impressive some of them were.

Till his eye fell on one. It came under the group heading 'Second Class'. Amy's class. Sure enough, there was one signed Amy, in bright pink neon crayon, her favourite colour. But there were four Amys in the class, Luke thought. Could this be his Amy? He bent down to look at the picture more closely. It was a crudely drawn sketch of a woman with brown hair and blue eyes, dressed in white and with wings, sitting up on a big puffy cloud.

He read the caption and the breath froze in his mouth.

'My Mummy,' it read, in that babyish, wobbly writing that he recognised instantly. 'With the angels, where she is now.'

His heart twisted and the pain was like a kind of torture. Fresh pain, new pain, like nothing he'd felt before. He prided himself on never crying, ever, but at the sight of something as simple as this, sharp, stinging tears filled his eyes and blurred his vision. That was the killer thing about grief, he was fast learning. The big things washed over you. It was the little things that killed you.

'She's quite a talented little lady, isn't she?' came a sudden voice from behind him, making him jump. 'I think she must take after her father. You're an architect, isn't that correct, Mr Wright?'

Twisting around, there she was, Stella Mackey, principal of

the junior school. The woman with the power, the woman who every parent for miles kowtowed to.

Luke had met her a handful of times before, but 99.9 per cent of the time, it had been Helen who'd dealt with her, just as Helen had dealt with pretty much everything. She was young to be a principal, maybe early forties, not that much younger than Luke himself. Practically dressed in a khaki green trouser suit, with light brown hair clipped back into a neat low bun, she was someone who dressed far older than her years, almost as if she was going out of her way to seem age appropriate and to fit the part. Everyone called her Miss Mackey, parents and kids alike, and Helen always said that there was a heart of steel under there. 'Forget that at your peril,' she used to warn the other parents, whenever they'd all meet at the school gates for drop-off and collection.

'Miss Mackey,' Luke said, blinking his eyes clear and hoping she didn't notice that he'd just had an emotional wobble.

She didn't say anything, just looked keenly at him, scanning his face.

Luke filled the silence.

'Yeah, look, I'm so sorry about earlier. About Amy, I mean. We... that is, she and I... well, let's just say that the day got off to a bad start and went downhill from there. Obviously, you know what she's going through, and all I can say is it won't happen again.'

'Oh, but it's not Amy I wanted to speak to you about at all, Mr Wright,' she replied, formal and polite as ever. 'Amy will take her cue from you and therefore it's you I'm concerned about.'

'Me?' Luke repeated, having difficulty keeping up with her.

'I'd like you to come inside,' said Miss Mackey with great finality. 'I want you to take a seat, and then all I ask is that you hear me out.'

6

CONNIE

'Seriously? You're actually being serious?'

'Insane and all as it sounds, yes, I'm being serious.'

'Oh, really?' Kate, Connie's best pal, said to her, concerned.

'It's just...' Connie began, but at that, she sat back and sighed deeply, not having a clue how to finish the sentence. How was it possible to convince anyone what had just happened? She was having a hard enough time convincing herself. *I heard my dead mother's voice chatting away to me on a broken mobile phone.* Thank God for Kate though, who at least had the decency not to laugh in her face.

'On that gobshite-looking yoke there?' Kate said, pointing to the battered, thick-as-a-brick ancient Nokia phone that sat on the kitchen table between them.

'Heard her clear as day. No mistake.'

The two were sitting at Connie's kitchen table with a half-drunk pot of coffee in between them. And propped up beside the milk jug and a plate of Hobnobs was *the* phone. Connie just stared blankly at it, while Kate tried her best to make sense of it all.

'OK, let's just drill down into this a bit,' Kate said, taking a sip of coffee. 'What did you really hear, when it boils down to it? Wind? A bit of whispering? That could have been anything. Absolutely anything at all.'

'I know.'

'And nothing since?'

'Not a thing.'

'So you were up in the attic when it happened. Come on, Connie, it *must* have been the wind you heard. You were in the attic, it was probably draughty.'

Connie shook her head firmly. 'It was her,' she said. 'It was very definitely my mum. Wanting to know what was happening in all her soaps and what was on Netflix. Come on, Kate, you knew Mum so well. That's exactly the kind of thing she'd say to us if she were sitting here with us right now.'

'The woman did love her telly all right,' Kate said thoughtfully, rocking her youngest son in the buggy beside her as he slept peacefully. Next thing, loud, vicious screams broke out from Connie's living room, sounding uncannily like someone being murdered. Kate's two older boys were squabbling over whether to watch a Disney movie on an iPad she'd given them, or something else about dinosaurs.

'Will you keep it down, you pair?' Kate whispered in at them, picking up the baby, who'd begun to stir. 'Your Auntie Connie is losing her marbles and Mummy is trying to get her to see a bit of sense. And if you wake the baby, then there's no pizza treat for either of you tonight!'

'But Tommy won't let me read about dinosaurs and now he's ripping Connie's house apart!' Toby, her ten-year-old, wailed.

'I don't want to watch this any more!' Tommy, aged eight, chipped in. 'It's boring! I want to go outside and play football!'

'We don't have a football, you moron!' Toby snapped back.

'Well, then, let's play with these!'

Then there was a deep thudding sound, just as Connie leapt to her feet and ran in to check on them. But one quick glance told her everything was OK. Normally the house was reasonably tidy, but right then, the two boys were standing in a river of discarded old-lady clothes and shoes, ancient magazines long yellowed with time, box after box of discarded make-up and Christmas decorations that didn't sparkle any more, all destined for either the charity shop or else the skip outside the front door.

'Don't worry, all's good in here,' she called back to Kate in the kitchen. 'No one's hurt. It's just some of the junk piles for the charity shop that toppled over, that's all.'

'Sorry about the mess, Connie,' Toby, her godson, said, looking up at her, his saucery blue eyes full of worry.

'No need to be sorry at all.' Connie grinned back down at him.

'You really don't mind that we knocked over all your mum's stuff?'

'How could I ever be cross with you pair?' Connie said, patting their two little heads playfully. 'It was an accident, that's all.'

'Thanks, Connie, you're so nice and you never get cross,' Tommy said, beaming a gap-toothed little smile at her.

'Make as much mess as you like, lads.' Connie smiled indulgently. 'It can't get any worse than it already is, can it?'

'You're cool,' said Toby approvingly. 'You never give out to us, like... ever.'

'Yeah, it's impossible to get in trouble here,' Tommy chimed in, picking up a pile of jumpers and throwing them high in the air. 'I wouldn't mind living here.'

'Tell you what, though,' Connie said. 'If you're really, really good, just so me and your mum can have a grown-up chat for a little while longer, then I'll take you out and buy you each an ice cream later on. How does that sound?'

'Yay! Ice cream!' the two of them cheered.

Then Toby piped up, just as Connie was on her way back to the kitchen, 'And, Connie? I like the mess. I think you should live here always.'

I wish, she thought, smiling and saying nothing.

'If that pair are trashing the place, then I'll drag them out of here.' Kate sighed wearily, placing the baby back into the buggy where, miraculously, he slept on.

'Oh, let them be,' said Connie wryly, sitting down at the kitchen table again. 'Sure, look at the state of the place! With all the crap I'm trying to get rid of before we sell, this is probably the only house in Dublin where a Seal team could break in and I'd barely even notice.'

'So how are things with the estate agent?' Kate asked worriedly. 'Arsehole Donald still putting pressure on them to sell up in the next twenty minutes?'

'You said arsehole, Mum,' Tommy shouted from the living room. 'I heard you! Arsehole, arsehole, arsehole.'

'Leave her alone,' Toby answered him back. 'She's just stressed. Like when she has wine at home and says it's because she's stressed.'

'Sweet Jesus,' said Kate, rolling her eyes as the kids ran off. 'That pair can't hear me calling them for school, but they can hear me using bad language through a wall? Never have kids, do you hear me, Connie? If you ever get broody, just borrow my lot for twenty minutes – that'll cure you.'

'They're dotes and you know I adore them,' Connie said firmly. 'They've certainly put the smile back on my face today and that's really saying something.'

'So the house sale is definitely going ahead?'

'And short of winning the Lotto, there's not a damn thing I can do about it.'

A silence fell. Then Kate did the following in no particular order: bit her lip, stared blankly down at her hands, started peeling her nail varnish off, twiddled with her wedding ring, then scratched at her head and scalp to the point where it looked as if she had nits. All nervous gestures she'd been doing for years, ever since they were both in school together, but ones that Connie knew the meaning of only too well.

'What's wrong with you, love?' she asked. 'Come on, spit it out. There's something on your mind, I can tell.'

'All right, here goes,' Kate said, looking anywhere except directly at Connie. 'The thing is, honey, you've got so many major stresses going on in your life right now, it's unreal. First bereavement, then a house move and all within weeks of each other. It's a helluva lot for anyone to have to cope with, one on top of the other. And I just think that…' but she trailed off here.

'You think what?' said Connie.

This time, Kate forced herself to focus directly on her.

'Put it this way. I think the stress you're going through is possibly making you see and hear things that aren't necessarily there. This phone business, for instance. When you start imagining that you're hearing voices from beyond the grave—'

'But I didn't imagine anything!'

'Come on, love,' Kate insisted, 'I'm in your corner here. Grief transference, psychologists call it. When you lose someone, then start to imagine you're seeing them everywhere you go. Or in your case, hearing your mum's voice when you can't possibly have done. I'm just saying, it turns out there's an actual clinical term for it. It's common and it's normal and it's all part of what you're going through.'

'And where did you come across this?' said Connie.

'Google.'

Connie rubbed her fingers to her forehead, as if she had a blistering headache coming on. 'Look,' she said, 'if I were you, I wouldn't believe me either. I'm just telling you what I experienced, that's all.'

'Oh – and by the way? Here's something else I found online for you,' Kate said, scooping up the baby's changing bag from the floor and rummaging around at the bottom of it. 'Printed it out for you and all. It's just something that might be of interest.'

At that, she fished out an A4 printout and shoved it across the table to Connie, who stared back at her, puzzled.

'Have a read of it,' Kate said firmly. 'That's all I'm asking. It doesn't cost a penny and I thought it might help.'

Connie was just about to take a look when from the living room there was yet another round of yelling and screaming. Instantly, both of them were on their feet, bolting into the living room to find out what the hell was going on now.

Connie didn't know whether to laugh or cry at what she saw. There was Toby, dressed head to toe in her mother's 'good' going-out pink woolly coat, and her 'really, really good' high shoes, that the woman only ever wore once, the time she was summoned for jury service. Meanwhile Tommy had decided to help himself to some of her mum's old make-up, so now his face was plastered with orange-y foundation with purple lipstick smeared all over his cheeks and lips, all put on completely skew-ways.

'Gimme that coat!' he was squealing at his brother. 'It's not fair! It's my go to try it on now. You've had it for ages!'

'Get lost, I'm having it,' said Toby, twirling around in the high heels, far better able to walk in them, Connie noted, than her poor mum had ever been.

'What the hell do you pair think you're doing?' Kate thundered as Connie looked on, bemused. 'Those things belong to

Connie's mum. Take them off immediately and you can start tidying some of this mess up!'

'But look at us, Mum! We've found the perfect costumes to wear for next Halloween!'

'Yeah! We're going to go as scary, horrible, ugly, evil, witch trolls from the olden days! What do you think?'

* * *

Later on that evening, when Connie was by herself, she read the printout Kate had given her.

The Daily Chronicle/features/checkitout!
The Bereavement Cafe

So how come we don't talk about death? It's the one thing we're all guaranteed to experience, yet we do everything we can to avoid even saying the 'D' word. Instead, we 'pass on', we 'rest in peace', 'push up the daisies', or, for those of a more religious bent, we've 'gone to meet our maker' or 'gone to a better place'.

We don't talk.

Which is where the idea of a Bereavement Cafe comes in. There are roughly eleven thousand dotted all around the world and with that number rising steadily. They're open to anyone, young and old. Admission is always free. And there is always cake.

'And before you ask, no, Bereavement Cafes most definitely aren't grief counselling groups and chats about politics or religion aren't encouraged. Other than that,' says Will Kempton, organiser of one of Ireland's Bereavement Cafes, 'the event is entirely focused on you and your late loved one.

There are no holds barred whenever we meet up. There's absolutely nothing that's frowned upon. Anything goes.'

So what do people come to talk about? Lots, as it turns out. They talk about how grief can be masked, yet still manifest itself in a hundred different unexpected ways. They talk about hospice care, about funeral customs and about nursing homes versus home care. About living wills and flowers and Facebook pages you somehow can't bring yourself to delete after a loved one has passed away. And there's more, much more. They talk about crying and not crying, movies and TV shows, life insurance, kids and grandkids and that strange, weird phenomenon of grieving deeply for someone you barely know. Because as Will so aptly puts it, 'Death and grief are complicated, but confronting them somehow robs them of their power over the rest of our lives.'

And all for the price of a cup of tea? Cheap at the price. Oh, and by the way – believe the hype. There is always cake.

7

LUKE

Luke so did not have time for this. It was a warm spring evening and he felt sweaty and cross that he'd had to somehow carve out time for this utter nonsense in the first place. What the hell was he doing here anyway? he wondered, pulling his car up on Leeson Street and parking outside a hodgepodge row of shops, two pubs, a sandwich bar, a dry cleaners and, oddly, a late-night music venue that went by the slightly bonkers name of the Sweet and Salty Club. He had about a thousand other demands on his time, with Amy at the very top of the list, and frankly didn't think for one second that showing up at some gimmicky 'Bereavement Cafe' was going to do him the slightest bit of good at all. No matter how much he'd been emotionally guilted into doing it.

One hour, he thought. *I'll give this crap exactly an hour, then make my excuses and get out of here. Try stopping me.*

Just on the drive to get there, he'd already had to fend off five calls, each more urgent than the last. The McKinsey job, a massive new office build that he was project manager on, was turning into a nightmare, to put it mildly. Luke calculated that even if he worked an eighteen-hour day, flat out, he'd still struggle with the sheer scale of the project. Then when you factored in Amy and his main priority of keeping her little life as normal as he could, it seemed nigh on impossible.

He was clinging on to the project, not to mention to his job, by the very skin of his teeth and he knew it. Ever since his meeting with the boss a few days ago, the word seemed to have gone around the office that his days working there were numbered. 'So you can focus on your family, man,' as Dave had put it, in his clumsy attempt at being compassionate.

Already Nick, Luke's right hand on the project, clearly had sights on taking over. He was even holding on-site meetings without bothering to tell Luke till it was too late. 'Didn't want to stress you out, not with everything else you're going through,' he'd said when confronted about it, so smugly that Luke had to clench his fists and try his damnedest not to sock him one.

Jesus, didn't these people realise how badly he needed this job? Unlike his colleagues, Luke didn't spend the tiny chink of down time he got in pubs and clubs and late-night bars and off on lads' weekends in Vegas, Instagramming the shite out of it. He loved his career and wanted nothing more than to bring his A-game to the table, but how was it possible when there were only twenty-four hours in the day and when he was already stretched so thin? He had a mortgage to pay and a home to run, not to mention school fees and all manner of treats and little mini breaks away he had planned for Amy during her school holidays, just as he and Helen had always done before.

He sighed deeply, not even able to complete that mental sentence. Enough to say 'before'.

Luke had become a leading expert on compartmentalising grief – it was a whole can of worms that he just hadn't the time to open. *Don't go there* had become his motto. Every single time he missed Helen, which was most of the time really, all he could think to himself was *don't go there*. Was this his way of coping? Burying himself in work, so he could somehow get through this? Well, if it was, then what the fuck else was he supposed to do?

Now, he thought, silently fuming as he grabbed his phone and clambered out of the car, he had to waste precious time away from Amy and away from his desk, to sit listening to a load of navel-gazing gobshitery from a bunch of strangers in some run-down cafe where he wouldn't even be able to get a decent beer, to calm him down a bit. And all for what? Because he'd been guilted into it by Stella Mackey, Amy's school principal, that was why. He and Helen had moved heaven and earth to get Amy into St Teresa's school in the first place. Competition for places was ferocious and, whatever else was going on in Luke's life, however little time he had, the school principal had to be kept onside at all costs. So Stella Mackey was the only bloody reason he hadn't weaselled out of having to do this hours ago.

'Forgive me for calling you in here at short notice, when I know you're a busy man,' she had said to him a few days ago when she'd hauled him into that poky little principal's office to see her at the end of a school day. A space almost designed to depress you, he'd thought, with only one light source, a tiny window positioned at a terrible angle and with zero chance of direct sunlight. *Give me five minutes with my drawing pad and I could transform this whole space for you,* he'd thought as Miss Mackey had sat behind her desk in front of him.

'None of my business of course,' she'd said, 'and there's no delicate way to put this, I'm afraid.'

At that, Luke had sat up.

'It's just that I see you coming in and out of the school regularly,' she'd continued, 'and – again, tell me if I'm overstepping the mark here, but I do have concerns about how you're coping. You're always rushing, always so stressed, you never seem to have any time. I've noticed, the staff have noticed, and we're concerned for your well-being. Amy is young and she will take her cue from you. If she doesn't see you functioning and coping, then how can you expect her to?'

'She and I are getting there,' he'd replied, trying to sound reassuring. 'It's going to take time, but we *are* getting there.'

'Hmm,' Miss Mackey had replied, looking doubtfully across her desk at him. 'Anyway, the whole reason I asked to see you is because I'd like to offer a suggestion. There's somewhere you should consider attending, on as regular a basis as you possibly can. Somewhere that I can guarantee will help you. Just as it's helped me.' Then she'd scribbled down an address on a notepad in front of her and passed it over.

'I'm sorry... what is this place anyway?' Luke had asked, puzzled. 'Some kind of bereavement support group? Because I've already been for grief counselling, thanks. I even took Amy to a child psychologist.' For all the good it did either of us, he could have added, but didn't.

Stella Mackey hadn't taken the hint, though.

'Next meeting is on Thursday evening at 7 p.m.,' she'd replied gently.

'Can't do next Thursday,' Luke had quickly replied. 'I've got a site meeting and unfortunately it's vital I'm there. Then by the time I collect Amy and take her home, that's the whole evening gone. I'm sure you understand.'

'Mr Wright,' she'd replied, her voice stern, and there it was – that glint of steel that Helen had so often warned him of. 'Just try it out, that's all I'm asking. For your own good and, ultimately, for Amy's too.'

Fine, Luke had thought, smiling politely and taking the address she'd held out for him while thinking to himself, *Yeah, right. Over my dead body.* He'd come up with some last-minute excuse, but no way in hell was he turning up to this place, wherever it was.

'Oh, and just to forewarn you, so you're not surprised,' she'd added, rising to her feet as if she'd considered the meeting over, 'I'll be there myself too. I look forward to seeing you.'

Shite. And just like that, he was trapped.

* * *

Right, then, Luke thought, clambering out of his car, striding down Leeson Street, looking for the right place and wondering how quickly he could make his excuses and scarper. *I'll just do this one meeting.* Amy was at his sister Clare's house and he had to collect her as soon as he possibly could, then get her home to bed.

He pulled out his phone to give his little girl a lightning-quick call, just to hear her voice, just to cheer himself up. After all, she was the reason he got out of bed in the morning, she was the reason he was working as flat out as he was and, now that Helen was gone, she was the only person in his whole world who could put the smile back on his face.

Clare answered immediately and, in the background, Luke could hear squeals and giggles as Clare's two girls, Poppy and Holly, fussed and faffed over their youngest cousin, who the pair of them treated like a real-life doll come to life. For her part, Amy looked up to her older cousins like the big sisters she'd never had and was always in heaven whenever she got to hang out with Auntie Clare and the girls.

'Can I just say a quick hello to her?' Luke asked Claire.

'Of course,' Clare said, laughing. 'Although I think she's having far too much fun with my lot – it might be a bit of a job getting her to the phone!' Luke waited patiently on the pavement as he overheard yet more hysterical giggles and tittering, then Amy's little voice eventually came on. Just the sound of her pulled at his heart like he could barely believe. She sounded happy. She sounded safe and minded and cared for and all the things he was falling down on so spectacularly these days.

'Hi, Dad!' she said and already he was beaming stupidly down the phone.

'Hello, pet, how are you getting on? You're having fun with Holly and Poppy?'

'Oh, Dad, it's the *best* here! We're playing make-up salon and they put lipstick and mascara and this red stuff all over my eyes and my cheeks and it's brilliant and Auntie Clare is making yummy lasagne for dinner and then we're going to play make-y-uppy musicals and it's amazing!'

'Well, I'll be there to collect you later, honey.' Luke smiled. 'So I'll see you soon, OK?'

And then came a sentence guaranteed to sink his heart like a stone.

'But I don't want to go home, Dad! You're always working at home, always. It's miles more fun here. Why can I not just stay here?'

8

CONNIE

'So tell us what you think you can bring to the part, please. In your own words.'

It's an ad for toilet bleach, Connie answered in her head. *What exactly is there to bring to an ad for toilet bleach?* Depth of character wouldn't exactly be top of the list here. But she needed the money and she needed the work, so she bit her tongue and swallowed her pride and forced herself to beam and gush like a pro. After all, it wasn't every day you were called to audition for the mighty Pearl Hamilton, the biggest casting director in town. This woman was huge, she cast every single thing going, movies, big juicy TV dramas, you name it. So if Pearl Hamilton asked you to read for a toilet bleach ad, then you bloody well did it with a big, happy smile plastered to your face.

'It's a wonderful commercial,' Connie raved. 'And you know, I'm a huge fan of... all toilet products. With a good, strong bleach right at the top of the list.'

'So what's your unique take on this character?' Pearl asked from the other side of a Zoom call. Connie was sitting at her kitchen table, the only space in her entire house with a clean white wall directly behind her, so it actually looked as if she were living in some kind of minimalist haven and not a soon-to-be-sold house with half its contents piled up in storage boxes and bin liners, and mounds of discarded crap destined for the charity shop just out of shot.

What's the right answer here? Connie thought. *I dunno, my take on the character is that this is a woman who wants a sparkling toilet?* But then she quickly reminded herself that on a Zoom casting call like this one, all they really wanted to know was what you looked like, how you came across on camera, and if you were capable of learning the one single line demanded of you.

'Oh, I love this character so much!' She beamed, really giving the hard sell. 'She speaks to me and indeed to any woman who's a big fan of... hygiene. After all, we all know that if you want your bathroom to smell sparkling fresh, then Ultra Loo is your only man!'

'Good, that's very good.' Pearl nodded from the other side of the Zoom call as she looked distractedly down at notes that were out of shot, then whipped her glasses off her head so she could read them properly. 'In your own time, then, please, Bonnie.'

'Umm... it's actually Connie.'

No reply to that, so Connie took a deep breath, double-checked that she was bang in the dead centre of the Zoom shot, then went for it.

'Now my bathroom smells like a summer meadow!' she trilled happily, gesturing around her like a fifties gameshow host, just as she'd been rehearsing in front of the mirror all morning. 'And yours can too, with new Ultra Loo!'

Silence. More silence. And now Pearl was looking at her a bit more keenly.

'Mmm.' She frowned, taking off her glasses and chewing on the end of them. 'Not a bad effort, but can you give it a bit more, I don't know, zza zza zoom?'

I'm thirty-four years of age, Connie thought. *I'm the perfect age to play Hedda Gabbler or Lady Macbeth. But yes, of course, I'll sit here with a rictus grin plastered to my face and give a bit more 'zza zza zoom' to the notion of selling your toilet bleach for the sake of a few quid. No problem, Pearl. Delighted to, Pearl. Three bags full, Pearl.*

'Of course,' she said obligingly. 'A bit more oomph. You got it!'

'Once again, please, in your own time,' Pearl said, with a dismissive wrist-wave.

Connie took a deep breath and launched straight back into it, with even more high-octane hysteria this time.

'Now my bathroom smells like a summer meadow... and yours can *too*, with new...'

But just then came the unmistakable sound of a phone ringing, and ringing good and loud too. Mid-line, Connie froze. Jesus, she thought, had she been stupid enough to leave her mobile switched on when she was doing the first casting she'd had in months? She glanced around distractedly, but no – her mobile was on the kitchen table, well out of shot and it was resolutely on silent *and* aeroplane mode. But wherever that infuriating ringing noise was coming from, it persisted.

'Am I hearing a phone ringing?' Pearl asked impatiently. 'We kindly request that all phones be kept on silent for the audition process, please.'

'No, no! I promise, wherever that noise is coming from, it's not me,' Connie said, flustered and confused now.

'Well, it's certainly not coming from this end either. Can you find it and turn it off, please? We're running out of time and we need to record you once more.' Gone was Pearl's initial professional friendliness and now she sounded curt and narky.

Still that annoying ringing noise persisted, getting louder and louder, but this time sounding as if it was coming from somewhere very, very close to Connie. Dangerously close. Panicking, she glanced all around her. How the feck could this be happening?

Then, out of the corner of her eye, she spotted it – that very, very faint light that she'd only ever seen once before. Sitting on a dresser at the opposite end of the kitchen table, just out of the Zoom shot.

No, no, no, no. This. Couldn't. Be. Happening. Not now. Leaping up out of her chair, she almost dive-bombed to grab the shagging thing urgently and with both hands shaking.

'Just switch it off so we can resume, please,' said Pearl tetchily. *But it could be Mum*, Connie thought wildly. Same as when she was up in the attic the other day. Super quickly, her addled mind weighed up the options. A possible job? Or another precious chance to hear her mother's voice?

A no-brainer. 'Excuse me one moment,' she said down the Zoom call to Pearl. 'It's just that... I really do need to get this.'

She scooped up the precious phone and, with trembling fingers, clicked on that clunky green button and answered.

'Oh, please, fire away. I'll just sit here waiting for you.' She could hear Pearl's voice dripping with sarcasm in the background. 'I've got absolutely nothing else to do all day. Take your time, Bonnie.'

But by then, Connie was utterly tuned into the phone, straining to hear something, anything. Then there it was, that same, scratchy, whooshing, wind-rushing noise, just like before.

'Hello? Hello? Anyone there?' she said, stress sweat starting to pump out of her. 'Mum? Mum, can that be you?'

A faint cracking, and then came that unforgettable voice. Loud, distinct and unmistakable.

'An ad for toilet bleach?' she heard her mum say, as clearly as if she were in the same room as Connie. 'Seriously? Ahh now, pet. Is this really what you want? To be the face that reminds people all over the country that they need to have a wee?'

9

LUCASTA

'Oh, do bugger off, you ridiculous man,' Lucasta said into thin air as she and her long-suffering assistant, Phoebe, stepped out of the car onto Leeson Street. No driving for Lucasta and as she so often explained to people, 'driving only ever gives me stress headaches, so after Johnnie passed away, I gave it up completely. Besides, how can I possibly have a little drinkie if I'm stuck behind the wheel of a car? Far too boring for words.'

'Now who are you speaking to?' Phoebe asked flatly as she double-checked that they were at the correct address, courtesy of Google Maps.

'It's only Johnnie again,' Lucasta sighed theatrically. 'I said *kindly desist*, you annoying man. I most certainly will not have "dirty talk" with you now. Really, darling. I'm out in public and the very last thing I want is to be arrested for lewd behaviour.'

'Come along, then, we're already late,' Phoebe said crisply, scanning around the street for the right place, till her gimlet eye lit on it. 'Ah, yes, here we are. This way, please. Don't dawdle and please remember we're only staying here for one hour, tops.

You're way behind on your editing deadline as it is and, like it or not, you've got to put in a minimum of two more hours of work when we get home.'

Lucasta was well used to Phoebe's nagging and barely even registered it. Instead, pulling layers and layers of her trademark long, swingy cardigans tightly around her, she glanced up at the cafe and nodded approvingly.

'Yes, yes,' she muttered to herself. 'I'm most definitely feeling something... a most deliciously positive vibration... The spirits are here, mark my words...'

'Is that you talking or is it the double gin and tonic you had before you left the house?' Phoebe replied tartly, walking briskly ahead and holding the door open for her. It rang with a most satisfying jingle and the moment they stepped inside, they found themselves in a delightfully old-fashioned coffee shop, just like something out of Dickens.

Well, well, well, Lucasta thought, drinking it all in, completely absorbing the atmosphere and breathing huge gulps of cinnamon-scented air. Just being in that space almost made her feel as though she were going back in time. There was a large bay window to the front with neat little sash panes and wooden floors underfoot that were well polished and shining, with good, solid mahogany tables dotted everywhere – none of those ghastly Formica things with wobbly legs that you saw in all the coffee shops now, she noted, deeply gratified. The chairs and chintzy armchairs that were scattered throughout looked cosy and inviting too, and were already filled with about a dozen or so people who'd got here before them, all sitting throughout the room. The turnout seemed to be mostly women, but there were two or three gentlemen there; the guests seemed to be from all possible age groups and from all walks of life too.

Utterly lost in thought, Lucasta swished her way around the perimeter of the room, shoving her long grey hair over her shoulders and letting her multi-layered cardigans trail behind her like a cloak. As she did, the whole room went silent and every head swivelled her way, drinking in this mad-looking stranger from head to foot.

'Let me find free seats for us, then just sit down and try to be unobtrusive,' Phoebe hissed in her ear, nodding politely at everyone assembled there ahead of them. With Lucasta, however, there was sod all chance of that. This was a lady who simply didn't do unobtrusive.

'Oh, sweet Lord,' said one elderly, white-haired lady with a bright pink face and a bright pink jumper the exact match of it, clasping her hands over her mouth as if she'd just seen a vision. 'It's you, isn't it? *The* Lucasta Liversidge? Oh my God, I can't believe I'm actually in the same room as you!'

'We've read all your books,' a younger woman beside her, who could have been her daughter, they were so alike, tittered happily, nudging the mother. 'We love the Mercy stories so much! I'm reading *Mercy at War* just now and I really think it's your best yet!'

'Oh, I'm *loving Mercy at War*!' came another voice from the back of the room, a middle-aged woman in yoga pants and a baseball cap, with her hair tied back into a ponytail and wearing so much of that dreadful fake tan, Lucasta noted, that most of this lady's bare skin – and there was quite a lot of it on show – was a most peculiar shade of caramel. 'I'm halfway through it now and I can't put it down! The bit where she's nursing at the Battle of the Somme and accidentally meets the man she's going to marry in a field hospital, where he's wounded and dying...'

'Wonderful, we love it too, don't we, love?' the pink-faced lady with the head of white hair squealed excitedly to the daughter beside her.

'My favourite bit is the part where he proposes to her,' the daughter gibbered to Lucasta, 'just as he's about to be shipped back to Britain suffering from shell shock and a broken leg—'

'And it takes her till the very end of the book to realise that he's the Duke of Marlborough – so romantic!' the mother finished for her.

'No plot spoilers, please!' The woman with the ghastly fake tan laughed. 'I still haven't finished it yet!'

'We're all reading them in my class right now. *Big*, big fans,' said a very young girl shyly, sitting on her own at a table much closer to Lucasta. She was still in her school uniform and looked no more than sixteen years of age tops. Lucasta caught the girl's eye and graciously nodded back, only to be rewarded with a shy little smile and a big thumbs up. 'My English teacher says it's amazing how those books never once dated or aged, even though they were written *decades* ago... like, the nineteen-eighties or something. Even Alex reads them, don't you, Alex?' Then she twisted around to another teen sitting on the floor at the very back of the coffee shop, who was wearing jeans and an oversized hoodie, but who looked utterly identical to her in every other way. This one, however, was staring down at her phone, and when the focus of the whole room turned to her, she just pulled the hoodie down even further to cover her face, positively radiating venom and studiously ignoring everyone.

'In the lockdown, my comfort read was *Mercy and the Marlboroughs*,' came another voice from somewhere at the back of the room, Lucasta couldn't see where, she was so inundated with all these lovely, wonderful compliments. 'Where she's already married to the duke, but then she has to run this falling-apart stately home, with all his family being so snooty to her, because, as far as they're concerned, she's only a nurse who got lucky marrying into their family. Not a born aristo like the rest of them.'

'Well, thank you, thank you all.' Lucasta beamed delightedly, waving at the room like Queen Camilla on a royal walkabout. 'How very lovely of you.'

'I just wish my wife were here to meet you too,' an older, well-preserved-looking gentleman in a cravat and with a walking stick clamped to his hands said, a little sorrowfully, Lucasta thought. 'She'd die and go to heaven if she ever got to sit in the same room as the one and only Lucasta Liversidge. Only she's already dead, of course.'

'It's always lovely to welcome new faces to our little gathering,' said a younger man sitting at the top of the room, who looked very much as if he was in charge, with a clipboard in his hands and a sheaf of notes on his knees. Mid-thirties, Lucasta guessed. Quite nice-looking too, but not in an obvious way, with good thick dark hair tied back into a practical bun and striking brown eyes that seemed to jump right out at you. 'Please,' he said, addressing Lucasta and Phoebe, 'come on in and join us. Everyone is welcome here.'

'Oh, well, now,' Lucasta trilled, taking in this nice young gentleman with a quick, practised scan. 'Aren't you terribly handsome? Who are you, now?'

'I'm Will.' He smiled back. 'I'm the facilitator here and it's great to see you both. You're Lucasta, I take it?'

'Oh, never mind me, dear. Do you have a girlfriend? Because if not, I'll have you matched up with one of my nieces in no time. The amount of time they both waste on that dreadful app thingy, Twindler or Swindler or whatever it's called, is perfectly mortifying. And they only ever meet complete idiots, you know. There are times when I despair.'

There were titters around the room at that, but Will just looked embarrassed and changed the subject.

'And may I have your name too?' he said to Phoebe, who stood stiffly by Lucasta's side, completely po-faced, as if she had to deal with these types of Lucasta love-ins every single time they went outside the hall door.

'I'm Phoebe Keane,' she replied curtly.

'You're most welcome too, Phoebe,' said Will warmly, jotting both names down then jumping to his feet to guide them to a free table over by the window, with two very comfy-looking chairs just waiting for them. 'We're all super-casual here, so please feel free to grab a tea or coffee, or whatever you fancy. Oh – and tonight's cake treats are courtesy of Mildred here,' he added, with a friendly nod towards that older, pink-faced lady with the shock of cotton-wool-white hair who seemed to want to turn the whole evening into an impromptu book club.

'Never mind your old cups of tea and coffee.' Lucasta waved dismissively. 'But if by any chance you had a little gin and tonic, I'd absolutely bite your hand off.'

'Just sit,' Phoebe hissed in her ear, strong-arming her boss towards the table and almost shoving her down into the chair Will was holding out for her. 'You've made your grand entrance, now it's time to be quiet.'

'So it seems we've got a grand total of three new faces joining us here tonight,' said Will. 'Lucasta, Phoebe, and Luke over there in the corner.'

Lucasta glanced over to an unobtrusive table by the wall, where a lone gentleman appeared to be texting or emailing away furiously on his phone, with absolutely zero interest in what was going on around him. Instead he was surrounded by a stack of notes and utterly focused on the screen in front of him; an appalling habit and one Lucasta had always despaired of, particularly when in company. Honestly, whenever she was out to dinner with chums and mobile phones were produced at the table, she wanted to hurl them out of the nearest window.

Yet there was something about this chap, she thought, intrigued, as she eyed him up and down, taking a good, long look at him. A sadness, yes, but an anger too. And something else that she tried to put her finger on but couldn't. At least, not yet she couldn't.

Then Will spoke again, distracting her.

'So just before Lucasta and Phoebe joined us,' he was saying, 'Lucy here was sharing some wonderful memories she has of her dad. Would you like to continue, Lucy?'

He nodded warmly towards the young teenage girl who was still in her school uniform, so Lucasta turned to look at her, same as everyone else.

'Yeah,' Lucy said shyly, playing with her long, straight red hair, sensibly parted right down the middle. 'You know what I forgot to say? Father's Day is really soon and we always used to celebrate that together, me, Mum, Dad and Alex – that's my twin, by the way,' she added helpfully.

All eyes drifted towards Alex, who was still sitting cross-legged on the floor over by the window, about as far away from everyone else as she could get and radiating hate waves.

'Is there anything you'd like to share with us, Alex?' Will asked her gently and sympathetically. 'Maybe about Father's Day and how you feel about it coming up?'

Nothing. Total silence from Alex. Instead, Will was rewarded with a hot glare that was bordering on venomous.

'She's... Well, let's just say Alex wouldn't really be into something like this,' Lucy replied on her behalf. 'Mum made her come with me. Thought it might be good for her. For us both, that is.'

Understanding nods from around the room as Will tactfully steered the chat back to Lucy.

'And is Father's Day a particularly special memory for you?' he asked softly.

'It used to be,' said Lucy. 'There's only the four of us in our family – sorry – I mean there *were* only the four of us and we always used to make the biggest fuss of Dad. Me and Alex would take over the kitchen and try our best to bake him a cake, even though we're both brutal bakers. Aren't we, Alex?'

Again, silence from Alex, except this time she didn't even bother looking up from her phone. Lucasta could barely keep her eyes off the poor girl, madly trying to read her aura. So much negativity for someone so young, she thought.

'You know what I think, though?' Lucy went on. 'Now I just think Father's Day is cruel and mean. There's ads for it everywhere, every single time I go on my phone, something pops up about "celebrating Dad". It's horrible, that's what it is. What happens if you've no dad to celebrate with?'

There was a tiny smattering of applause and nods of approval from around the room.

'Well said, love,' Mildred with the snow-white hair chipped in, the same legend who'd apparently made tonight's cake. 'You're a great young one.'

'For what it's worth,' said a forty-something woman sitting at a table over by the door, speaking slowly and clearly, 'I heartily concur about any and all Hallmark holidays. I'd gladly have the lot of them banned, if only I could.'

Ahh, now here was an educated voice, Lucasta thought, almost immediately getting a mental flash of this woman sitting alone in some sort of classroom correcting a towering pile of copybooks. She had light brown hair neatly tied back and was plainly dressed in a khaki trouser suit with a simple white T-shirt on underneath it. Interestingly, though, she wore a silver pendant necklace, which was dangling around her neck and which she kept fingering. There was something about that pendant, Lucasta knew in a flash. It had been given to her by someone very dear, who wasn't with her any more. A parent, perhaps? No, she decided, immediately dismissing the thought. Someone younger. Considerably younger too.

'Tell us more, Stella,' Will said.

Whoever this Stella person was, she held the room, warming to her theme.

'Mother's Day is a particular torture in my house,' she was saying. 'I think we can all agree, it's tough enough getting through milestone events like Christmas and Easter, without the added awfulness of entirely manufactured days, like Mother's Day and Father's Day. Maybe we should all start a campaign here to end them, once and for all?'

Another smattering of applause, but just as the conversation moved on Lucasta suddenly became rooted to her seat. The chatter in the little cafe became louder and more animated, but now all Lucasta wanted to do was stand up and hiss at them all to be quiet, that she couldn't hear, that she needed total and utter silence – and that this was terribly, terribly important.

Because she was here again. The voice, that light, ephemeral, floaty voice that Lucasta had only ever caught once before – back at home the other day in her little garden shed.

'Shh, everyone, please,' she urged as a huge wave of chatter rose exponentially.

'Oh, and by the way, everyone,' Mildred was saying at the top of her voice, 'I made a few tiny little walnut cakes for you all – and as they say, there's one for everyone in the audience!'

A round of applause now, as the chatter grew ever louder, till suddenly Lucasta could barely hear herself think any more. She rose to her feet as Phoebe looked on, alarmed.

'Please, people!' she said at the top of her voice, and, because it was Lucasta Liversidge speaking, everyone paid attention to her. 'There's someone here, someone who's desperately trying to contact one of you, but I can't possibly hear her with all of this racket! I need total and utter silence – just for a few moments, please!'

'Well, this is a bit irregular,' said Will, looking across the room at her.

But then Lucasta completely tuned out. It didn't happen very often, but when she was able to drift into that sacred space in her mind where it was just her and whoever was trying to reach out to her – my word, she thought, it really was powerful.

The room was silent. Now every eye was fixated her way and you could hear a pin drop. Only one person was paying absolutely no attention at all, and, with sudden and absolute certainty, Lucasta knew that this was exactly who the message was intended for.

'Yes,' she muttered, almost to herself. 'Yes, I understand what you're saying. Yes, I think I see who you're talking about too. You,' she whispered, coming out of her trance and pointing at the middle-aged man, the one who sat alone at a table over by the wall, who'd been so utterly fixated by his mobile phone and the huge sheaf of work notes in front of him. 'She's here for you. Her name is... Dearest, might I ask you to speak up?'

The man looked up at her, confused and clearly not knowing what to think.

'Your name is Luke, dear, isn't that right?'

Luke nodded, mystified and looking as if this were some kind of cheap vaudeville act that he was a most unwilling audience participant in.

'Yes, yes,' Lucasta said under her breath. 'Yes, I do understand. And, of course, I'll do exactly as you ask. I've got someone here to speak to you,' Lucasta said to him. 'She says her name is Helen... and I really think she's trying to reach out to you... and to someone called Amy too. Do either of those names mean anything to you, dear?'

10

LUKE

Exactly one hour earlier, Luke had been in a foul humour. Just get it over with, he'd thought, the minute he'd first arrived at that coffee shop place for this 'Bereavement Cafe' lark, whatever the hell that entailed. Get in, make damn sure he was seen by Stella Mackey, do a can-can in front of her if that was what it took to make sure she knew he'd bothered to turn up, then get out of there as quickly as was humanly possible. He even had it worked out in his head what he'd say to her when they met.

'Miss Mackey? How can I thank you enough for encouraging me to come along this evening? The whole experience has been more valuable than I know how to put into words. Already I feel like a better parent and whaddya know? My grief has magically disappeared – all thanks to you. Sorry I won't be able to come back here again, but I'm all cured now, so that's the end of that. Bye for now and see you at Amy's next parent-teacher evening!'

He'd lay the insincerity on with a trowel if need be.

What had surprised him was how intimate the whole thing felt – he'd counted no fewer than a dozen people sitting around the coffee shop in total. Another plus: it all seemed very comfy and cushty in there, with a kind of neo-Victorian vibe going on; good south-west-facing light source, he'd noted professionally, taking the place in, with ample tables and armchairs dotted throughout the room. As a space, it felt – OK. Inviting. Not weird or 'ick', as he'd imagined it would.

Luke had expected to see a few doddery pensioners on Zimmer frames but that had been yet another surprise: the age range was wider than he'd predicted. Two school kids had even turned up, twins it seemed, roughly about sixteen or so. One of them, by the name of Lucy, was open and chatty and engaged, but the other one? Needed help of a far more professional nature than a gathering like this could possibly have provided. That much was obvious, even to Luke. It seemed their dad had died, but where was the mother? Did she seriously think that sitting around yakking and drinking tea with a complete bunch of strangers would help her kids?

The sullen one, Alex, sat on the floor over in a corner, glued to her phone, pointedly not engaging with anyone or with anything. Poor kid, Luke had found himself thinking, determined that, whatever else happened, Amy would never end up sulky and moody and so obviously unhappy. Kid was crying out for help – and would you blame her?

Aside from the twins, there was a mother and daughter who dressed like carbon copies of each other in garish pink and who'd spent every chance they got plugging some kind of cake they'd brought with them. What do the two of you expect, Luke had wanted to say to them, an entry form for *The Great British Bake Off*? Then there was a guy in his early thirties, Will someone, who dressed like a hipster, in cargo shorts, an oversized check shirt and God help us, a man-bun. Will seemed to be running the show, he was the one who got everyone seated and who acted like a kind of MC for the evening, coaxing people to chat and share memories and whatever other useless time-wasting crap they all frittered their time away with once a week. He was asking everyone for email addresses: good luck with that.

And then, of course, there was Stella Mackey. She'd already arrived by the time Luke had got there, sitting alone at a table up against the wall. He'd made a beeline for her when he'd first arrived, making a concerted effort to put on his politest and most engaged face. Just as he did every single day of the week with Dave and that dickhead Nick he worked with at the office. When it came to acting the hypocrite, he'd had lots of practice.

'Miss Mackey.' He'd fake-smiled at her, reaching out his hand to shake hers. 'Good to see you. Delighted to be here and thank you so much for suggesting I come along this evening. So kind of you.'

She'd taken a good long look at him before answering.

'I'm very glad to see you here,' she'd replied evenly. 'I really do think you'll find this useful. It takes time, of course, but I sincerely hope you'll benefit. I know I did.'

'I'm sure I will.' He'd smiled confidently back at her. 'But I hope you'll forgive me if I need to dash off a little early, it's just I need to collect Amy from my sister's house…'

However Stella Mackey was having none of that. 'Our meetings generally take up to about two hours,' she'd firmly cut across him. 'So I'll chat to you afterwards.'

Bugger, Luke had thought, skulking off to a less obtrusive table tucked in a convenient little alcove, about as far away from her as he could get. That meant any hope he'd had of slipping out of there early had just gone up in smoke. He'd put his work phone discreetly on his lap, so he could answer a couple of urgent emails that had just pinged in for him. He'd taken a notepad and pen from his briefcase too, with every intention of breaking down some of the costings on the McKinsey project, so at least the time he was wasting here wasn't entirely for naught. Hopefully he was sitting far enough away from Stella Mackey that she wouldn't notice he was scribbling away on his notepad the whole time.

The evening from hell had eventually kicked off, with a long, meandering welcome speech from that hipster guy with the man-bun, Will. Predictably enough, a whole barrage of white noise had followed. As ever, at any group meeting, there were too many people too fond of their own voices who dominated, including that mother and daughter dressed in lurid pink, who it seemed were called Mildred and Dee and who, half an hour in, had still been wittering on about their homemade walnut whatever-the-feck-they'd-baked. Luke had just kept willing them to shut up, then eventually schooled himself to completely tune them out.

Otherwise the whole evening had basically been just a bunch of lonely people sharing some of the most boring memories imaginable. Some old man had kept talking about a stray cat who had been visiting him since his wife passed away and who he was now convinced was her dead spirit trying to contact him. *Give me strength,* Luke had thought, desperately trying to keep his focus on the costing sheet on his lap that he'd been working on under the table, so the mighty Stella Mackey wouldn't get on his case about it.

Oddly, though, Miss Mackey herself had stayed quiet, for the initial part of the night anyway. *What's your story?* Luke had found himself thinking, his eye automatically wandering over to her. She'd lost one or possibly both parents, more than likely.

Which, let's face it, was nothing out of the ordinary for anyone over the age of forty. And certainly nothing compared with what he'd just been through. Not even close.

But then, out of nowhere, there had been an interesting development. Roughly ten or so minutes into the meeting, the coffee shop door had swung open with an annoying tinkly bell ring and in had breezed what Luke could only describe as a sheer force of nature. A mad-looking older lady, eighties at a guess, had suddenly appeared in their midst and, without even trying, been the instant focus of every eye there. Hard not to look at her: she had straggly, matted, long grey hair that looked as though it hadn't seen the inside of a hairdresser's in decades, and she was dressed in floaty layers of dark-coloured clothes, as if she'd just come from a jumble sale and had dressed in the first items of clothing she'd grabbed. She looked like a combination of Miss Marple, as played by Margaret Rutherford, and Iris Apfel, in a pair of oversized, dinner-plate-shaped glasses in bright red that frankly made her look a bit barmy. Luke had found himself unwittingly staring across the room at her, same as everyone else. It seemed cruel to say that she looked like a bag lady, and yet that was the only way to describe her.

Whoever she was though, she seemed to be some kind of celebrity. No sooner had she come into the coffee shop than she was being inundated with all manner of compliments and effusive gushing about how brilliant she was. A writer, Luke had gathered, which had instantly given him a pang of sadness. He never read himself, apart from the odd historical biography he might skim through on holidays, and how long was it since he or Amy had been on an actual, proper holiday?

No, Helen had been the reader in their house, the most astonishing, insatiable reader that Luke had ever come across. She'd worked as an English and History teacher and read all the time, always, non-stop. Helen's idea of heaven was to spend the whole day in a bookshop and for Christmas and birthdays she'd never wanted jewellery, handbags or clothes; all she'd ever say was, 'Buy me more bookcases and I'll be happy.' She'd even been able to read and walk around the house simultaneously, something that had never failed to astonish Luke, to the extent that he'd thought, if they ever moved house, he'd have to design a custom-made home especially for her, with an actual library, where he knew she'd be so happy.

Practically from the moment Amy had been conceived, Helen would read to her in the womb and, right up to the day she'd passed away, that had been her 'thing' with Amy. How many times had Luke walked in on the pair of them cuddled up in bed together, with Helen reading aloud from a Roald Dahl story that she herself had loved as a child? Not even through the worst of chemo, and God knows it had got hellish towards the end, not even when she'd had to be hospitalised in palliative care had that ever, once, stopped Helen from reading to Amy.

Luke had tried his best to keep up the tradition after she'd gone, but even in the whole of his strength, he couldn't do it. It was too much for him and way too emotional for Amy. Books had been Helen's thing, books had been Helen's department and books, he'd often thought, had been the love of her life, next to her family, that was.

If you were only here now, he'd said silently in his head, where he held so many conversations with Helen these days, *you'd know exactly who this new arrival is. You'd have read some, if not all, of her books. You'd be able to engage with her and chat to everyone else here just like you were able to engage with every single human being who ever crossed your path.*

It was a gift Helen had – she could walk into a room of total strangers and, within minutes, each and every one of them would think of her as their new best friend. Up until her very last, agonising days, there hadn't been a day or night care palliative nurse on her ward who hadn't thought of her as one of their own. One of the NCDs, the incredibly hard-working non-consultant doctors who looked after Helen right up to the bitter end, had even invited her to his wedding.

And still the love-in for the bag lady had continued – Lucasta someone or other. Everyone had been fangirling over her, even one of the older men, a guy in a cravat who looked as if he'd just stepped off the set of a Noel Coward play, had been bellowing at the top of his voice about what a colossal fan his late wife had been.

'Oh, how very lovely of you!' Lucasta had said, in an astonishingly posh, cut-glass accent. Only then had Luke noticed that another, younger woman had come in with her, who seemed to be either her daughter or her assistant. She was probably in her fifties, but seemed far older; long, lean, thin-faced, dressed neatly all in black and completely unsmiling. Whoever she was though, she seemed to have a bit of control over Lucasta Liversidge, which he'd discovered was her full name – and a more made-up name Luke couldn't possibly imagine.

Quickly enough, this long, skinny woman in black had steered Lucasta to a table, sat her down and clearly instructed her to shut up, so at least the meeting could warble on in peace. Meanwhile Luke could get back to his work.

But what had happened next was beyond description. The room had settled down and Luke had been beavering away, minding his own business, when, out of nowhere, this Lucasta famous-author one, had seemed to drift off into some kind of trace. He'd never actually seen a person go into a trance before, but there'd been no mistaking it; this seemed to be the full-on works. Her glasses had fallen off and her eyes had looked as if they were almost rolling into the back of her head as she'd swayed back and forth on her seat, mumbling and groaning until even that posh, cultured Anglo-Irish voice of hers had begun to take on a totally different register.

The whole room had gone silent and all anyone could do was stare over at her – it had been impossible not to. She'd been muttering and throwing out names and dates and random images that had seemed to be hitting her as the sideshow had gone on.

The assistant, however, had seemed blithely unconcerned, staying cool and calm and acting as though this kind of thing happened on a regular basis.

'I assure you all, she's absolutely fine,' she'd said, trying to take everyone's focus away from what had been unfolding – a nigh on impossible task. Even Luke had found himself glancing up from his notes.

Then, to his astonishment, Lucasta had pointed over his way with a snow-white face and the most astonishing pair of turquoise eyes he'd ever seen. 'Your name is Luke, dear, isn't that right?' she'd said directly to him.

He'd stared across the room at her, unable to reply. Then she'd muttered something incomprehensible, but after that she spoke quite lucidly and clearly.

'I've got someone here to speak to you,' she'd said. 'She says her name is Helen... and I really think she's trying to reach out to you... and to someone called Amy too. Do either of those names mean anything to you, dear?'

And in that single moment, everything changed.

* * *

Soon, far too soon for Luke's liking, their little gathering broke up, with cheery promises from Will, hipster-guy himself, that, 'we look forward to seeing you all next week – as you've all seen for yourselves, anything and everything can happen here at our little Bereavement Cafe. Don't forget to leave those email addresses, people! And who knows? If we're all very good, Maybe Mildred and Dee will spoil us rotten with more of their gorgeous cakes!'

Spoken like a true kids' TV host, Luke thought irrationally. Jesus Christ. Cake. Was that all this guy could think about? His dead wife's spirit, if you believed in that kind of thing, had possibly tried to reach out to him and this fella seriously was all about cake?

After Lucasta had spoken Helen's name, and for the rest of the evening, Luke had stared at her fixatedly, itching for the chance to get a bit of one-on-one time with her. Not much chance of that though. No sooner had she looked at Luke and said Helen's name – literally, no sooner had she spoken the words – than the flood-gates seemed to open. All of a sudden the chat in that little coffee shop went to almost deafening levels and, in spite of Lucasta pleading with them all to be quiet so she could tune in, there was no hope. Instead, she looked across the room at Luke and shrugged her shoulders, as if to say, *No chance now. Sorry.*

Luke sat there, poleaxed with shock. How would this total stranger have known the names Helen or Amy? There was absolutely no rational explanation for it, none whatsoever. He sat there, dumbstruck and madly trying to process it all as the chat around him meandered on. Since Lucasta had spoken, the conversations certainly had become deeper and far more interesting too. Whether Luke believed it or not, it seemed that signs from the dead were quite the thing.

'With me, it's my phone,' one of the young twins said, Lucy, the more likeable one, who sat in the middle of the room in her school uniform and who had seemed so engaged with the whole evening. 'Sometimes the home screen on my phone just freezes on me – but the weird thing is that it's always on a photo with my dad in it. Just today, it froze on a photo of me, Alex, Mum and Dad on the last Christmas we ever had as a family before he died. It's not even that special a photo, it's a selfie Mum insisted on taking of us all playing this Sherlock Holmes board game we used to love. It's just – we're all laughing and... happy. Do you remember, Alex?'

She turned back to her twin, who was still sitting on the floor over by the window, still with her phone glued to her hands. Alex looked up with dead eyes, but, just for a moment, Luke thought there was something there, a flicker of... something. Interest? The urge to join in and maybe share something of her own? But then the barriers came down just as fast and, with a dismissive eye roll, she went back to that bloody phone.

The 'sharing' was coming thick and fast now, from all sides. It seemed as though the whole room wanted to get a word in as they battled it out for airtime.

'Funny you're talking about your phone, because with me it's electrical things too... Lights in my house keep coming on and off in rooms I'm not even in...'

'My laptop sometimes freezes on an image of my late husband... God, he was so handsome! At first I found it upsetting, but now I feel like he's trying to get through to me somehow... It's kind of comforting in a weird way...'

'I keep hearing my sister's favourite songs on the radio... She was an eighties kid, and literally every time I turn it on, I can guarantee I'll hear early Madonna or The Cure, sometimes The

Clash… which always makes me think of her… I'm sad of course, but it brings up lovely memories of her…'

Meanwhile Luke tried to get a word in. He had to. He couldn't not. He waved his hand in the air for ages till Will eventually spotted him and opened up the floor to him.

'Thanks for letting me talk,' he began tentatively. 'The thing is, I have a question for Lucasta if that's OK.'

'Of course, dearie,' Lucasta said, seemingly fully back to herself now, with no eye-rolling or mumbling or anything scary. 'Fire away.'

'You mentioned two names, both of which mean everything to me. Might I ask if you're hearing anything else? Is there more?'

A silence fell and it was as if he heard the words leaving his own lips. Had he seriously asked this batty old lady who was hearing voices if she by any chance had another message for him? Before setting foot in this place, he'd have laughed at the very notion.

Lucasta looked across the room at him, deep in ponderous thought.

'No, my love,' she said firmly. 'I'm afraid not. At least, not now. But then that's the thing about the spirit world, they tune in and out and I need to concentrate extremely hard so I can pick up anything at all. I do most definitely think that you and I should come back here next week though. Don't you?'

Not long after, Will called the meeting to an end and suddenly everyone was gathering themselves up to go. Not Luke though. Instead he sat there, trying to make sense of it all. He wasn't sure what had gone on here tonight, but something had most definitely happened.

'So what did you think?'

He looked up to see Miss Mackey standing in front of him,

pulling on the neat jacket of her khaki trouser suit and looking down at him.

'I don't know,' he said truthfully, unable to move. 'I honestly don't know what to think.'

'Common enough reaction to your first visit.' She nodded. 'But are you glad you came?'

He just looked up at her. No words would come. None.

'Till next week, then,' she said gently, then turned on her heel and was gone.

11

CONNIE

It's cheaper than therapy, Connie told herself. *Here I am, hearing voices from an ancient mobile phone – clearly all the grief and stress and pressure I'm under is leading to some kind of mental breakdown and I badly need to talk it through with someone. Anyone who'll fecking listen to me.*

Seeing a grief counsellor, she knew of old, cost anything from €70 upwards, depending on the therapist you went to see. And she didn't have it, simple as that. Not only was she big, fat unemployed, but after her self-tape disaster that week, it was highly unlikely that Pearl Hamilton, by far the most influential casting agent in town, would give her the time of day from hereon in.

This is starting to get seriously scary, Connie thought, panic rising in her every time a new household bill plopped onto the doormat, or she had to do a supermarket shop. Because if work didn't start to come in, she'd have to swallow her pride and ask – no, beg – for any kind of job anywhere. Stacking shelves in Tesco, waitressing, anything just to make ends meet, at least till the house could be sold.

But that was the very least of her worries. Because it

happened again. Beginning that very night, when she was invited to a production of *Hamlet* at the national theatre in Dublin for the opening night. One of those cutting-edge, zany, off-beat 'out there' productions with gender- and colour-blind casting, the cast in modern dress and, for some reason, the entire production set in a carnival theme park, with an actual carousel onstage, as well as bumper cars and slot machines. Which of course meant that the cast had to leap and bounce all over a pretend-y funfair for the full duration of the three-and-a-half-hour show. One of Connie's pals was in the production, a hugely gifted actor called Simon Yeates, but, although she'd auditioned for it herself and given it her all, she'd got absolutely nowhere.

'*So* sorry about this, Connie,' an assistant director, who looked as if she'd barely left school, had explained to her on the day she'd been called in for an audition. 'But it's your age, you see. You're early thirties, so you're too old for Ophelia and too young for Gertrude. Just age, that's it. Nothing to do with you as an actor at all!' Then, with a fake smile, she'd added, 'We love you here, you know that. Love your work, can't wait for you to join our team, just as soon as the right part comes along. So best of luck and close the door on your way out, will you? Thanks so much.'

'But if the production is gender-blind,' Connie had tried to argue at the time, 'then can't I read for some of the men's parts?' Why she'd bothered arguing she wasn't sure, because with this particular casting department, she'd never got anywhere anyway. They were always lovely to her face, but never, ever gave her jobs. 'Maybe Horatio?' she'd suggested bravely. 'Or either Rosencrantz or Guildenstern?'

'Mmm, no, don't think so,' came the response, polite, professional, but very, very firm. 'How do I say this without causing offence? You're just not the *right fit* for this. Hope you'll come and see the show though, we really appreciate your support!'

So come the opening night, there Connie was, sitting in row three with one of her best pals, Mbeki, who'd also auditioned for the show, but again without success. They were both considerably cheered up by the overwhelming buzz and the sense of excitement that seemed to fill the whole theatre. The great and the good had gathered for the big night, the audience was distinctly celeb-heavy and, from where they were sitting, you could spot a daytime TV presenter, a runner-up from last year's *Love Island*, a bona fide movie star who was rumoured to be in town on a location shoot, and three very well-known legends of the Irish and international theatre scene, who Connie was far more excited about seeing in the flesh than any amount of TV stars.

It was a glittering occasion and it seemed as if the whole of the national theatre was packed to the gills. This particular production of *Hamlet* was their centrepiece for the entire summer season and audience expectations were sky-high. Not only that, but Simon had been cast in the pivotal role of Laertes, a huge break for him, and to cheer him on was the main reason Connie and Mbeki were there in the first place. He'd insisted on getting them the tickets for the big night and had even invited them to the after-show cast and crew party, which, of course, they were up to high doh with excitement over.

'Let's just forget that either of us auditioned.' Mbeki beamed cheerfully, but then Mbeki was one of those people who was never down, ever. 'Let's put it to the back of our minds that one of us could have been up there with Simon, on the brink of a huge career break. Let's just cheer him on every step of the way and make sure we all have a great night out afterwards.'

'Best idea I've heard all day.' Connie grinned back at her. 'It's terrific that at least one of our gang got cast in such a huge show. And I don't know about you,' she added cheekily, 'but I fully intend to enjoy every moment of the after-show party.'

'You said it.' Mbeki laughed as the lights began to dim and an authoritative voice welcomed patrons to the national theatre and reminded them to switch off all mobile phones. 'After three and a half hours of blank verse, we sure as hell will have earned several very large glasses of vino.'

Connie settled into her seat. This was her first big night out since her mum's funeral and it felt so good to be there, among her friends, her colleagues, her 'tribe'. The show took off at a cracking speed and she was loving every minute of it. The first and second interval had come and gone and she'd barely even noticed the time passing. Because Simon was brilliant. Simon was on fire. All around them, you could hear audience members raving about him, wondering who this hot young newcomer was.

'Newcomer?' Connie whispered to Mbeki as the pair retook their seats for the third and final act. 'Simon's fifteen years in this business – that's even longer than me!'

The show had already run for longer than three hours, and, feeling exhausted but exhilarated, they settled down, full of anticipation for the battle scenes, yet more soliloquies and Simon's biggest moment of the whole play, the epic sword fight still to come. Time whizzed by and you could have heard a pin drop as Laertes and Hamlet finally locked swords. The King and Queen were already dead, the body count was high and after such a long, emotional, exhausting show, now all you could hear was the sharp clink of metal clanging off metal.

Until a phone rang. Loud and clear, fully audible throughout the whole auditorium. There were more than a few exasperated 'tsk tsks' from all sides as Connie and Mbeki turned to look at each other in horror as if to say, 'Bloody hell, right in the middle of Simon's moment of glory?'

It kept on ringing. And ringing. Faintly at first, but clearly whoever it belonged to hadn't made the obligatory mortified deep-dive into their bag to try to silence it. The cast battled on, even though there was no way they didn't hear it the same as everyone else.

And then a slow, vomit-making realisation began to dawn on Connie.

Oh, dear God, no, she thought as the penny finally dropped that the sound was coming from somewhere very close to her. Dangerously close. Like, from the handbag she'd abandoned on the floor at the very start of this act. Moving slowly, in utter shock she fumbled around for it, zipped open the bag and, sure enough, there it was. That infamous Nokia brick-sized phone that she'd taken to carrying everywhere with her, like a kind of talisman, its tortured ringtone squawking away. Mbeki was staring at her in panic and, from all around, faces were turning to her in disgust.

'For God's sake, will you switch it off?' Mbeki whispered, as the cast onstage valiantly struggled on.

Trembling, Connie grasped the phone in sticky, sweaty hands, her mind in a boiling panic. 'I'm so sorry,' she said to Mbeki, pushing madly at buttons on the keypad, anything to stop that awful ringing noise. It was pitch dark though, and she couldn't see what she was doing, so still the bloody thing kept on ringing. It had gone beyond an irritation now, and more people were glaring at her murderously. Connie rose to get the hell out of there, squeezing her way past people's legs, still punching wildly at buttons on the phone, anything to make that horrible noise stop.

'You can't leave!' she heard Mbeki saying to her, sotto voce.

She was aware of filthy looks zooming her way from all sides as, somehow, she made it to the end of the row and stumbled her way up the sloping aisle towards the blessed relief of the emergency exit.

'Will you kindly switch your phone off?' an usher caught up with her to fume in her ear. 'You're causing a huge disturbance!' Too late though. Somehow, she hadn't the first clue how, Connie managed to wrench the emergency exit open and was just stepping out into the bright lights of the main foyer when, finally, she found the right button to press to answer the bloody thing once and for all.

'Hello?' she whispered shakily down the phone, as soon as she'd made it to the peace and quiet of the bar area, where staff were busy setting up glasses for the post-show drinks party.

The usher, who by then was red-faced and incandescent with rage, had followed her and was standing right in front of her with his arms folded and his face thunderous.

'I do not believe this,' he said to one of his colleagues who'd come over to see what was going on. 'First, she lets her phone ring during the most pivotal moment of the whole play, then she comes out here to answer it? If I had my way, people like that should be banned from the theatre, full stop.'

'I really am so sorry,' Connie stammered at them both, utterly mortified. 'I can't explain...' Then she pressed the phone to her ear. And there it was. That voice. Again.

'Well, that was... interesting, I suppose,' her mum said, instantly sending a familiar chill down Connie's spine.

'Mum? Is that you?' she replied stupidly, her logical mind saying, who else did you think it was going to be?

'A call from her mother,' the usher was bitching about her in the background. 'Now I've heard it all. She ruins the whole last act of the show on the opening night to take a call from her mother? Seriously?'

Yet Connie's mum kept on talking. Loud and clear, as if she were in the room with them.

'Now, Connie, love, I mean, nothing against your nice friend Simon, who's very good in the play, I grant you,' she was saying, 'but, honest to God, that show is so, so long. And it's still not even over! To be honest, I think I'd have preferred to stay in and watch the telly tonight. If it's all the same with you, the next time you're going to the theatre, then how about a decent comedy instead? Can't remember the last time I had a good laugh.'

* * *

The following morning, Connie found herself sitting at her kitchen table, still in her dressing gown and with a mug of coffee in hand, this time taking a very serious look at the A4 sheet of paper that Kate had insisted on leaving for her the previous day. She read it carefully. Reread it. Wavered. Thought about it a bit more.

Feck it, she thought. *I have to do something. I can't go on as I am. I need help.* She'd made a holy, mortifying show of herself the previous night. Throughout the after-show party, all she could hear were snippets of chat among the great and the good, including actors and directors she admired and respected: 'Can you believe some idiot let their mobile ring during the most critical bit of the whole show? And then left the auditorium to go and answer it? Honestly, some people!'

Even Mbeki had words with her, albeit gentle ones.

'I know you're going through a lot,' she'd said to Connie as the pair of them had worked their way through the throng to queue up at the bar for drinks. 'And that forgetting to switch your phone off is something I'm sure you didn't do on purpose. But leaving the theatre to take the call? Seriously, Connie? What is going on with you?'

'I know, and I'm so sorry,' was all Connie could say, grateful for two things in that exact moment. That the darkness in the auditorium meant no one had recognised her, and that Simon had been so immersed in his epic sword fight that, as he'd said afterwards, he'd been aware of a disturbance in the audience, but not that one of his best friends was the cause of it.

'If I could explain it to you, I would,' she'd added as Mbeki had looked back at her, real concern written on her face. 'But I just can't. You'd have me put away if I told you what was really going on.'

In the bright, warm summery sunshine of the following day, however, Connie was beginning to see things more clearly. She was still rooted to her kitchen table with the famous Nokia phone clamped to her hands, as it had been for most of the previous night. Just in case it rang again. Just in case it was her mother's voice again. Just in case.

Look at me, she thought. *I'm slowly cracking up here. I need to talk to someone.* Paying for a therapist was a complete non-runner. But this 'Bereavement Cafe' lark? She'd snorted at Kate for even bringing it up. Now, though, she was starting to think very differently about the whole thing. *I could ring them,* she thought. *I could find out when their next meeting is and ask if I can tag along.*

After all, she reasoned, what was the worst that could happen? For the price of a cup of coffee and maybe the chance to be told she wasn't losing her marbles? Cheap at the price.

Without a second thought, she picked up her phone and dialled the number.

12

LUCASTA

'Are you paying attention? It's important that you actually listen to me, instead of drifting off like you usually do. And then informing me that you're bored.'

'Of course I'm paying attention, Phoebe, you goose. Impossible not to, isn't it? You're standing right in front of me with that ghastly spreadsheet and, might I add, you're ruining my evening tipple.'

'It's your schedule for tomorrow,' Phoebe sighed, rolling her eyes. 'And as it's going to be a full-on day, I really need your full attention, please.'

Lucasta took a long, cool, soothing sip of her gin and tonic and really tried her best to focus on what Phoebe was saying. It was damn hard to concentrate though, given that she had a thousand other, far more important thoughts converging on top of her. Worrying thoughts. Thoughts that had kept her awake long into the previous night and probably would in the night to come.

It was a warm, balmy evening and as soon as Lucasta had finished up her writing day, she'd emerged from her little garden shed looking forward to a bit of peace and a good, stiff G & T back at the main house. But then Phoebe had pounced on her, full of bossy-pants efficiency and insisting they comb through the minutiae of what lay ahead. So now the two of them were in the kitchen as Lucasta sat at the top of the table with Phoebe hovering by her shoulder, droning on with all this boring nonsense about times and schedules. Meanwhile Lucasta just sat there, petting Sausage, who clearly wanted to go for walkies, and wishing dear old Phoebe would go home for the evening, so she'd have the house to herself to think clearly. Properly.

Small chance of that though. The following day, the two of them were due to travel to a book festival all the way down in County Kerry, a wonderful part of the country and one Lucasta and Johnnie had always adored visiting together. Phoebe was nothing if not thorough though, and was point-blank refusing to leave until they'd been back and forth over the day ahead, like an army sergeant-major drilling schedules into lowly cadets who were only half listening.

'So we'll be leaving here at 7 a.m. sharp,' she was saying, harking back to those wretched spreadsheets she was so fond of.

'So early?' Lucasta piped up. 'You know me, dear. I'm absolutely no use at all until I'm on my second mug of coffee.'

'It's a four-and-a-half-hour drive to Ballybunion,' Phoebe answered primly, 'so you can have your coffee in the car and be ready to leave bang on the dot, please. You're the guest speaker at the festival, so the very least you can do is be punctual. We've got to be there extra early because you've got a lunch with the organisers beforehand, which I've allowed two hours for. And no alcohol, please.'

'Like hell,' Lucasta muttered, but Phoebe overrode her.

'Your event is scheduled for 3 p.m. and the good news is that it's already a sell-out with a long cancellation list. The event will be recorded too, which of course means your hair and make-up will need to be particularly well attended to,' she added pointedly.

'Hair and make-up?' Lucasta snorted into her gin. 'Nonsense. I'll splash some cold water on my face in the morning as I always do and they can take me as they find me.'

Phoebe shook her head, but said nothing, sensing where and when to choose her battles.

'Rex Clarke from Channel Six will be interviewing you,' she went on, 'and his researcher will need to brief you thoroughly beforehand.'

'Rex Clarke?' Lucasta perked up momentarily. 'Oh, I'm glad, such a delightful young man. A genuine book lover too, you know. Last time he interviewed me, he told me that he'd read every single line I've written, ever since he was a teenager. Wonderful to hear. It's all about being relevant to a younger generation these days, you know.'

'As I was saying,' Phoebe harped on, still glued to those ghastly, never-ending spreadsheets, 'I've allowed ninety minutes for your conversation with Rex, plus a thirty-minute Q and A with the audience afterwards. Then I've scheduled a meet and greet with your readers and fans immediately after your event. Lastly, you're expected to go up to the main house for dinner and then stay overnight. As you can see, it's a full-on day, so you should try to get a good night's rest. You need to be firing on all cylinders tomorrow.'

The Mount Herbert book festival was one Lucasta took part in annually and, normally, one she would greatly look forward to. It took place in the grounds of a glorious old stately home and the family who ran it, the Herberts, were an utter delight. Every single one of them was completely bonkers, which suited Lucasta down to the ground, but then people with slightly different reference points from everyone else were her very favourite type.

The Herberts were passionate about books and reading and best of all was that Lucasta was always invited to spend the night as their guest in their stately home, which was a particular high point that she and Johnnie would look forward to.

Not that the house was grand, not at all. It dated from the early eighteenth century and, although it was stunningly impressive to look at from the outside, as soon as you got inside, you could see that the entire house was held up by the wallpaper. The whole place stank of damp, there was zero heating to speak of and if it rained, saucepans had to be dotted about the floors to catch the water. Not that Lucasta cared about any of that nonsense in the slightest. What intrigued her was that the house had a wonderfully benign spirit presence – the whole place was positively alive with the ghosts of all those wonderful Herbert ancestors. Many's the ectoplasmic manifestation she'd witnessed there over the years, to her great delight and Johnnie's amusement.

Normally Lucasta would be brimming with excitement about what the following day would bring. Normally it would be a high point on her calendar: the thrill of meeting so many lovely old and new readers alike. Normally, that was something very dear to her heart. Events like this, she often said, were the best part of this strange and wonderful job she did for a living, no question about it.

So why was she feeling so preoccupied? she wondered, taking another sip of her G & T and wishing Phoebe would either shut up or else join her for a drinkie. Why was she so worried and concerned? The fact was that the most ghastly feeling had been hanging over her since she'd been to that 'Bereavement Cafe' place yesterday. She couldn't stop thinking about that chap who'd been there, Luke, who'd been sitting alone at the back of the room, and for whom she'd received such a clear message.

He was a widower, Lucasta had subsequently discovered when he'd sought her out after the evening had wrapped up. With a little daughter too. Sad beyond words, she thought. There was a most worrying aura from this chap too, one of deep anxiety, and stress levels that were off the charts.

'How did you *know*?' He'd come up to Lucasta, genuinely baffled. 'You said both my wife's and daughter's names so clearly, it was as if you knew them. How did you do that?'

'Oh, I can tell you, it's not some kind of party trick,' she'd rushed to reassure him. 'I only wish it were. No, this is something that I've got absolutely no control over, none at all. The spirit world just seems to use me as a sort of channel or conduit. There's no rational explanation for it. You either believe in this sort of thing, or you don't.'

Luke very definitely didn't believe it though, that much was glaringly obvious. Instead he'd just nodded, thanked her very politely and disappeared a moment later, something about the little girl who had to be collected. Such a shame, Lucasta thought. When people were so blocked and unreachable. They didn't know what they were missing and clearly his late wife, Helen, was anxious to get in touch, some way, somehow. The strength of the voice Lucasta had tuned into the previous night was quite astonishing. Spirits tuned in and out with her all the time and, as with her late husband, Johnnie, most of the time she barely batted an eyelid when it happened any more. Not this Helen though. There had been a real urgency, a strong, vital force – something Lucasta had only encountered very rarely.

At the crack of dawn the following day, and during the whole drive to Kerry, she was still preoccupied with worry over this Luke fellow. She just couldn't stop thinking about him. Even Phoebe remarked on how quiet she was.

'Not like you to have unspoken thoughts,' as she put it, in her own Phoebe-like way, as she pulled into the Barack Obama Plaza for a little pit stop. 'Normally, it's hard to get you to shut up for two seconds together. Anyway, come on. I've scheduled exactly ten minutes here for something to eat, so let's get going, please.'

'Hmm?' said Lucasta distractedly. 'What did you say, dear?'

'Brekkie and an Americano?' Phoebe offered. 'You haven't had breakfast and on a day like this, I strongly suggest you keep your strength up.'

'Oh... emm... no, thank you, all the same,' Lucasta said, still utterly lost in thought. 'Not now, I just need to... think clearly, that's all.'

'Then I suggest you think about your copy-edit deadline.' Phoebe sniffed, unstrapping herself to get out of the car. 'I drew up a schedule for that too and you're already well behind on it. There's much to catch up on when we get you home.'

'Oh, must you nag, dear?' Lucasta said. 'I really do need quiet time and you're giving me the most dreadful headache.'

Phoebe sighed and left her in peace, but still nothing would distract Lucasta from the cloud of worry that hung over her.

Hours later, when they finally pulled up though the imposing gates of the Mount Herbert estate and when the event organisers emerged from tents scattered around the grounds to welcome her, she was perfectly polite. She smiled, she shook every hand, she told them all how very happy she was to be back again. She put on a jolly good show and possibly Phoebe was the only one who might have sensed that something was amiss.

The time for the book event came. Rex Clarke bounced out onstage and it took him several attempts before he could calm the crowds down, such were the fever-pitch levels of excitement in the main marquee.

'I know you're all thrilled to be here today,' he began, expertly building up the anticipation, 'for what's surely the hottest ticket going in the entire book festival. Well let me tell you, she's here, she's in the house and she's backstage right now, dying to meet all of you too. So without further ado, please give a warm welcome to a true icon of the Irish book world, a legendary figure both here and overseas, whose novels regularly sell over a million copies and whose books have inspired no fewer than five academy-award-winning movies, fourteen hit TV shows, three online series, eighteen plays with five Tony awards between them, and a record twenty-nine book awards over the decades. Ladies and gentlemen, here she is, the doyenne of the Irish fiction scene, a real living, breathing national treasure, please give a warm welcome to one of my very favourite guests, the one and only Lucasta Liversidge!'

The applause was thunderous, off the scale and normally Lucasta would have been lapping up every moment. Normally she'd have been twittering about, flirting shamelessly with the crew backstage and knocking back a pre-show G & T as a hairdresser wrestled to comb her hair and the sound people struggled to get her attached to one of those dreadful radio mic thingies.

But today, she was like a different person. Instead, she slipped out onto the stage quietly, giving a tiny little wave to the audience, who cheered raucously back at her, then she shook hands with Rex, who kissed her fondly on each cheek, before taking her seat. The two had done many interviews together in the past and he'd always been so friendly and warm to her during the long, meandering chats they had on his prime-time radio show. Rex was young, late thirties, but still baby-faced and so passionate about his work and, above all, his guests that it was generally impossible not to get swept up in all of that youthful enthusiasm.

Not this evening though. While Lucasta smiled as best she could both at him and at the packed audience, she most definitely was not at the races. She was edgy, tense and with the most splitting headache she'd been nursing all day and for most of the previous night too – in fact since she'd been to the Bereavement Cafe.

Oh, do snap out of it, she lectured herself sharply, stealing a quick glance out into the audience at all the eager, hopeful, happy faces smiling back at her. *Look at all these lovely people who've made the effort to come out today, just to listen to you warble on, you big goose. You've got a duty to perform for them, to entertain them and hopefully send them home intending to read everything they possibly can, not just by you, but by any other author they can get their paws on too. So, as Johnnie used to say, get on with it and cop the hell on!*

The marquee was packed to the gills and it seemed as if everyone there was gaping back at her, beaming in the full expectation of being royally entertained. Lucasta had a reputation for being effortlessly funny in interviews, and the fact that she came without any kind of filter whatsoever delighted people the world over. Rex's preamble all done, he shushed the audience, and launched into his very first question. Lucasta could feel the audience's anticipation, which was already sky-high and mounting, as the whole marquee dutifully hushed down.

'Look at you.' Rex beamed admiringly at her, like an adoring grandson chatting to his granny. '*The* Lucasta Liversidge, a true legend. Many readers are familiar with your career, but can I begin by asking, how did it all start? Am I right in thinking that at one point, many, many years ago, your life might easily have taken a very different turn?'

But just as he posed the question, the killer headache Lucasta had been battling all day suddenly became excruciating, almost blinding. The lights that were beaming straight into her face were only making it worse.

'Oh yes, indeed,' she heard herself saying, trying her best to smile at him even though her voice sounded as if it were coming from another room. 'You see, when I first left a rather fancy Swiss finishing school that my parents had sent me to – utter waste of money, if you ask me – all I really wanted to do was be a journalist.'

'Why was that?' Rex probed.

'Well, you know, people assume it was for all manner of altruistic reasons, bringing hard news to readers and giving them the truth, all of that, but actually it wasn't at all. I thought it would be a very jolly way to travel the world and to meet nice men,' Lucasta said truthfully, to big laughs from the audience.

'So at the tender age of twenty you managed to land a job as the features editor at the *Daily Chronicle*. Tell us a little about that.'

'Oh, the *Chronicle* was terrific back then, I did adore it. Every journalist kept a small bottle of gin in their desks, you know. It was far too civilised for words.'

'But then is it fair to say you had a bit of a run-in with senior staff?'

'To put it mildly,' Lucasta said, rubbing her temples to try to ease the acute throbbing and hoping no one would notice. 'But then I was sent to interview a very well-established movie actor who had just starred in one of those terribly tedious "swords and sandals" films that were all the go back in the sixties. Something about gladiators in the Roman Empire and slaves and, oh, dearie me, it was hours too long and far too boring for words. Even though the whole ghastly thing was widely tipped for Oscars.'

More titters from the audience as Rex ploughed on.

'So what happened?'

Lucasta launched into a story she'd told a thousand times before, sensing the audience would have expected no less of her than to be funny and self-deprecating and, at all costs, never, ever boring. Even though she felt wretched and now, for some godawful reason, the whole room was beginning to sway in and out of focus. It was nauseating, the pain was unbearable, but somehow she willed herself to go on.

'Well, he hit on me, you see,' she said to Rex, 'as I believe all the young ones say now. Locked me into his hotel suite, pinched me on the arse, and tried it on in a perfectly shameless way. As if the old perv had some sort of *droit de seigneur* over me, just because I was young and he was famous. Well, I was having absolutely none of it, so I kneed him in the goolies then leapt out of a balcony window, screaming for all I was worth. And then instead of writing a gushing, adoring piece about how wonderful this big movie star was, I wrote – and published – the unvarnished truth. Which did *not* go down well with my editor, let me tell you. He fired me on the spot.'

Gasps from around the audience, so Lucasta turned to speak to them directly.

'Oh, my darlings,' she said, trying her best to sound coherent, given that she actually felt like passing out. 'You must understand, these were very different times. This was in the sixties, when feminism and women's rights were in their infancy. The most dreadful things went on – which makes me so grateful for the wonderful Me Too movement we see happening now. I applaud the brave women who've brought this about, and I'd urge you all to keep up the terrific work.'

There was a thunderous round of applause at that, but then just as Rex was about to launch into another question, it came over her. The exact same sensation she'd had in the cafe. It was the most extraordinary thing imaginable and although Lucasta willed herself not to succumb, not now, not here – she knew she was wasting her time. She was utterly helpless.

Suddenly she couldn't hear a single thing, just a loud high-pitched ringing noise in her ear. She wasn't aware of it but, at the very same time, her head began to loll uncontrollably from side to side as her eyes rolled to the back of her head. Dimly, from miles away, she was vaguely aware of Rex asking her something, she couldn't hear what though. It sounded like gibberish, almost as if this respected Channel Six presenter were speaking in tongues. A second later she was lifeless and limp and utterly powerless to stop whatever was happening to her.

And then that voice came to her again. Just the same as before. A gentle, clear, soft voice, speaking slowly but with far more urgency this time. *You're getting stronger,* Lucasta thought through the semi-hypnotic trance she'd slumped into.

'Lucasta?' she could have sworn she heard Rex saying to her, sounding as if he were miles away. 'Are you still with me?' Then her eyes rolled out over the audience, but instead of gazing up at her adoringly, now the expressions on all their faces had changed. Dimly, from the part of her brain that was still conscious, she could read anxiousness on some faces, worry on others, with some gaping up at her in absolute horror. Lucasta Liversidge passing out live onstage? This was most definitely not what any of them had bargained for.

Last thing, right before she went under, she caught Phoebe's eye backstage, lean and pale and with a horrified look on her face that said it all.

Not this. Not now. Not again.

'Hello?' Rex was saying, looking at her, white-faced. 'Lucasta, are you OK?' Then, twisting to the wings, he said, 'Can someone help her, please? Can someone get a glass of water? She's not well.'

Phoebe strode out onto the stage, trying to calm everyone

down. 'Nothing to worry about,' she was saying, 'and nothing to see here. She's quite well, I assure you. This will pass, trust me.'

Lucasta was dimly aware of her body being lifted by what felt like burly men, stage crew, she assumed. 'Get her backstage, get her to a dressing room where she can lie flat. And for God's sake, someone ring an ambulance!' one of them said to no one in particular.

'*No*, there's no need!' Phoebe was protesting, but by then it was too late.

'There you are now,' Lucasta muttered to herself, as she could finally hear the new spirit who clearly needed her help – badly. 'Speak to me. How can I help you? What do you need from me?'

It's Helen here. You've got to help me. You're the only one I can ask. It's Luke and it's Amy. They need me and I'm stuck here and I don't know what to do. Or who else to turn to.

And then, nothing – as Lucasta passed out, lost into sweet, delicious oblivion.

13

LUKE

'Hope you don't mind me interrupting you,' said Nick, a young, up-and-coming architect at Luke's office. Nick was ruthlessly ambitious, driven and, as far as Luke was concerned, an obnoxious pain in the arse who spent most of his time snapping at Luke's heels, almost willing himself into his job.

Momentarily, Luke looked up from his desk, where he'd been beavering away all morning, ever since he'd dropped Amy off at school. He'd had feck all sleep the previous night and had been up since 5 a.m. working from home, so he was shattered and the very last person he was in the mood for now was Nick.

'Something up?' he asked as politely as he could, even managing a terse smile.

'Yeah, no, it's just that I noticed you were using the photocopier for something you're working on,' Nick said, shifting awkwardly from one foot to another, 'and I think you left this behind.' At that, he held up a few sheets of A4 paper, covered in notes and numbers and figures. 'Couldn't help noticing what it is – it looks to me like a draft of the costings pitch for the McKinsey project,' he added.

'Thanks,' said Luke, pointedly grabbing back the sheets he'd stupidly left lying inside the photocopier. But Nick still wasn't budging.

'Course, I didn't mean to look, man—' he half laughed '—but just so you know? Already I've spotted two miscalculations. You've underestimated the number of joists we're going to need and I think you're miscalculating some of the insulation costs on the basement floors too.'

He said it casually, almost lightly, as if it were perfectly normal office behaviour for a newly qualified architect with virtually zero experience to start pointing out a minor slip-up his project manager had made – someone with almost two decades more experience than him.

Luke's jaw clenched and it was a real effort not to bite the little shit's head off. *Oh, yeah? Way to watch my back, you little prick,* he wanted to yell at him. He pulled himself together though, reminded himself of just how dispensable he was in this job and somehow managed to hold onto a professional tone of voice.

'Thanks for pointing that out, Nick,' he replied curtly. 'As you can appreciate, though, this is still very much a work in progress. It's not a final draft by any means.'

He'd only said that to save face, though. The fact was, this *was* his final draft and a quick glance down at the A4 sheet Nick handed over confirmed that, yes, indeed, he had made two pretty glaring mistakes. Stupid errors that he'd have been hauled over the coals for. A result of extreme tiredness bordering on exhaustion – there was no other reason for it.

The fact was, though, ever since Luke had that unsettling experience at the Bereavement Cafe, he'd hardly slept a wink. Well, how could he possibly? How could anyone after something like that? His mind was chock-a-block and even concentrating on work was a major challenge. For the past few nights, as soon as he had Amy happily in bed and sleeping soundly, he'd taken to spending hours and hours online, looking up anything and everything he could about the notion of signs from the afterlife.

Just look at yourself, he'd thought. *If anyone saw me, I'd be locked away*. The whole thing was a load of hokum, of course it was, there was no other possible explanation for it. Luke had never been religious and not for two seconds did he believe that his late wife's spirit was trying to contact him from some kind of spirit plane. It was complete bollocks. He'd just wanted it confirmed, that was all.

'Hey, no worries, buddy,' Nick said breezily, shoving his hands deep into his pockets and rocking back and forth on his feet. 'We all know you're going through a lot in your personal life right now and I'm here to help any time. You can trust me.'

'Cheers, Nick, but everything is well under control here, thanks.'

So you can go back to spying on me behind my back and the best of luck to you.

Nick still wouldn't budge though. 'Can I ask what you're working on right now?' he asked. 'Because if it's costings, then maybe I can give you a hand?' he added, sneaking a quick look over Luke's shoulder at the screen of his desktop computer.

Fuck it, Luke thought, not able to click off the page he'd been on quickly enough. Too late for that. Nick had already seen quite enough and, predictably, was straight in to remark on it.

'Jeez, man, what was that?' Nick half laughed. 'Are you by any chance looking up something about the occult there? Did I see something about seances?'

'No, absolutely not,' Luke quickly replied, punching at keys in a panic until he'd wiped the page and brought back up the costings database.

'Because that's what it looked like to me,' Nick persisted. 'I could have sworn I saw something about spirit guides and the dead trying to contact you.'

Which, no doubt, you'll have spread all over the office in the space of about twenty minutes, you little shit.

'Oh, that?' Luke said, cursing the fact that he was no actor and was rubbish at trying to worm his way out of awkward situations. 'That's just something that my daughter is working on for a school project that I was printing off for her, that's all.' *Nothing to see here, so piss off, why don't you?*

'Oh, yeah?' Nick said, folding his arms, seemingly determined to pick holes wherever he could. 'Thought your kid was only about six or seven and still in primary school. Stuff about the occult is a bit advanced for kids that age, I'd have thought?'

'Well, you're not a parent, are you?' Luke tried to smile and seem friendly and professional, but this fecker was so bloody persistent it was a real struggle to be civil. *So please, will you just get lost?* He wanted to snap at him.

'Course, sure, man, didn't mean to interrupt you.' Nick shrugged. 'But just so you know, I'm here if you need me.'

'Don't you worry, I'm well aware of that,' Luke muttered darkly as Nick finally peeled himself away. Feck it anyway. He'd been working around the clock, day and night, on those costings and had literally just taken his eye off the ball for a minute, no more than that.

The fact was, he couldn't put what had happened the other night out of his mind, try as he might. That batty novelist old lady with the made-up-sounding name, Lucasta whoever it was, had sounded so sure and certain when she came out with the names Helen and Amy. How could she possibly have known those names were so significant to him? There must have been some kind of trick to it, there was no other possible explanation.

The website that Nick had spotted him on was interesting and one he'd get back to when he had a bit of peace and privacy. It was all about how easy it was to 'lead' people at seances. How a skilled scammer could get a 'read' on a person just by looking at him. There were all sorts of tells they could then throw back at you, purely by taking note of the way you spoke, dressed and behaved around other people. We were all giving away information about ourselves without even realising it, which made life easy for complete chancers like Lucasta to hoodwink you into thinking whatever they wanted. In Luke's case, that his dead wife was trying to reach out to him.

He'd been googling this Lucasta Liversidge too. There were literally thousands of entries for her; it seemed she wasn't just famous nationally, but was something of a global superstar in the publishing world, even if Luke hadn't the first clue about her. The woman even appeared on Ireland's Rich List. So why had she set out to hoodwink Luke? Why would she be bothered doing something like that in the first place? What was in it for her? Even if she'd looked him up and read Helen's death notice online, she'd had no possible way of knowing Luke would pitch up at the cafe the other night.

It was weird and it made no sense and Luke really hated things that made no sense. He sat back and rubbed his eyes wearily just in time to spot Nick over by the Nespresso machine, deep in huddled conversation with two other junior colleagues. They were all looking over his way, but when he glanced up at them, they quickly looked away.

Yup, Luke thought, *I was right.* He glanced down at his watch. Three minutes. That was how long it took for Nick to start spreading it around the office that he was losing it.

A record, even for a dickhead like Nick.

* * *

Later that afternoon, Luke hurriedly left a site meeting out in a huge industrial estate off the M50 motorway, having made his excuses to the client, then leapt into his car, panicking that he was already late and, by the look of the traffic, would be later still. He needed to get to Amy's school, collect her, make sure that she was happy and that her day had gone well before dropping her off at his sister Clare's. Just for a few hours max, he promised himself. Then he'd hotfoot it back to the office, hopefully before anyone noticed he'd been missing, catch up on yet more project deadlines, then finally, finally, finally zip back to Clare's to collect Amy so he could get her home to her own bed for the evening.

Poor kid, he thought, being passed from one carer to another, day in and day out. Then he sighed deeply and dabbed away beads of sweat on his forehead as his car ground to a halt in bumper-to-bumper gridlocked traffic. Why was his life like this, he wondered for about the thousandth time, when he was only trying to do his best? When was he ever going to get a bit of quality time with his little girl? When was he ever going to get quality time, full stop?

It was as if he were stuck on this ridiculous hamster wheel: get up, then get Amy up in the morning. Get her breakfasted, washed and into school, then work, work, work at the office, then collect Amy, spend maybe twenty minutes in her company on the drive to Clare's if he was very lucky, then zip back to work, where he'd chain himself to his desk till it was finally time to collect Amy for the evening. Then he'd play with her, providing the poor child wasn't too banjaxed, then bathtime, bedtime, before heading straight back to his desk at home till he was falling asleep. Literally.

More than once, he'd actually woken from a deep sleep with

a sharp jolt, only to find himself still fully dressed and crashed out over his desk, surrounded by his laptop, notes and mounds of architectural drawings that were acting like a kind of pillow. Never enough time with Amy and never enough time to keep up with all the pressures of his job either. It was starting to give him chest pains when he was only trying to do his best by everyone and somehow keep the show on the road.

Way past school collection time, he finally got to the school gates, where he saw the heartbreaking sight of a white-faced Amy holding Stella Mackey by the hand, the very last child to be collected. He double-parked outside, leapt out of the car and raced over to the pair of them, brimming over with apologies.

'Miss Mackey, please forgive me for being late,' he almost tripped himself up saying, before turning to Amy. 'Hey, sweetheart,' he said, bending down to give her a kiss. 'I'm so sorry I'm late. Silly Daddy got held up at work.'

Amy said nothing and barely even looked up at him. Normally her whole face would light up whenever she saw him; she'd rush over to him and give him a big, warm hug, which quite literally was one of the best moments in his whole day. Now though, she just picked up her bright pink schoolbag from the ground and automatically made for her booster seat in the back of the car, without uttering a single word. *She's sulking with me,* he thought. And this was a child who never, ever sulked.

Cursing that it was Stella Mackey here and not Amy's class teacher instead, Luke turned his full attention back to her. 'I can't apologise to you enough,' he said respectfully. 'I was at a site meeting out of town and you've no idea what the traffic is like at this time of day.'

Stella didn't respond though, instead she did that thing of looking evenly at him for a moment or two before answering, 'I think you and I need to have another chat soon.'

Luke sighed. Of course, Amy and her well-being came first. It was just he had no shagging time for any of this now – none whatsoever.

'The thing is, I'm a bit snowed under with a work project,' he said politely. 'How about if I make an appointment to come in and see you in a week or two?' As if on cue, his phone rang – the office, doubtless wondering where he was and why he wasn't back from being on site yet.

But Stella Mackey was having none of it. 'This is more in the nature of an unofficial conversation,' she said, nodding over in the direction of Amy sitting waiting for her dad in the car. 'Somewhere little ears won't hear us. How about I see you at the cafe later this week for another meeting?'

'Ahh, yes, that cafe place,' Luke said, all set with his excuses. 'I'm afraid I'm not going to be able to make it this week. Or the week after either. It's a bit of a problem for me finding any time to go there at all, with everything that's going on in my life right now, you see.'

'Just remember, you're ultimately there for Amy, as well as for you,' she said firmly, looking him square in the face. 'And this is one meeting you can't be late for.'

14

CONNIE

The following Thursday, Connie stood nervously outside the cafe, drumming up the courage to go inside. It was in an area she knew well, as it happened, at the very top of Leeson Street, beside the Sweet and Salty Club, a popular spot among actors for a very late-night drink, when all the bars in town had turfed them out. But she'd never taken a good look at the inconspicuous little coffee shop with a paned-glass bay window that looked right out over the street and a discreet handwritten sign on the door saying 'Closed for private function'. A nothing-to-be-scared-about kind of place, the kind you passed in the streets a dozen times a week and you never gave a second glance to.

She texted Kate, desperate for a bit of reassurance.

They'll think I'm a right nut job

Seconds later, Kate called her back.

'Now just remember what you said yourself,' she said firmly. 'This could well turn out to be a pile of shite, but it's a helluva lot cheaper than therapy.' At least, Connie could have sworn that was what she said. In the background, her boys were playing indoor soccer and the yelling and the shrieking were at fever pitch. Connie had to shout so loudly just to thank Kate for calling, people waiting at a bus stop nearby stared over at her. She hung up, promising to ring Kate the minute she got out of there, then she patted her handbag, feeling the deep, comforting weight of the ancient Nokia phone that she was carrying around permanently with her now. Literally every place she ever went. These days she even took it to the loo just in case it might ring and she'd miss it. Just in case.

The coffee-shop door clanged open with a cute bell sound, all very retro chic, all very *Homes & Gardens* magazine. So far? Not too weird, Connie thought, slinking into a quiet seat by the door, at a discreet corner table. It looked as though she was the first here, and she was just about to start messing around with her iPhone, trying to make it look as if she were a very busy employed person with an actual job, when a guy about her own age in cargo shorts and a man-bun came out from behind the counter.

'Hey.' He smiled, coming over to her and shaking hands. 'A new face. Always great to see new faces here. You're very welcome to the Bereavement Cafe. If that doesn't sound too maudlin,' he added dryly. 'I'm Will and I run the cafe, so if there's anything you need, just holler.'

Will seemed nice and normal, Connie thought, shaking hands and smiling back up at him. So far, this was aeons from the icky experience she'd been gearing herself up for. In fact, this was no different from coming into any other ordinary coffee shop in town to meet a bunch of pals.

'I'm Connie,' she said. 'Good to meet you too. I heard about this place from a friend and just wanted to check it out for myself.'

'Not easy coming here for your first time,' he said and she smiled back, glad that he seemed to get it.

'Some people come back regularly and one or two we never see again, after their first visit,' Will chatted away amicably while Connie had a good look at him. There was a good, strong hipster vibe from this guy; the man-bun was a dead giveaway, but aside from that, he was dressed casually in a T-shirt, shorts and a barista-style apron. Man-buns were generally a tough look to pull off for any fella, in her experience, but somehow Will seemed to manage it.

'So how are you feeling?' he asked. 'Bit nervous?'

'Just a bit.' She half laughed, but the truth was she was quietly petrified, not that the Bereavement Cafe regulars wouldn't be perfectly polite and friendly, but that they'd all piss themselves laughing when they heard the real reason she was here.

'Thing to remember,' Will said warmly, 'is that an evening like this won't be to everyone's taste, but for anyone who's grieving, which is pretty much everyone you're about to meet, it can give great comfort. And sometimes one or two surprises along the way too. You've lost someone close to you, I take it?'

He looked down at her with big brown eyes and she felt she could trust him, so she nodded yes.

'My mum,' she said, with that same wobble she got in her voice every time she had to tell strangers. 'Barely two months ago, so it's all a bit... you know...'

'You don't need to tell me.' He nodded sympathetically. 'It's raw for you. It's still very early stages. But for what it's worth, I do think you've come to the right place.'

You might not say that when I start talking about the fact that my mother is ringing me on an old mobile phone.

'And just so you know,' Will added reassuringly, 'there's no rules here, no set formula that we follow every week. Everyone here has something in common, we've all lost someone very dear to us and we're here to chat about it, nothing more.' He shrugged. 'So don't be nervous, this isn't group therapy or anything like it. All we're here to do is share our experiences. Sometimes we laugh, sometimes we cry and sometimes the maddest and most unexpected things can happen. Believe you me, between all my regulars, you're going to see a huge range of grief tonight. You might well be surprised.'

'Certainly sounds intriguing,' Connie said.

'What I mean to say is, some of the stories you'll hear this evening are genuinely moving,' Will explained. 'Some are downright hilarious. And one or two might give you a bit of a shiver down your spine.'

Then, the coffee-shop door clanged open and slowly the place began to fill up.

'So what can I get you, Connie?' Will asked her, changing the subject. 'Tea? Coffee? Juices, water? No booze licence here, I'm afraid, but we've got everything else and the first drink is always on the house.'

'Hey, that's nice of you.' She smiled, slowly starting to feel a bit more confident in herself. 'Just a tea would be great, thanks.'

'Stay where you are, it's on the way,' Will said, disappearing behind the counter where a queue was starting to form. Meanwhile, Connie took the chance to have a good people-watch of everyone else who'd come in. To her surprise, they all looked relatively normal. Just like her. Ordinary people with extraordinary stories to tell. She could be in any Costa or Starbucks anywhere in the country, except that the new arrivals were all table-hopping and chatting to each other, greeting each other almost as if they were old pals meeting up.

But if Connie thought she could sit in the background nice and quietly, she was badly mistaken. Pretty soon, she was spotted.

'Oh, Dee, look!' chirruped an older lady with a big shock of white hair cut short, pointing at Connie and immediately bustling over to her. 'We have someone new here this evening, isn't that nice, now?' Hot on her heels was another woman who looked like her absolute dead ringer, right down to the cropped white hair and the red, round, smiley face. The two of them even dressed alike, in Birkenstock sandals with white ankle socks and long, loose, oversized flowery dresses in lurid colours. Sisters? Connie wondered. Whoever they were, the pair of them had quickly enveloped her, commandeering her, bending down to hug her and generally acting as if they were long-lost friends who'd known each other for decades.

'Always lovely to welcome a new face,' one of them tittered as Connie looked from one to the other, like Tweedledum and Tweedledee. 'I'm Deirdre, by the way, but everyone calls me Dee, and this is my mother, Mildred – we're long-standing regulars here, aren't we, Mother?'

Mother and daughter? Jeez, Connie thought, the pair of them looked exactly the same age. They were both carrying large serving dishes covered in tinfoil and before she knew it, they'd plonked down at her table on either side of her and were plying her with all manner of cakes and treats, talking over each other and tittering away non-stop.

'So what's your name, love?'

'I'm Connie,' she replied, with a little smile.

'Oh, we love that name! Constance. So elegant. And isn't Connie such a pretty girl, Mother?'

'She's gorgeous! I'd say you have all the young fellas chasing after you, Connie.'

'Emm... well, no, not at all actually—' Connie began to say, but they barely let her get a word in edgeways.

'Anyway, we always like to bake before we come here, don't we, Dee?'

'Absolutely! A good sugar hit helps everyone to open up that bit more!'

'Go on, Connie, love, have a frangipane blondie, fresh out of the oven...'

'Or try a nice piece of raspberry fool, it's very popular here, isn't it?'

'Oh yes, you have to try the fool, it's well laced with brandy, so that'll get rid of any inhibitions you might have!'

All the while, the cafe door kept clanging open as more and more new arrivals breezed in, filling up the place to capacity. Connie was just tucking into a particularly gorgeous-looking slice of frangipane when the door chimed open yet again, except this time, both Dee and her mother started squealing like two fangirls.

'Oh, look, Mother, she's come back! Now, isn't that marvellous? You owe me a fiver – you said we'd never see her again.'

'Quick!' said Mildred. 'Get her books out and ask her to sign them all for us. Come on, love, move! Now, before the meeting starts!'

Connie looked over to whoever the pair of them were talking about and, sure enough, she spotted a very familiar-looking face in the throng. An elderly woman, with long grey straggly hair that fell almost to her waist, who'd just bounced in and who already seemed to be the centre of attention. She wasn't alone either; there was a younger woman stuck to her side, reed-thin, dressed head to toe in black and with a snooty, disdainful expression on her face, as though she'd rather be anywhere else than here.

'Of course, you recognise who it is, don't you, Connie?' Dee, the daughter, twittered excitedly. 'Can you believe we get actual celebrities in here? Isn't it exciting? And Lucasta is so nice too. She was so easy to chat to last week, wasn't she, Mother?'

But Mildred had already scooted over to the new arrival, laden down with a SuperValu bag she'd dragged in with her, stuffed full with paperback novels. Dee was hot on her heels and now the pair of them were plying the grey-haired lady with paperbacks and all manner of treats. The room was crowded and Connie could only catch glimpses of whoever they were love-bombarding, but as soon as she did get a decent look, she instantly recognised who it was.

That's Lucasta Liversidge, she thought. It was easy to be a gushing fangirl of Lucasta Liversidge. Even if you'd never picked up one of her books in the whole course of your life, it was almost impossible not to be aware of who she was. The woman seemed to be a semi-permanent guest on late-night TV chat shows as well as all the prime-time radio programmes and she was never out of the magazines her mum used to buy. Lucasta Liversidge was a real media darling, famous for going on shows like *The Graham Norton Show* without any kind of filter, where she'd curse her head off, knock back the G & Ts, have the studio audience in absolute hysterics and find herself trending on X for days afterwards.

Connie sat back quietly and took the chance to have a really good look at her. After all, it wasn't often you were up close and personal with a living, breathing national treasure. From what she could see, Lucasta Liversidge seemed like a born natural with people. She was shaking every hand, signing every single book that was shoved under her nose, which was a surprising amount considering that this wasn't a book signing, and yet she still had a kind word for everyone. *She's gracious,* Connie thought, studying her. *That's exactly what I want to be like, if I ever do become famous.*

There was one late arrival who really caught Connie's eye, mainly because, whoever this fella was, he seemed like the only person she'd spotted tonight who very definitely looked as if he didn't fit in or want to be there in the first place. He was roughly about ten years older than her, forty-something, she guessed, dressed in a suit and tie like a real corporate type. He slipped quietly into an alcove, laden down with a briefcase and a stack of notes, which he dumped at an empty table, checking his mobile almost non-stop as he did so.

To her surprise though, the minute the awkward-looking guy spotted Lucasta, he was straight over to her and, for her part, she lit up when she saw him. Lucasta led him aside and very quickly the two seemed to get into an intensely private conversation, which, try as Connie might, she couldn't overhear a word of. In an evening of weirdness, this was particularly strange. Whoever Mr Corporate was, he certainly didn't look as if he was a fan of Lucasta Liversidge books. Mind you, she thought, he didn't exactly look like the type to pitch up at a Bereavement Cafe either, but then, as she was fast learning, there really was a whole spectrum of grief here tonight. Will had been on the money about that.

Pretty soon, Will was calling everyone to order, plonking himself back to front on a chair, as relaxed and laid-back as if this were nothing more than a chilled-out coffee amongst pals.

'Welcome back, everyone.' He smiled warmly, waving at one or two that he hadn't said hi to yet. 'Well, we certainly seem to be gaining in popularity; this place is getting busier and busier every week, which is very encouraging to see. So, who'd like to get the ball rolling this evening?'

Normally at any group meeting like this, Connie had found that people were a bit shy and hesitant to be the first to take the floor. But this was like nothing she'd ever come across as, almost instantaneously, there was a huge show of hands in the air, with everyone clamouring for airtime.

'Mia, how about we start with you?' Will said, nodding at a woman sitting at a table to the right of Connie. She twisted around to see this Mia; a complete gym-bunny as it turned out, with long, swishy blonde hair extensions tied up into a high ponytail, a very definite spray tan, dressed head to toe in Lululemon gear, with a sports bag lying at her feet, as if she'd just come out of a particularly hefty workout. She could have been any age from forty to sixty, but when you looked as cool as this one, who cared?

'Thanks, Will,' she said, flashing a perfect Hollywood smile, delighted to have been given the floor. 'So here's a weird one for you all. Those of you who know me will know that I lost both my parents this year, within a few months of each other.'

There were a few sympathetic mutterings from around the room, and she made a little 'namaste' bowing gesture to thank them all. 'Here's the thing though,' Mia went on, kicking off her trainers and sitting cross-legged on the chair, with the most perfect posture Connie had ever seen. 'Mum and Dad specified in their wills that they wanted to be cremated. So because they'd died so close to each other, the undertaker suggested I get both sets of ashes mixed together in the one urn.'

'Saved you a few quid too,' Mildred chipped in. 'Those urns are a fortune.'

'Yeah,' said Mia, 'but here's my dilemma. Where do I scatter them? My dad loved the sea, but Mum hated it and the one time he talked her into going on a cruise together, she spent the whole holiday in the bathroom vomiting. On the other hand, Mum was a real city girl who loved zipping off to London or New York on her shopping trips. Which Dad said made him come out in hives – he couldn't even go to Tesco's with her for half an hour to do the weekly shop without getting into a bad temper. Dad loved golf, Mum hated it. Mum loved the theatre, Dad said it bored him rigid. So what do I do? How do I keep them both happy?'

'Jeez,' said a voice from the back of the room, but Connie couldn't see who it was. 'Did your folks get on at all?'

'They actually got on great.' Mia smiled. 'A case of opposites attract, I guess.'

'Where are they now?' someone else asked.

'In a huge urn under my kitchen sink. It's the only place I have room for it.'

'Well, you have to get them out of there for starters, love,' Dee piped up, 'otherwise they'll come back and haunt you.'

'Don't laugh,' said an older lady from somewhere over by the loos; Connie couldn't get a proper look at her, the place was so packed. 'But I keep my fella's ashes in a big Pringles tube. It was his food of choice and the only thing I could ever get him to eat, so it just seemed right.'

'A tube of Pringles?' said a young teenage girl with big saucery eyes who was sitting right at the front, couldn't have been more than fifteen or sixteen, Connie figured. Lovely looking young one too, with pale freckly Irish skin and long reddish hair that came well past her shoulders.

'Oh, Joe would get through three tubes a day, no bother,' came the reply. 'Probably a lot of the reason why he keeled over from a heart attack at the age of forty-eight, but there you go.'

'My dad was a mad keen golfer,' this red-headed teenager said quietly, flushing to her roots. 'So he wanted his ashes scattered on his favourite golf course, right at the eighteenth hole. The golf club were lovely about it when we asked them; they even let us have a little ceremony out on the green. Dad would have loved it and Mum says it gave her great peace.'

'Is your sister not with you tonight?' Mildred piped up.

The girl didn't answer; instead she pointed over to the window with her thumb and it seemed as if every neck in the whole room swivelled around to have a good look outside. Sure enough, you could see her exact double through the window, another flame-haired teenager with AirPods stuck in her ears deep in conversation on her phone and vaping on an e-cigarette. But she seemed to have some sixth sense telling her that the whole room was looking her way because she turned around, gave them all two fingers, then moved well beyond the window, so no one could see her any more.

'Alex still not interested in joining us, then?' Will asked gently.

'Not a chance,' teenage girl replied. 'The only reason she comes here is because she can spend as much time as she wants on her phone without Mum getting on her case. If Mum knew she vaped, she'd be, like, grounded for weeks. Please don't any of you tell her when she comes to collect us, will you?'

'Not a word, I promise,' said Will kindly. 'So, back to Mia, and her dilemma. Any suggestions where Mia can have her parents' ashes scattered, somewhere that would have kept both of them happy?'

Lucasta spoke up, in a cut-glass accent that made her sound posher than Camilla Parker Bowles. 'Can't beat your own back garden, dearest,' she said with great authority. 'That's where my Johnnie is buried, along with Hugo.'

'Who's Hugo?' Dee asked. 'Is it a family member?'

'I never knew you had kids,' Mia replied, crinkling up her

forehead and clearly showing she'd never been near a Botox needle in her life.

'Oh, dear me, no.' Lucasta beamed broadly. 'Hugo was our Labrador. My late husband, Johnnie, adored him, you know. I often think he preferred the dog to me. In fact, he often comes back to me to let me know how peaceful he finds it being buried at the bottom of my garden. Doesn't much like being near the compost heap, but there you are, you can't have everything. Even in death.'

'Your late husband comes back to you?' someone said, Connie couldn't see who, but Lucasta replied graciously. 'Oh, I get messages from the dead all the time, that's par for the course. Generally at the most mortifying moments. My Johnnie, for instance, has a dreadful habit of speaking to me whenever I'm on the loo. But then lately, a brand-new voice has started coming to me, someone I've never heard before, someone who's desperately anxious to make contact—'

And then a phone rang. Loud and annoying and insistent. People dived to pockets and bags, double-checking it wasn't them, but Connie stayed rooted to her seat, completely frozen.

'Just to let you all know,' Will said, 'we don't encourage phones here. If you can all make sure they're switched off, we'd really appreciate it.'

And still the phone rang and now Connie found herself reaching down into the depths of her own bag, which was on the floor at her feet. That awful, squawking ringtone alone gave it away. *It's her,* she thought. *And for once, she's calling at the most perfect time in the best place I possibly could be.*

'Hello?' she answered, pressing on that heavy, faded green 'answer' button. 'Mum? Mum, is that you?'

She was aware of more than a few vexed looks coming her way, but this time, she didn't care.

'Well, this place is certainly interesting,' came her mother's voice, loud and clear. 'Do you know, love, I even think there might be one or two single men here this evening? Wouldn't that make a nice change for you, now? Meeting someone in real life, instead of all those roaring eejits you keep picking up on those rubbishy aul dating sites you're so obsessed with?'

15

LUCASTA

'Well, now, this isn't something you see every day,' Lucasta said under her breath, just as the young woman Connie's phone rang and she picked it up to answer it. 'There really is the most remarkable energy here tonight, mark my words, Phoebe.'

'There may well be enough energy here to power the entire city,' Phoebe whispered back, glancing down at her watch and looking bored and pissed off. 'But just a gentle reminder: we're leaving in exactly thirty minutes. And as soon as we get you home, you still have a redraft of your book edits to finish for the US publishers. Because of the time difference, you have until 11 p.m. tonight to deliver it and on no account can you be a moment later. I won't let that happen.'

But Lucasta couldn't possibly focus on work and deadlines at a time like this. As if! She was on edge with excitement and could barely contain herself – when in her entire life had she witnessed even close to this before? There were some truly astonishing forces at play right in this very room and she badly wanted to help in any small way that she could.

In a blink, she was out of her seat and making a beeline for the terribly pretty young woman sitting right at the back of the room clutching the most unwieldy-looking mobile phone, which was roughly about the size of a brickbat and which the poor thing was clinging on to for dear life.

'My dear girl,' Lucasta said, slinking into the free seat opposite her and deliberately keeping her voice good and low so no one would overhear them. Not that it made much difference as the entire cafe seemed to be watching them. 'Is she still there? Is your mother still on the other end of the telephone?'

'No,' this young lady replied, shaking her head. 'She's gone. This is what's been happening. The phone rings and it's her, I know it's her. And she'll chat to me and then just as quickly she's gone. I know that sounds insane,' she added almost apologetically. 'Believe me, I'm starting to think I am losing my mind here.'

'Oh, my darling girl,' said Lucasta, gripping her hand and holding it tightly. 'That's not the case at all. Sometimes the dead want to reach out to us so badly that they'll use any means necessary to gain our attention. For your mother, it seems a terribly old phone is what works for her. She must have loved you so very much.'

'Are you OK, Connie?' Will called out worriedly from where he was sitting at the top of the room.

Connie, so that was her name, Lucasta thought. Aware that everyone was now staring her way, Connie seemed as if all she wanted was for the focus to be off her, more than likely so she could digest what had just happened. And who could blame the creature?

'She's absolutely fine,' Lucasta answered for her. 'Might you all have the goodness to give us a moment or two?' That young chap who was running the show, Will, seemed to cop on that she needed a little space, so he nodded, then expertly steered the meeting back to what they'd been chatting about before the phone rang. Some kind of group discussion about urns and ashes and what on earth to do with them, which Lucasta simply tuned out.

'How often has this been happening, my dear?' she said in a nice, low voice, resolutely not letting go of Connie's thin little hand until she was quite happy the poor girl was all right.

'A lot,' Connie confessed to her. 'More and more frequently now. And just like you were saying earlier, usually in the most embarrassing places.'

'And what sort of messages is she passing on for you?'

'Exactly the kind of thing she'd say if she were alive and sitting here right now.' Connie shrugged. 'Asking about what's on TV. Or calling to tell me she's got no one to talk to and she's bored. That's what's so weird about this – it's all so *normal*.'

'But of course it's normal, my dear. The dead trying to leave little signs for us is the most normal thing in the world.'

'Like just now?' Connie went on. 'Mum was telling me there's a few single men here this evening and that I might even get lucky. As if that's what I came here looking for – a fella!'

In a flash, Lucasta got a strong sense that this was the very first time Connie had confided in someone who didn't laugh in her face or tell her she was insane.

'Our dear departed,' she said thoughtfully, 'can often be the most wonderful matchmakers, I've found.'

'Anyway,' Connie said with a smile, 'thanks for taking this seriously. No one else does, let me tell you.'

'Not only do I believe you, I actually think it's a great privilege to be able to get these signs from beyond. Clairaudience, it's called, you know.'

'Clairaudience,' Connie repeated, genuinely intrigued. Unlike so many people in Lucasta's orbit, with Phoebe top of the list – the sort of folk who instantly wrote her off as batshit crazy the minute she spoke about anything to do with the other side.

'What *is* clairaudience?' Connie asked innocently.

'It's when you can hear the dead, quite as clearly as if they're in the room with you,' Lucasta said. 'Not to be confused with clairvoyance, which is when you can actually see the dead. Or clairsentience, which is what I believe I experience myself, before I feel and hear the spirits who visit me.'

'Clair... what?'

'That's when you get a perfectly clear sense that a spirit is in the room with you. Just like in this room this very evening. Happens to me quite a lot, actually.'

'You think there are spirits here?' Connie asked, mystified. 'For real?'

'Oh, darling, I've never known anything quite like it. From the very first moment I came in here, I could feel it. Spirits clamour for our attention all the time, you know, but the energy in here is off the Richter scale. Now, you mustn't be frightened,' she hastily added, clocking the look on Connie's face. 'This isn't anything scary or spooky at all. This is a dearly departed loved one simply wanting to maintain contact with you. That's all. Time was when they'd let us know they were present by knocking on walls or furniture or banging doors open and closed, or even by pushing ornaments off shelves, anything to attract our attention. But nowadays, it's as though the spirit world has become more sophisticated; as if they've realised we all spend so much time in front of those wretched computer screens and mobile phones, that that's the best possible way for them to reach out to us.'

Lucasta was suddenly aware that the room around her had gone silent. She quickly glanced up to see that just about every eye was riveted to her. Except for Phoebe, of course, who sat in the corner, tapping on her watch and making impatient 'it's time to go' gestures.

'Didn't mean to be earwigging,' said a terribly dapper-looking older gentleman wearing an actual cravat with an open-necked shirt, who was sitting in the dead centre of the room. 'But I'll tell you something. Whatever the two of you were talking about sounded *very* interesting to me. Far more interesting than urns and ashes and what the hell to do with them.'

Lucasta was just about to answer when, out of the corner of her eye, she spotted Luke staring over. His face was pale and drawn and exhausted-looking and as she locked eyes across the room at him, she knew in an instant exactly what needed to be done here.

'You know, I think this particular coffee shop must have been built on the most extraordinarily powerful ley lines,' she said, addressing everyone. 'That's energy lines, you know,' she added helpfully. 'The sense that we're not alone in this room really is quite palpable. Surely I can't be the only one to pick up on it?'

'You're wasting your time asking me, I'm afraid,' said cravat-man. 'To me, it's just an ordinary coffee shop where we come to chat about our late loved ones, that's all. No offence.' He nodded politely in Will's direction.

'None taken.' Will smiled. 'I've had the lease on this place for over a year now and no one has ever spoken about any kind of spiritual presence here.'

'For those who believe,' Lucasta said thoughtfully, 'no explanation is necessary. For those who don't believe, no explanation is possible. But I really think there's only one thing to be done – and must be done soon, too. The spirits are very anxious to make contact. Helen, most particularly,' she added, with a respectful little nod in Luke's direction.

'What's that?' Connie asked her, still gripping tight to that brick-like mobile telephone of hers.

'Oh, I would have thought that was perfectly obvious, dear. I've got to conduct a seance, I've got to do it on this very spot and you've simply got to be here for it. I won't take no for an answer.'

16

LUKE

As soon as the meeting broke up, Luke found himself drifting back outside into the warmth and sunshine of a summery May evening, automatically taking his phone off silent and checking messages. Two from Dave at work, which was always going to be bad news. Any message from Dave at this time meant a particularly late night ahead of him, ironing out whatever glitch the McKinsey clients had thrown back in his face now. But on the plus side, there was a very reassuring message from his sister Clare, who was minding Amy like the sainted angel that she was, texting to say that all was well, that Amy had great fun with her cousins, had eaten a good dinner and was now cuddled up in the top of a bunk bed with Holly, sleeping soundly. Her text continued:

> Want to leave her with me for the night? Seems mean to wake her up just to take her home and put her into her own bed. What do you think? We love having her here, you know that!

Luke hesitated. It was late for Amy, well past nine, and the poor dote must have been exhausted. He hated not getting to see her for the whole evening, but Clare was right, it was probably far better to leave her. The main thing was that she was safe and minded and happy.

He was just about to reply when none other than Miss Mackey fell into step beside him. It occurred to him he didn't even know her first name.

'Hey,' she said, momentarily distracting him.

'Oh, hi,' he said, glancing up from his phone.

'I'm glad you turned up tonight, that's a step in the right direction. I was afraid you wouldn't come at all.'

'Afraid it would all be a bit "out there" for me?' he asked wryly.

She looked him up and down appraisingly. 'I know you have a lot of demands on what little spare time you do have,' she said smoothly, 'and, of course, it must be tough having to leave Amy for any length of time, just so you can be here.'

'It is,' he answered honestly, still thinking about Amy and weighing up what was best for her.

'Last thing you needed was me insisting you pitch up here tonight,' she added, with a little smile. 'I know that. So I really hope you didn't think it was a complete waste of time.'

They strolled down Leeson Street together, until she came to a stop beside a bike chained to railings and immediately produced a thick set of keys to unlock it. Even the bike, Luke thought, was so very her. Sturdy and sensible with absolutely no bells or whistles or anything else that she'd probably consider frippery.

'Messages from the other side,' he said thoughtfully, staring ahead of him as she undid a heavy-looking padlock. 'Phones ringing with dead people on the other end of the call. Seances. Mad stuff! If you'd said to me two weeks ago that I'd have crossed the threshold of a place like that, I'd probably have laughed in your face.'

She stopped unlocking her bike and looked up at him.

'Don't suppose you fancy a quick drink?' she asked. 'Unorthodox, I know, for the principal of your daughter's school to suggest it on a school night, but, if you don't mind me saying, you really look like you need to talk.'

He wavered for a moment before making up his mind.

'Go on, then,' he said. 'A quick one is no harm.'

'How about over there?' she said, pointing down the road to a quiet-looking bar with lots of outdoor tables sitting empty and with soft music playing in the background. It looked like a private kind of place, somewhere where you could speak freely.

'Drinks on me.' He smiled. 'Mind if I just call my sister, to make sure Amy's OK?'

'Of course. I would have been surprised if you didn't.'

* * *

Minutes later, they were sitting at a private, secluded corner table as a friendly young waiter bounced over to take their order.

'Just a fizzy water for me, thanks,' Miss Mackey said, while Luke ordered a non-alcoholic beer. It felt strange beyond words for him to be sitting down like this, actually out in a bar, socialising, when his whole life for months now had been work, collect Amy, home, repeat.

'So,' she began as soon as their drinks arrived. 'How are you doing? For real? You don't need to put a brave face on it, not with me. Remember, as a fellow Bereavement Cafe regular, I've been there too.'

She looked right at him, but without any of that fake concern that Luke had seen so many times on so many faces over the past few months. He could spot faux sympathy a mile away at this stage. People who asked you if you were OK, but really only wanted to hear the answer, 'Yes, I'm fine. Nothing to worry about here', so that they could virtue signal and feel as if they were being a caring friend, while at the same time giving nothing more than superficial lip service to whatever it was you were going through.

Luke took a sip of beer before answering and really considered the question properly. Miss Mackey was certainly a good listener, he'd give her that much. She seemed like a genuinely caring person too, which was quite rare in his orbit right now.

'Honestly?' he asked her.

'The truth and nothing but, please.'

'In that case,' he eventually said, 'I think I'm still a bit numb, to be honest.'

A silence fell as she digested this, while he looked straight ahead. At a far table, a Thursday evening after-work brigade were setting into a few drinks and, by the sounds of it, getting into a serious bitching session about a co-worker who was pissing them all off in a major way.

'The thing is,' Luke said after a long, long pause, 'at the moment and for the foreseeable future, all I'm trying to do is keep the show on the road. Make sure Amy is OK, stay in touch with family, both Helen's family and mine, and keep up with work deadlines. And that's it. That's my life. This hamster wheel I'm stuck on is just the way it is for me now. In fact, the last two meetings at the Bereavement Cafe have been the first time I've even been out since Helen passed away.'

'So how have you found the meetings?' Miss Mackey asked. 'You can tell me the truth. Not to everyone's taste, that I know.'

'Lucasta... the author with the long grey hair who looks a bit like...'

'Who looks a bit eccentric,' she tactfully finished the sentence for him. 'That much I can agree with.'

'Well, she completely freaked me out last week. I mean... how did she know Helen's name and Amy's too? How did she just come out with it like that? There's no possible way she could have known. Then tonight she told me privately that she'd had another message from Helen, right in the middle of some book festival she was speaking at.'

'Yes, I saw the two of you deep in conversation after the meeting ended tonight and I wondered about that. If you don't mind my asking, what exactly did she say to you?'

'That Helen's spirit was strong and anxious to make contact with me,' Luke tried to say, only then he found himself laughing bitterly. 'I'm sorry,' he said, 'but did I really just say that? All that nonsense about the spirit world? I'm a non-believer in anything otherworldly.'

'And yet,' she said quietly, 'you still came back this evening.'

He shrugged. But then it was hard to find a polite way of saying, 'Mainly because you told me you'd see me here and I'm anxious to keep onside with Amy's school principal.' He thought it best to go for a complete subject change instead.

'Enough about me,' he said firmly. 'You know all about me and about my stuff. You must be well sick of me. What about you? If you don't mind my saying, you've been so quiet in meetings – you never talk about your own loss or about how you're coping with grief. You've lost – a parent maybe, I'm guessing?'

'I lost my mum some years ago,' she replied quietly. 'But I'm glad to say my dad is alive and well and hale and hearty. He's a teacher too, although he's retired now.'

'He must be so proud of you.'

She smiled and blushed and pushed her hair behind her ear with her finger. This time, Luke looked properly at her, really taking her in. She was wearing another one of those trouser suits, he noticed. Made her look older, more like she was in her mid to late-forties. Yet she was a lot younger than that, you could tell. Did she go out and buy three or four of the same austere-looking suits in different colours, just to dress older, in case any of the parents complained that she was too young to be a principal? Certainly looked like it.

'You must still miss your mum an awful lot,' he said to her.

'I do,' she said. 'But I've lost someone else far more recently and that's what first took me to the Bereavement Cafe.'

'Another family member?' he asked.

'No. We weren't family.'

'So, if you don't mind my asking...' he persisted.

'I lost my fiancé,' she said simply.

Luke did a double take, but then he'd had no idea she'd ever been engaged. She was a deeply private person, he was fast learning.

'I'm so sorry to hear that,' he said. 'How long since he passed away? He must have been young.'

'He was thirty-nine, the same age as me,' she replied. 'He'd be forty now. Melanoma. Quite aggressive too. By the time it was found, he was at stage four and the treatment, I'm sorry to say, caused him untold pain and yet hardly prolonged his life at all.'

'I had no idea,' Luke said quietly. 'That must be heart-breaking for you.'

'We were due to get married within months of his passing away,' she went on, quite calmly and without a trace of emotion, 'so, as you can imagine, last year isn't one I'd like to repeat.'

'I wish I'd known – Helen and I would have gone to the funeral, just to be there, just to support you.'

'I don't like to talk about it in school,' she said, with a firm shake of her head, 'not to the rest of the staff, in fact not to anyone outside my family and close friends. When I go into work, I need to have my "work face" on. Work is work and my private life is just that – private. In fact, you're the first parent I've spoken to openly about it.'

'Do you find going along to the Bereavement Cafe meetings helps?'

'In a strange way, yes,' she said thoughtfully. 'We're all at different stages of grieving and it's been like a balm to me, to see other people coming out of it on the other side. Like that mother and daughter, Dee and Mildred. Last year, they were both in a very different place; poor Mildred could barely mention her late husband without bursting into tears. But this year, even I can see that they're both healing and doing so much better. Now, the pair of them come into the cafe laughing and skittish and sharing lovely, warm, deeply personal memories – Mildred about her husband and Dee about her dad, who they both adored. What can I say?' She smiled, shrugging her shoulders. 'It gives me a feeling of there being light at the end of the tunnel.'

'You must miss your fiancé so much.'

She didn't answer. Instead, she bent down to the floor, rummaged around in her briefcase and produced her mobile phone. Then she flipped it open and held it out for Luke to have a look. It was a selfie on her screensaver, a photo of a younger version of herself with a round-faced guy in shades with an absolutely euphoric smile, both of them beaming at the camera and looking as if the photo was taken up the peak of a snow-capped mountain. They were swaddled underneath very professional-looking North Face-style mountaineering gear and looked so happy and proud that they'd managed to reach the summit.

'That's him,' she said with a tiny smile. 'That's Tom. We'd planned to do the Seven Summits together, but, sadly, that didn't come to pass.'

'That's just awful,' Luke said gently, feeling deeply sorry for her and, at the same time, half flattered that she'd opened up to him. 'At least Helen and I had fifteen happy years together and at least we got to have Amy. You and Tom didn't even get that much. For what it's worth, I'm really honoured that you confided in me.'

'I'm honoured that you confided in me too, Mr Wright.'

'Oh, come on,' he said lightly. 'We're not in school now. It's Luke, please.'

'In that case, don't you think it's high time you started to call me Stella?'

17

CONNIE

The estate agent was bright, buzzing and absolutely brimming over with enthusiasm. She introduced herself as Karen with a dazzlingly confident smile, took Connie's hand warmly in a tight, professional grip and shook the bejaysus out of it.

Karen was fifty-something and looked super-cool too, dressed in a smart black and white patterned dress that hung so well on her, Connie decided, it could only have been from COS. That, with the chunky, bang-on-trend flatforms she was wearing and big black oversized glasses, made her look sassy and funky, the kind of woman you wanted to take as your style icon and slavishly copy every single thing she was wearing.

There was just one little caveat. *Don't be too good at your job,* Connie found herself silently praying, the minute she greeted Karen on her front doorstep and welcomed her inside. *I'm in no rush to sell this house – truth be told, I don't want to sell it at all. So the worse you are at selling houses, then the bigger a favour you're doing me.*

No such luck with Karen though, who barged through the hall door, all 'sell, sell, sell' like some kind of thundering tornado.

'Well, well, well, what have we here now?' She beamed professionally, scanning the tiny entrance hall up and down. 'Isn't this absolutely charming? Perfect for a young couple. Close to all amenities too – and within walking distance from the city centre, which can instantly add tens of thousands on to the asking price, you know.'

'Emm, well, as you can see,' Connie said, shuffling awkwardly on her feet and looking doubtfully around her, 'the place hasn't seen a lick of paint in a very long time. I'm afraid when Mum and I were living here together, money was a bit tight for us.'

'It's a fixer-upper,' Karen said firmly, before breezing into the living room without having been invited to and, again, giving a lightning-quick, up-and-down appraisal. Next thing, she produced a digital measuring tape and automatically started measuring up the square footage of the room, jotting down notes at the speed of light. 'But you know,' she added with a flash of a high-wattage smile, 'that's exactly what people want now. They want a place they can gut and then renovate to the very highest standards with absolutely no expense spared. Floor-to-ceiling windows, underfloor heating, combi-boilers, that's all pretty standard now. Buyers want a blank canvas so they can put their own unique stamp on the place.'

Connie winced, hating the idea that the home her mum had loved and adored ever since she was first married, this comfy, warm home with all its memories, would soon be gutted and renovated, with floors dug up and walls blithely knocked down, so it could end up looking like an identikit copy of every other Dermot Bannon-inspired build out there. When Connie was alone in the house, she often used to play 'fantasy redecoration' in her head, where she'd try to visualise exactly what she'd do to the place if she owned it outright and if money were no object. She'd upgrade, of course, give it a good freshen up, repaint and get a more modern kitchen and bathroom put in. But she'd do absolutely nothing that would destroy the character of the house, which was a railway cottage dating back to 1860. What was the point in living in an old house otherwise? she'd often ask herself.

But then, the same reality check would hit her square in the face, as it did every single day now. Whether she liked it or not, the house was going to be sold and there was pretty much sweet damn all she could do about it. Of course, it was Donald, her older brother, who was the prime instigator of all this. He was the one who'd got in touch with the estate agency and arranged for Karen to come out for a viewing today; he was the one who wanted a quick sale so he could cash in his half of the proceeds as fast as humanly possible. Pointless for Connie to have the same roundabout conversation she'd been having with him for months now: that she didn't want to sell and had nowhere else to go.

'Yeah.' Donald would sniff uninterestedly down the phone from his luxury three-bedroomed apartment on the 5th arrondissement in Paris. 'But just think: with your share of the proceeds, you can buy somewhere else. Easily. Dunno what you're whingeing about, Con, it's a win-win situation for both of us.'

No, it's really just a win-win for you, Connie had to restrain herself from snapping back at him. *You and your wife both work for Google and both make a fortune and you have a fabulous apartment that you jointly own. Bottom line? You're rich. I'm not. So where exactly do you suggest I move to, with my non-existent earnings and with the way house prices are in Ireland now? With my share of the proceeds, I'll be doing well to afford a mobile home in a caravan park in the back arse of nowhere a good two-hour drive away. And that's if I'm very lucky.*

Connie hated the situation so much she wanted to vomit, but

the fact remained: she and Donald were equal co-owners of the house. She couldn't afford to buy him out, so this was the only option open to them. Nothing for it but to put a brave face on it and suck it up.

'As you can see, I'm still in the midst of decluttering,' she said to Karen, trying her best to be positive and to give some kind of explanation for the stacks of boxes and bin liners that were piled high everywhere. Karen ignored her though and kept on powering through, flinging open the double doors that led into the kitchen, which was, to put it mildly, a complete pigsty. Huge storage boxes from IKEA were stacked along one wall while on the kitchen table, piles of cardboard boxes towered one on top of the other, almost reaching up to the cheap, shiny lampshade that dominated the middle of the room.

'I have just two words for you,' Karen said bossily, taking it all in with a quick, professional glance. 'Charity shop. Take my advice and just dump it all. You can always buy brand-new stuff. After all, that's what those discount homeware stores on the Long Mile Road are for. Staging a house for sale is all part of the process now, you know!'

'Bit of a problem there, I'm afraid,' Connie was quick to say. 'Buying a shedload of new things might not be a runner, in my case. I'm an actor, you see, and not working right now, so dosh is a bit tight.'

'An actor?' At that, Karen stopped dead in her tracks, looking at Connie with renewed interest and giving her a quick up-and-down glance. 'But that's fabulous! We can market the property as belonging to an actual celebrity! That'll pack out all our viewings – buyers who are fans of yours will be dying to see where you live. Can I ask – what would I know you from?'

'Oh,' said Connie, always delighted with a chance to chat about what she loved most. 'Well, I've done theatre work mostly.

Lots of Shakespearian plays. I was in the whole Henriad, that's Henry IV Parts One and Two, as well as Henry V and Richard II. We had gender-fluid casting, which was great because it meant women got to play men and vice versa—'

'Yes, that's all very well,' Karen interrupted, 'but were you ever in any TV shows or big-budget movies? Or anything online that people might have actually heard of?'

'Okaaay,' said Connie, temporarily wrongfooted. 'Well, on screen I've done commercials mostly, and a small part in a series set in Viking times that was shot here last summer.'

She didn't get a chance to say, 'Blink and you'll miss me,' because Karen had completely barrelled over her like a force of nature.

'"Artisan dwelling,"' she said, thinking aloud, as if she were reading from an imaginary estate agent's online listing, '"owned by star of stage and screen, Connie Cassley." Yes! I love it. We already have our media tagline and I'm barely in the door! See how good I am at my job?' she added with a light-hearted wink. 'I'll have this house sold with a snap of my fingers, wait till you see! I hope to have this place signed, sealed and delivered to new buyers in less than two months.'

Connie was seriously starting to panic now. She didn't want the house sold in the snap of some total stranger's fingers. Two months? Two months was ridiculous. She needed time, lots of it and the more, the better. To find somewhere else to live, for starters.

'Well, you know, Karen,' she said, back-pedalling furiously as Karen busied herself measuring up the kitchen, even whipping out a compass to check the orientation. 'Although I love the house myself, it might just turn out to be a far harder sell than you anticipate.'

'Did you say a hard sell?' Karen turned to look at her, puzzled.

'Don't be so ridiculous. I've never come across a hard sell, not once, not in the course of my whole career.'

'Well, look at how tiny the kitchen window is,' said Connie, vainly hoping to put her off a bit. 'Even in broad daylight, you still have to switch the lights on in here and you never, ever get the sun.'

'"Kitchen a blank canvas, ready for a stunning makeover,"' Karen said, again conjuring up ads for an imaginary estate agent's website out of thin air. '"With gorgeous views overlooking a delightfully mature garden."'

'What views are they?' Connie said, rushing to the window and opening it up. 'The only view from here is of my bike leaning up against the wheelie bins.'

'"Scope for buyers to let their imaginations run riot,"' Karen countermanded.

'If you were to start knocking walls down and getting floor-to-ceiling windows in here,' said Connie, gesturing frantically all around her, 'then the only view you'd be able to see is of my next-door neighbour, Charlie, and his wife, Breda, who are both practising nudists, just so you know. Even in winter.'

'"Charming local views,"' Karen fired back.

'And take a look at the low ceilings and the mildew growing up the walls,' Connie said, pointing over to the skirting boards between the fridge and the cooker. 'That's going to be a horrendous sell.'

'Nonsense,' Karen said dismissively, brandishing her measuring tape like a weapon. 'Lots of character, that's how we describe that. Covers a multitude from damp patches to actual holes in the ceiling. Believe you me, I've seen it all. And sold it all.'

'But the house is so small!' Connie almost pleaded. 'Mum and

I used to be on top of each other!' To that though, Karen just shook her head.

'It's never small in my game. We say "cosy".'

'*And* the plumbing in the upstairs bathroom is wonky. Sometimes you have to hammer on the pipes to get hot water.'

'Then we describe the property as a "diamond in the rough".'

'Mum and Dad never once invested in the house, not in all the decades they lived here!' Connie was clutching at straws now, and still Karen kept bouncing back at her. 'Then it's "lovingly maintained". Wow,' she enthused, getting more and more excited the more she saw. 'This just keeps getting better and better!'

'There's no amenities nearby at all,' Connie said, thinking of a fresh excuse. 'You have to walk miles to the nearest Tesco Express and even then, it's in the local train station, so they have feck all to speak of.'

'"Fond of exercise? This gem is perfect for the fitness addict."'

'And wait till you see the state of the bedrooms – they're like shoeboxes!'

'Ah, yes, the bedrooms. Come on, let's have a good look at them,' said Karen, barging past her straight out of the kitchen and striding up the stairs. 'Do they have built-in wardrobes?' she called back over her shoulder to Connie, who was frantically trying to keep up with her.

'Ehh... yeah.'

'Then they're not small, they're "compact, but with ample storage".'

'But for any new buyer,' Connie pleaded, 'there's just so much work to be done!'

'"A rare opportunity to put your own stamp on the property,"' Karen replied, breezing into what had been Connie's mum's room and which still had all her clothes, shoes, make-up and perfumes scattered about everywhere, waiting for Connie to sort through them.

'Oh, you know what?' Connie said, as a fresh argument struck her. 'This probably should have been the first thing I told you.'

'What's that?' Karen replied, busy with her measuring tape.

'Even if you do sell this place—'

'There's no "if" about it. *When* I sell this place, I think you meant to say.'

'In that case, when you sell this place,' Connie went on, 'you need to be aware of a slight problem. Which is that I haven't found anywhere else to live yet. New owners might want vacant possession and I can't leave till I've got somewhere to go, now, can I?'

'Then it's your lucky day!' Karen grinned at her. 'Because I don't just think of myself as an estate agent; rather, I like to describe myself to clients as a sort of matchmaker. My job is to match you up with your perfect home. So as well as selling this place for you, I will take it as my personal mission to find you somewhere wonderful to live. Somewhere far, far better than here, let me tell you!'

Oh, dear God, Connie thought. *What have I unleashed?* She glanced down at her mother's bedside table at a photo of her with Connie as a baby in her arms and Donald aged about five, and felt the weight of the famous Nokia phone that was zipped tight into the pocket of her fleece top.

Which was when inspiration struck.

'There's one last thing, Karen,' she said. 'Something that might just be a deal breaker for any prospective buyer.'

'Which is?' Karen replied, doubtless with a quick answer to whatever it was up her sleeve. Connie shoved her hand into her pocket and gave the phone a reassuring little squeeze. She even reminded herself to darken her tone of voice like actors did in old creepy movies.

'In the interests of fairness,' she said slowly and, she hoped, effectively, 'I really do need to tell you that there's every chance this house is haunted. A haunted house, Karen. Try selling that!'

For the first time since she'd got there, Karen was silent. Then she burst into gales of euphoric laughter, even waving her fists in the air in a triumphant 'I won!' gesture. 'But this is the best of all.' She laughed. '"This charming home may look ordinary but it is full of the most unexpected surprises!" Two months, Connie. Wait till you see, I'll have it snapped up in two months or less!'

18

LUCASTA

'I've brought you a Nespresso. Your very favourite. And if you promise to behave yourself today and get through all of the copy-edits I've scheduled for you to work on, then I may even bring you a gin and tonic later on. Provided you've earned it, of course.'

Lucasta lit up, greedily grabbing the coffee from the tray Phoebe held out for her. She'd been working terribly hard that morning, as it happened, beavering away on those wretched edits that Phoebe was being such a dog with a bone about.

'You've got a particularly busy day today,' Phoebe went on, pulling her neat cardigan tightly around her – black, of course. Honestly, Lucasta thought distractedly, why did the woman permanently have to look as though she were on her way to a funeral?

'I've arranged a transatlantic Zoom call at 3 p.m. our time with your US editor to discuss the upcoming book tour for the new *Mercy* paperback. They've scheduled to launch the book in the run-up to Thanksgiving, so that will mean a trip to New York for us closer to the time. Which I'll book and take care of today. Your usual hotel, of course.'

'Oh, I *do* love Thanksgiving,' Lucasta trilled. 'All that divine turkey and ham. And the sales in all the shops the next day too... We could go shopping, Phoebe, dear. I could stock up on more doggie treats for you, Sausage,' she said, bending down to pat the dog's head as he panted enthusiastically at her feet. 'And you could buy more clothes in black for yourself,' she added dryly.

Phoebe ignored her and, instead, referred back down to the iPad she had tucked under her arm. 'They're quite confident that Oprah will want to interview you again,' she added. 'It'll be your third interview with her and I hope to have confirmation of that later today.'

'Oprah? Oh, how very kind of her,' said Lucasta. 'Such a lovely lady.'

'Hmm,' said Phoebe, getting back to the day's schedule. 'Then at 5 p.m. our time, you've got another Zoom call, this time with the LA producers of the *Mercy* online series. As per your contract, you're not actually entitled to a say in casting, so if you do happen to have any suggestions, airing them during this call is probably not a good idea.'

'Oh, you know how easy I am about these matters,' Lucasta said, waving her wrist breezily. 'What do I know about actors and actresses and movie stars? You know my rule of thumb: as long as they cast a few complete unknowns, that's quite all right with me. Pointless casting big movie names; they're already rich and famous enough, thanks all the same. Let's give a chance to some poor, struggling actors out there – isn't that a far nicer thing to do instead?'

'Most altruistic of you.' Phoebe nodded, still tapping away on her iPad. 'Will there be anything else before I let you get back to your edits?'

Lucasta shifted in her seat. 'Well, yes actually, dear, there is.'

'Yes?'

'That nice man from the Bereavement Cafe the other evening,' Lucasta said, staring at the window as her mind wound back to the previous Thursday evening. 'The chap who ran the place,' she said, almost talking to herself. 'Wonderfully thick hair tied in a bun, lovely warm brown eyes. Such a lovely aura from him – he's definitely been here before. Possibly in one of the caring professions, nursing perhaps. I see him working as a nurse...'

'Will, I believe you're referring to. What about him?' Phoebe said, raising an arched eyebrow.

'Can you drive me to see him at that little coffee shop, please? I must speak to him face-to-face and it really is rather important.'

At that, Phoebe's whole expression darkened. 'Really? Please don't tell me this is about seances? Haven't you wasted quite enough time there as it is? You have work to do today and schedules to stick to. You have deadlines. Lots of them. This, you do realise, is time-wasting of the highest order.'

'My dear cynical Phoebe,' Lucasta replied, knowing perfectly well that she would run into roadblocks exactly like this, and fully prepared for them. 'Work is important and deadlines are important, of course they are, but even more so is helping other people. I realise that you're only doing your job, but you do know that I'm being called on here. You were there the other night. You saw for yourself the number of people who are crying out for guidance. That poor widowed chap, Luke, for instance. Think of him, Phoebe. And think of that young woman clinging to that ridiculous-looking telephone waiting for messages from her mother. I can help. Even if it's only in a very small way, then don't you see? That's exactly what I need to do.'

Phoebe rolled her eyes, knowing when she was beaten. 'You're not going to give me a minute's peace till I take you back to that wretched cafe, are you?'

'How well you know me, dear. That's the first sensible thing you've said all morning.'

* * *

Exactly one hour later, right in the middle of a spring deluge, Lucasta and Phoebe were letting themselves in through the door of the Bereavement Cafe, after a sum total of three separate rows about what a complete waste of time this was – Phoebe – a separate row about how some people really ought to just do their job and stop emanating such negative vibes – Lucasta – and a non-related row about whose job it was to make sure there was an umbrella in the car and who was now to blame for the fact they were both soaked to the skin.

The cafe door opened to the accompaniment of that now familiar clanging bell sound. Lucasta squelched in, drenched right through and with Phoebe hot on her heels. To Lucasta's surprise though, the place was half empty. One or two students sat in the gorgeously comfortable sofas with laptops propped up in front of them and backpacks strewn at their feet, but apart from them and a few bedraggled commuters coming in and out of the cafe looking for take-out coffees before they dashed back out into the rain, the place was tumbleweed empty.

'Will is serving a customer,' Phoebe said briskly. 'Let's just sit down here and wait till he comes to us.'

'Yes, yes, yes, whatever you say,' Lucasta muttered, looking all around her, savouring what an utterly different vibe the place had during daylight hours. 'Astonishing,' she muttered under her breath, 'really quite extraordinary.'

'What is?' Phoebe said, catching Will's eye and waving across the room at him.

'The energy today – don't you feel it?' Then, remembering

who she was talking to, Lucasta quickly corrected herself. 'Oh no, stupid question. Of course you don't, you're impervious to this sort of thing, aren't you, dear?'

'Thankfully, yes.'

'In that case, you just sit there and tap away on your iPaddy thing and let me get on with it.'

'As long as you remember that we're out of here and straight back to work in exactly ten minutes,' Phoebe griped at her just as Will approached their table, wreathed in smiles, looking genuinely delighted to see them.

'Ladies!' he said warmly, shaking each of them by the hand. 'Well, this is an unexpected honour. And we're not even scheduled to have a Bereavement Cafe meeting today! As you see, you've caught me on an ordinary Monday morning. Same old, same old. What can I do for you? Tea for you, if I remember correctly,' he said, pointing two index fingers at Phoebe, 'black, no sugar, right? And a double decaf expresso for you?' He smiled at Lucasta. 'Although you usually say you'd far prefer a gin and tonic.'

'Yes, yes, absolutely, dear, thank you,' Lucasta said, not letting go of his hand and almost pulling him down into the empty seat between them. 'Only I really would like to have a quick word with you first, if you've got a moment?'

'I certainly do have a moment,' Will said, gesturing around him. 'You can see for yourselves how quiet the place is this time of day. For you ladies, I have all the time in the world.'

'You poor old chap,' Lucasta said sympathetically. 'How on earth are you even doing business?'

'It's why I latched on to the whole Bereavement Cafe idea,' Will explained. 'I'm not exactly run off my feet here. Had to find some way to pay the bills.'

'Well, the thing is,' she said, giving his hand a reassuring little squeeze, 'I may just be able to help you there.'

'Just so you know,' Phoebe added acidly, 'I had absolutely nothing to do with what she's about to say.'

'I think I can guess,' Will said warily, lowering his voice and turning to Lucasta. 'You want to host a seance here, don't you? You mentioned something about it the other night.'

'Oh, my dear Will,' Lucasta enthused, 'this is your space and of course it's entirely your decision. Please trust me, though: if we do go ahead, then it really is going to be something very special. The moment I first stepped in, I could feel the vibrations practically pinging off the four walls,' she added, waving her arms theatrically. 'The energy really is palpable, like nothing I've ever experienced before. If I am to do a seance, then it needs to take place here, you understand. But it's not possible without your permission. This is, after all, your cafe and nothing can happen without your say-so.'

At that, Will folded his arms and looked unconvinced.

'Yeah.' He nodded thoughtfully. 'I have doubts, though. Major doubts. My very real fear is that this might just scare off some of my Thursday night regulars. They've been coming for well over a year now, ever since I began the entire thing, and I do have to think of them.'

'A perfectly reasonable point, if I may say so,' Phoebe interjected.

'Then we'll do it on another night,' Lucasta said, turning two big blue cornflower eyes back to Will, at the exact same time.

'You see, the whole reason they keep coming back here again and again,' Will said, 'is that they know they can chat freely about anything to do with the deceased. Funny memories, mad things as well as sad – it's not all maudlin. I don't think anyone would want it to be. You've seen that for yourself. Now, I can sense that you seemed to have channelled someone – or something – the last few times you were here. I just have to be careful that we're not getting into scary *The Exorcist* territory or anything like that. Bereavement Cafe is a safe space and I'm anxious to keep it that way.'

'Right, that's it, then,' said Phoebe, instantly rising to her feet, clearly considering their little chat to be at an end. 'You heard the man. It's a no. No seances are happening here, full stop. So come on, up you get, we need you to get back to work.'

But Lucasta seemed lost in thought, completely absorbed elsewhere.

'Did you hear me?' Phoebe said to her, a bit more sternly. 'Will has a cafe to run and we need to leave. Now, please.'

Lucasta had completely tuned out though. She barely moved a muscle and sat so still; it was almost freakish.

'Are you OK?' Will asked her, starting to get concerned.

'She's here again,' was all Lucasta said quietly, staring off into the middle distance. 'She's around right now.'

'Who?' Phoebe said witheringly. 'The ghost of the late Queen?'

'Don't be silly, dear, it's her. Helen. Luke's late wife, only there's nothing late about her. She's very much present, in this room with us, right now.'

'Bloody hell,' Will said under his breath.

'Oh, you mustn't be worried. All she wants is to speak to her husband. Just once. Just one time. And that nice young woman Connie – I know her mother is anxious to reach out to her too.'

Then Lucasta shuddered violently, as if she was snapping out of it.

'Are you all right?' Will asked worriedly, leaping to his feet. 'Let me get you some water.'

'No need, dear,' Lucasta said, sounding far more like herself again. 'This happens to me all the time. It's nothing to be alarmed about.'

'I can vouch for that,' said Phoebe caustically.

'Please hear me out though, Will, dear,' Lucasta went on. 'Your cafe appears to be a place where the bereaved can find peace. If a tiny seance gives even a bit of peace to anyone at all, then how can we possibly deny them?'

* * *

Later, in the car on the way home, Phoebe turned to Lucasta, while they were stopped at traffic lights.

'Well, that was very convenient, wasn't it?' she said.

'What was?' Lucasta asked innocently.

'Spirits coming to you, at the exact moment you were trying to convince Will to let you have a seance in his cafe?'

'Hmm, what's that, dear?' Lucasta replied, pretending to be distracted by a delightful view of roadworks all along Leeson Street.

'Almost like you were acting a part there, I'd have said.'

'Really? Is that what you thought?'

'Most definitely,' Phoebe said firmly.

'In that case,' said Lucasta with a sly little smile, 'as I say to journalists whenever they start asking awkward questions, I have no comment to add.'

19

LUKE

The email was forwarded on from Stella and pinged straight into Luke's phone as he sat beavering away at his desk that afternoon.

From: Stellamackeyprincipal@primary.com
To: Lukearchitectanddesign@Ireland.com

Hi there,

Quick one for you. I just had an email from Will at the cafe which he asked me to pass on to you. Check this out. Sounds spooky, I know, but then, as Shakespeare didn't quite say, we're in blood stepped this far. I can be there too, as I'm guessing this is something we'll all need to support each other through as best we can.

Would love your thoughts.

Stella

His eye darting at speed, Luke scrolled on down to the bulk of the attached email and quickly picked out the salient points.

Hi all,

Forgive the round robin email. As you know, we've had one or two developments in our weekly Bereavement Cafe sessions. It seems now that one of our newer members would like to take things a little further and conduct a full-blown seance at the cafe.

This, I completely understand, mightn't be something that everyone is all on for. Truth be told, I'm against it and I wouldn't be surprised if the whole idea freaked some members out. Honestly? I'm a little freaked out myself too.

However, I thought it only fair to at least run it by you all. If enough people are up for it, then maybe we can take it from there. It wouldn't be on a Thursday night, because that's our 'regular' Bereavement Cafe nights.

Would appreciate your thoughts.

Warm wishes and thanks for your continued support,

Will

* * *

Later on that evening, coming up to 5 p.m., Luke was winding up for the day, filling his briefcase with plans and drawings that he planned to work on that night, once Amy had gone to bed. Before then, though, he had something entirely different planned for the two of them, something he was determined to do.

So far, so good, he thought, heading for the staircase that led down to the ground floor below, then out of a quiet side door onto the busy street outside. This was better than good and with any luck, he wouldn't be spotted. It was a warm, sunny evening and, for once, he actually had a bit of time on his hands. His plan was to collect Amy, then treat her to a trip to the zoo he'd long since promised her. For bloody once, work could take a back seat;

feck it, he'd pull an all-nighter if he had to, just to keep up to speed. Amy was so looking forward to this and the truth was, Luke was too.

When Helen was around, they'd done spontaneous things like this all the time, just the three of them. Helen had been brilliant at that; even with Luke so flat out in work, she'd always made sure that family time came first. She'd forever been planning little picnic excursions in the summer, or trips to a movie that Amy would love if the weather was cold. No matter how busy Luke had been, she'd always insisted he drop everything and come with them. 'Just for a few hours,' she'd say. 'What's the point in having kids unless you're going to be together as a family?' What indeed?

Picking up the pace, he was just tripping down the metal and chrome staircase at the back of the office, praying he wouldn't bump into anyone, when, from right behind him, a voice stopped him dead in his tracks.

An all too familiar voice.

'Hey, Luke, my man!' Luke twisted around sharply, his heart sinking like a stone when he saw who it was.

Dave, his boss. Bloody Dave. Beard-stroking Dave. The worst possible person who could have caught him.

'Heading off early?'

'Yes, actually,' Luke said, determined not to explain or to apologise. Why would he? He so seldom took time out, he'd lost count of the number of holidays he had stacked up. That particular day, he'd been working from home from 5 a.m. before Amy woke up and would probably still be hard at it come midnight too. He worked his arse off for this company, but this was family time and far more important than anything.

'You didn't get the email?' Dave asked, puzzled.

'What email is that?' Luke got literally dozens of emails every single day. Often, it was late at night before he got a chance to respond, with the exception of urgent ones that needed his attention immediately. But there'd been nothing out of the ordinary that particular day, definitely not. He'd have spotted it immediately; he'd have known.

'Bad news, man,' Dave said. 'The McKinsey team wants to meet us at the site later this evening. It seems their quantity surveyor has a few issues around the last engineer's report and he wants us to walk him through it. It's a fine sunny evening, so we thought it would be good to get this over and done with now. The forecast tomorrow is for storms, which means the site won't be safe. So it has to be this evening.'

'But no one told me about this,' Luke said, baffled. He whipped out his phone to double-check he hadn't missed anything, and sure enough, no. There was nothing there, absolutely nothing about any unplanned site meeting.

'Oh yeah?' said Dave. 'Is that right? Because Nick definitely said he got in touch with you to let you know.'

The little shit did *nothing* of the sort, Luke thought, quietly seething.

'So we'll see you there?' Dave said. 'At the site, in one hour's time? We really need all hands on deck for this. It's a biggie for us.'

But Luke held firm. He had to. This was too important to him and to Amy. She'd been so excited that morning before school; she'd skipped into her class happily telling all her pals that later that day she was going to see 'a lion *and* a zebra *and* an orangutan'. It was perfect weather for the zoo too, warm, balmy and sunny. Amy was going to have a ball and that was more important than any fecking job.

'I'm afraid I can't be there at such short notice,' Luke said politely. Or, in my case, no notice at all, he could have added, but didn't. He also could have said, you know what, though? I could meet you all there later, about 8 p.m. or so tonight. But he didn't volunteer that either. That would have meant a rushed, pressured trip to the zoo, then abandoning Amy back at Clare's. That would have meant disappointing his daughter when he'd promised to spend the whole evening with her, with the added treat of McDonald's for dinner. *To hell with that,* he thought. *How is that fair on her, or on me?*

'It's none of my business, but have you got somewhere else you need to be?' Dave asked worriedly.

'As a matter of fact, yes, I do. And it's important.'

'OK, I get it – your private time is your private time. But just this once, could you possibly change your plans? You're the project manager on this and we really do need you there.'

'I'm afraid not,' Luke said firmly. 'Family, you understand.'

Dave said nothing, just looked down the stairwell at him. No, Luke thought. Clearly someone like him had absolutely zero understanding about what family meant. None whatsoever.

Then Dave started stroking the beard and looked anywhere except at Luke. Which meant that this was bad. Worse than bad.

'Look,' he sighed. 'I hate to come over all "bossy" on you. You know me; I'd be the first to give you as much time out as you need. We all know what you're going through and we all feel for you. But this really is an emergency. I know you're dealing with a lot, but all we're asking for is one evening of your time. Hate to say it, bro, but is there any chance you'd reconsider?'

* * *

'Noooooo! You promised me! You're so mean and I *hate* you... I *hate* you!'

The screams were murderous. Luke was kneeling down in

Clare's hallway face-to-face with Amy, who sat on the bottom step of the stairs, howling inconsolably.

'Sweetheart, listen to me,' he said calmly, trying to reason with her. Ha! part of him thought. Good luck reasoning with a bitterly disappointed six-year-old. 'Daddy has to work this evening. I can't help it. This is really important.'

'But you promised! You *promised*! I even wore my jumper with all the animals on it today,' she said, pulling at the end of the jumper as snot rained down on it. 'Because you told me I was going to see a hippopotamus! You told me a lie! You're just a big, fat liar!'

'Honey, please try to understand,' Luke pleaded with her. Again, trying to make a kid of her age understand something like this? Not a chance. Wrong word, wrong approach, wrong everything. 'You and I are still going to the zoo,' he said, his heart breaking at the sight of her little face all bloated and red from crying, 'just not today, that's all. We're going to go on Saturday instead. We're still going to see the gorillas and the hippopotamus and all the monkeys, just like I promised. You just have to wait a few days, that's all.'

'You said we'd go today! You promised me!' Amy wailed again as Luke pulled a tissue out of his pocket and tried to wipe her nose. She pulled away from him then slapped him hard on his hand. Which was fair enough, he reckoned.

'Amy, pet, I told you, I have to work. It's a very big meeting that Daddy has to be there for.'

'You're always working! That's all you ever do!' she screamed, slapping him repeatedly on his hands and arms and anywhere her little arms could reach, in sheer bad temper. Luke tried to grab her hands and gently restrain her, but she was far too hysterical for that. 'Mum never broke her promises to me! Ever!'

Then the words that cut to Luke's heart like a physical stab.

'I want my mummy! I don't want *you*. I want my mummy!'

With that Amy clambered back to her feet, wailing for all she was worth, then ran straight back upstairs to her cousins, Holly and Poppy, who Luke could clearly see staring down through the bannisters from the very top floor of the house. Both of their faces were glaring hotly down on him, emanating hate waves. Check out the bad dad. The useless parent. The total waste of space.

As soon as Amy joined them, the three of them grabbed hands and scuttled out of sight as Luke slumped against the bottom stair, holding his head in his hands.

This is it, he thought. *This is rock bottom.* Making his poor, lost little girl cry tears like that? It didn't – it couldn't possibly have got worse.

'That went well, didn't it?'

He looked up to see his sister Clare, all five feet two of her, arms folded and looking so uncannily like their late mum, it was remarkable. Clare was looking down on him in deep disgust and, for Luke, it was a bridge too far.

'Clare, don't you start,' he said wearily. 'You have to understand that I'm holding on to my job by a thread. Dave is just looking for any excuse to get rid of me and then what? You know how badly I need this job, otherwise Amy and I sink.'

'No, Luke,' she said, icily furious. 'You're the one who has to understand. You cannot *ever* make a promise to a child and then renege on it. Have you any idea how shitty that is? Ever since I collected her from school today, all Amy could talk about was her trip to the zoo with you. She was so happy and excited and then you went and crushed her. It's despicable to let a child down like this. Shame on you, Luke. *Shame* on you.'

Clare was by far the most equanimous person Luke knew and to see her lose her temper like this really was a sight to behold. It didn't happen often, but when it did, by Jesus, you'd better run and hide.

'Go back to your fucking job,' she spat at him. 'Go and lick Dave's arse and tell your clients how bloody wonderful they all are. Just get out of my house, please. I can't look at you right now. Or listen to your pathetic excuses any more about why your job is the be-all and end-all and Amy isn't.'

'Clare, you don't understand,' Luke said exhaustedly. 'You really need to listen to me.'

'No, you dickhead,' she said, her voice low and throbbing and pretty bloody terrifying actually. 'You're the one who needs to listen to *me*. I know parenting is tough. I know it's not easy adjusting to being a single parent, because when Helen was here she did everything and she made it look easy. But you have *got* to find a way. Amy needs you to be both father and mother to her right now and you're failing on both counts – failing spectacularly, if you ask me. Sort yourself out. Get on top of this. Farming the child out isn't good enough – it's *you* she needs. Now, I'm her auntie and I love her like my own, you know that. Poppy and Holly would have her stay here forever if they could, but still. She only has you now and you're hardly ever there for her.'

Clare was shaking with rage and now Luke started to feel his own temper flaring. 'So what would you suggest I do?' he asked her. Jesus, he was sick and tired of getting it from all sides. Not cutting it in work and, according to Clare, the worst dad on the planet. 'Seeing as you have all the answers.'

'I never said I had all the answers,' Clare replied curtly. 'I'm just saying something's got to give. Amy should be your number-one priority and she's clearly not.'

'You want me to quit my job and go on the dole? Have you any idea how many unemployed architects there are out there?

Give up our lovely home, give up all my savings to keep Amy in a good private school? Is that what you'd have me do?'

'At least you'd be there for her. At least you'd be a proper dad instead of someone she sees for an hour in the morning and the same again at night, and that's if she's lucky. At least you'd have time for her. It's you she needs, not your fancy home and private school. You think a kid her age gives a shit about things like that? You're dreaming. Your job shouldn't be your top priority and yet it is.'

At that, Luke lost it. This was the last straw, even for someone like him who'd already dealt with so much.

'Oh, give me a break, Clare, would you? Seriously, you'd have me quit my job and move Amy to some shitty little shoebox somewhere miles from her school and from all her friends?' He could have said 'and away from you and the girls too' but he was too furious with her.

Jesus, why was he getting it from every direction? He was trying to do his best by everyone – why was he getting hell for it? Easy for someone like Clare to talk about quitting work and being a full-time parent. What did she know? Her husband, Tony, sat at board level for a huge multinational tech-support company, he regularly pulled in a six-figure salary, not including bonuses. He and Clare lived the high life; she drove a four-wheel-drive BMW and Tony drove a Lexus sports car that probably cost more than Luke earned in an entire year. You only had to take a look around Clare's hallway to see all the photos of the family away skiing at five-star resorts, or else spending their winter breaks in the Bahamas. Tony earned so much, Clare was in the privileged position of having been able to give up her own job in the bank, so she could be there for her own kids. Best of all, she could afford childcare whenever she wanted, around the clock, on tap. How dare she lecture him like this? How fucking dare she?

Determined to hold his tongue, Luke rose to his feet and made to leave. But Clare was nothing if not a last-word merchant.

'Go on, then, go,' she said coldly. 'Back to work, back to your precious job that's so fucking important. I think it's best Amy stay the night with me tonight. She doesn't want to be around you right now. And you know something else, Luke? Neither do I. Now fuck off and come back when you're ready to apologise.'

20

CONNIE

On the same day, across town, Connie was standing in the queue for 99s from an ice-cream van parked at the very top of Stephen's Green. It was a blistering hot sunny day and she was out for a stroll with Kate and the boys and, as Kate said, 'The little feckers have already heard the tinkling of the van, which means we'll never get a minute's peace till they've each got a Mr Whippy in their hands.'

'You get the coffees for us, I'll get the ice cream.' Connie had smiled as the boys trailed after her, bickering over whether to get chocolate flakes on top or else 'colourdy sprinkles,' as Tommy, Kate's eight-year-old, put it.

'Later on, can we go for pizza, Connie?' said Toby, with all the wisdom of a ten-year-old who knew when to take advantage of his mum being temporarily out of the frame, even if only for a few precious minutes.

'Ice creams first,' said Connie, ordering for the two of them, 'then we'll see how we go, OK? And in the meantime, how about a game of football in the Green?'

'Yay!' Tommy squealed, punching his fists in the air. 'I love hanging out with you, Auntie Connie. It's like, there's no rules at all. It's brilliant!'

Kate caught up with them just then, wheeling the baby in his buggy and laden down with a coffee tray with blueberry muffins for her and Connie. It was just after the boys had finished up school for the day as they all strolled from the top of Grafton Street across to the Green. In no time, Connie and Kate found a conveniently shaded bench with a huge grassy area in front, where the boys could kick a football around and scream their heads off all they liked.

'Let them tire themselves out to their hearts' content,' said Kate, pulling the stroller up beside her as she plonked wearily down on the bench. 'It'll certainly make my life a whole lot easier tonight. So tell me this, hon, now that we can talk,' she said, changing the subject. 'Any more calls on that battered old Nokia you keep dragging everywhere with you?'

'No,' Connie said, shaking her head. 'Not one. And when the estate agent was at the house scoping the place out, boy, what I wouldn't have given for an otherworldly phone call, just to scare the bejaysus out of her, if nothing else.'

'That Karen one sounds terrifying.'

'You have no idea,' said Connie, shuddering. 'She's determined to have the house sold and me out on the side of the road within weeks. It's like she's on a mission.'

'Well, you'll always have a roof over your head at my house,' said Kate kindly. 'The boys adore you; they'd never let you out of their sight!'

'That's so sweet,' Connie said, genuinely touched. 'And I adore them too. It's a lovely offer and I hope you realise how grateful I am.'

Still though. A large part of Connie knew how overloaded Kate's life was with the kids. The last thing she'd ever want was to be in the way. Like it or not, if the house sale happened as fast as Karen confidently predicted it would, then she'd have to find a forever home for herself. It would probably be hours away from Dublin and far from all her pals, but then what other choice did she have?

Just then, an email pinged through to her phone, distracting her.

'Sorry, Kate,' she said, jumping as her mobile alerted her. 'Do you mind if I just check this out? I'm waiting to hear from my agent about a casting later on this week, so say your prayers that this is good news.'

'I'm praying, babes.' Kate grinned, taking a sip of coffee and a large bite of her blueberry muffin. 'I'm cosmically ordering a big jammy job for you on a huge, big-budget movie that makes you a household name and a millionairess into the bargain. Then I can bring the kids out to LA to visit you when you're living in the Hollywood Hills and you'll be so rich, you'll be able to afford round-the-clock childcare, so I can have a proper holiday for once.'

Connie's eyes quickly scanned through the email, which had been forwarded many times but, first of all, was from Will at the Bereavement Cafe. Then, without a word, she passed her phone over to Kate, who read it too.

'Fucking hell, an actual seance?' said Kate, when she'd finished.

'I know.'

'Did you hear that? Mum said fucking hell, I'm straight telling Dad!' Toby squealed, although how he managed to hear anything was a total mystery – the kid was at least twenty feet away, acting as goalie to his brother.

'That's the thing about my kids,' Kate said dryly. 'I always say they have selective deafness when I'm nagging at them to tidy up their bedroom, but they can hear me eff and blind from two streets away.'

'I had a feeling this might happen,' Connie mused, rereading the email as she scrolled up and down. 'That woman I was telling you about, Lucasta...'

'She sounds extraordinary,' Kate chipped in. 'I've seen her on TV so many times and I've read a fair few of her books, but I'd no idea she was into all this.'

'It's like...' Connie grappled around for the right words. 'It's like she's some sort of conduit. If you believe that the spirits of the dead are all around us, then they seem to want to communicate through Lucasta Liversidge.'

'That sounds batshit crazy.'

'It *is* batshit crazy. And yet you just read that email. She mentioned doing a seance at the cafe the other night and you know what? If this does go ahead, then I've got a chance to be there.'

'A seance conducted by one of the most famous women in the country,' Kate said thoughtfully. 'You could video it and post it on YouTube. Make yourself a fortune.'

'As if,' Connie laughed.

'Seriously though,' Kate said, rocking the stroller beside her, completely wrapped up in thought. 'It all sounds kind of spooky to me. If you do go, what do you hope to gain from it?'

Connie sat back, took a sip of coffee and really gave thought to her answer.

'If Mum wants to get in touch with me, if she has some message from the other side, then I want to make it as easy for her as possible. Plus, I'd seriously love to know that I'm not imagining things. If there is a message for me, then hopefully there'll be other people there who'd be able to witness it. Hearing Mum's voice again has been so… emotional for me. But I'd really love to know that I'm not going off my head.'

'Fair point,' Kate said. 'And I'll tell you one other thing.'

'Which is?'

'That Will fella who sent you the email? He sounds like a dote.'

Connie looked back at her, puzzled.

'Just saying.' Kate shrugged, getting up to referee a fresh fight that had just broken out between the boys. 'If you happen to meet a nice fella out of this Bereavement Cafe malarkey, then there's yet another result for you. Win-win, if you ask me.'

* * *

Not long afterwards, yet another email pinged through from Will.

From: Will_Kempton@leesonstreetcafe.com
Subject: Seance?

Me again everyone,

Just to say I've had a pretty overwhelming response from people and it seems enough of you would like to have a seance at the cafe, which Lucasta has agreed to host. As you know, I'm a bit reluctant, but happy to go with what the majority want.

So how's this coming Tuesday for you all? 7 p.m. OK?

With thanks for your continued support,

Will

* * *

In the end, the following night a grand total of ten people turned up at the Bereavement Cafe. As they came in nervously one by one, Connie counted. It was strange though; whereas the last time she'd been here, the atmosphere had been relaxed and congenial, now everyone seemed to be peppering. There was tension in the air and, much as Will did everything he could to make everyone feel welcome and comfortable, there was no disguising it.

'Connie!' he said, greeting her warmly when she stepped nervously inside, with her mum's phone buried deep in the pocket of her jacket, just in case. Just in case. 'You came back to us. I was afraid the whole seance idea might scare you off.'

'No chance of that.' She smiled shyly back at him. 'Not every day you get to witness something like this. So I thought, why not?'

'Not a bad turnout.' Will nodded and as they turned around to scan the room, he folded his arms. 'I had no idea how many of you would actually pitch up this evening.'

'Me neither.' Connie smiled. 'I was afraid I might be the only one here.'

'I was very reluctant myself, I can tell you. Terrified it might scare regulars. But let's just see how it all pans out.'

They stood side by side and both took a moment to look around them. The architect, Luke, had arrived just before Connie and was sitting at a table for two with a woman Connie recognised from last week too. Neat trouser suit and no-fuss hair and make-up, along with sturdy, sensible shoes. *She looks professional,* Connie decided, taking her in from head to toe. *Like she's a senior manager somewhere or else works in government buildings.*

'That's Stella,' Will leaned down and whispered to her. 'Sound woman, once you get to know her. Comes here regularly, but rarely opens up. She's a school principal, apparently, although she looks far too young to be running a whole school.'

A school principal. Connie nodded. She hadn't been too far out. At the next table were the twins with the beautiful heads of thick red hair, one still in her school uniform and the other one in denim shorts with a sweatshirt that said, 'fuck the patriarchy'. She had AirPods in and was sitting cross-legged on an armchair ignoring everyone and everything, except for her phone, which she was texting furiously on.

'That's Lucy and Alex,' Will explained, following her gaze. 'They've been coming pretty regularly for a few months now. Lucy is always so friendly and chatty and involved, whereas Alex...'

'She's the one who stayed outside the group the other night? Glued to her phone?'

'She's a teenager who's grieving,' Will said wisely. 'In my experience, she'll open up when she's good and ready to.'

'So how long have you been running these evenings for?' Connie asked, turning to him with genuine interest.

'Over a year, would you believe?' Will chatted away, seemingly in no rush to serve anyone before they got going, happy just to chat. 'It started small, and then it just snowballed. Seems people really do need a safe space where they can talk about anything and everything to do with death and grief, but without judgement.'

'Such as nutters like me who are convinced their late mother is calling them on an ancient mobile phone?' Connie said teasingly.

'We've all been there.' He smiled kindly.

'Really?' Connie asked, surprised. 'Getting mad messages from a dead person who's trying to get in touch with you?'

'Some time when it's quiet,' he said quietly, 'we'll talk. Preferably on a night when we're not about to conduct a seance.'

Just then the Lululemon lady burst in, looking fresh from the gym with her long fair hair tied up into a high ponytail and wearing the coolest-looking pair of trainers Connie had ever seen. The kind that cost about €400, but looked like you'd got them in Penneys. She found herself staring over half in awe at her and wondering how it was possible to do that flawless, perfect 'no make-up make-up' look.

'And here's Mia,' Will said, welcoming her warmly as she bounced over to join them, brimming over with health and vitality. 'Good to see you, glad you came.'

'Sorry I'm late,' she said breathlessly, opening up the Chilly's water bottle she'd been carrying and taking a long, cool gulp.

No wonder she has that perfect skin, Connie thought, vowing to take a leaf out of her book. Gym and water seemed to be her thing; a right pain in the arse to stick to, but you only had to look at Mia to see the results.

'I was babysitting my granddaughter today,' Mia chatted away, 'but then my poor daughter got held up in work, so she was a bit late collecting her.'

'Granddaughter?' Connie blurted out, shocked. 'How can you be a granny? Seriously?'

'She's two months old and she's the light of my life.' Mia laughed. 'If you're not careful, I'll start boring the arse off you with baby photos. You have been warned.'

Hot on her heels came Mildred and Dee, the pair of them each carrying a serving platter covered in tinfoil, oohing and ahhing as they came in the door like an old vaudeville double act.

'A seance?' Mildred was saying. 'Can you believe we're actually here for a seance? Done by *the* Lucasta Liversidge? Wait till I tell the girls at bridge this weekend, they'll all be mad jealous.'

'Come on, Mother,' Dee twittered excitedly, 'let's grab good seats so we don't miss any of the action. I bet it'll be exactly like in *Blithe Spirit*!'

'Hello there, everyone!' Mildred beamed at the room. 'Anyone hungry? Look what we have for you tonight – chocolate biscuit cake...'

'With about half a bottle of Kirsch liqueur in it,' Dee finished the sentence for her. 'I know there's no drinks licence here, but sure, Will, you can't stop us getting a tiny bit of alcoholic fortification into us on a night like this, now, can you?'

'Might loosen us all up a bit.' Mildred giggled like a schoolgirl.

'Don't know what we'd do without the pair of you.' Will smiled. 'You're a tonic, do you know that?' Then turning to the room, he added, 'OK, everyone, quick cuppa before we kick off? Come on over to the bar when you're ready and I'll get you all sorted. We're just waiting on Lucasta to join us and then we can start.'

As if on cue, voices could suddenly be heard having what sounded like a tiff outside, loud and clear. Every head swivelled towards the bay window that dominated the coffee shop and, sure enough, there was the one and only Lucasta Liversidge, clambering out of the passenger seat of a car and looking exactly as she always did on TV, Connie thought, with that long, waist-length grey hair streeling down her back, dressed in a sensible tweed skirt and flowing layers of brightly coloured cardigans that trailed all along the pavement after her. She was opening up the boot of the car and seemed to be taking out what looked like a carpet bag stuffed full with – something. Impossible to tell what. Then that middle-aged woman in black who never, ever smiled and who seemed to go everywhere with her got out of the driver's seat as the two of them picked up what sounded very much like an ongoing row.

'Lunacy,' the one in black was saying, loud enough that everyone inside could overhear. 'This is sheer and utter lunacy.'

'Yes, Phoebe, dear,' Lucasta said through gritted teeth, still rummaging around the boot of the car. 'So you've said. Ad nauseam, actually.'

'And another thing,' Phoebe replied, standing tall and erect on the pavement, arms folded and making absolutely no attempt to help with all the bags Lucasta was unloading out of the car boot. 'Did it occur to you that someone might just video this? Then post it on social media? Can you imagine the repercussions that would have for you? And for your career?'

'Name one,' Lucasta said, firmly slamming down the boot of the car and turning to face her.

'People may write you off as insane.'

'Let them. I'll devote a whole chapter to it in my memoirs. Now, dear, are you going to continue being such a brick wall of negativity? Or are you actually going to do your job and help me?'

21

LUKE

The minute the batty novelist came clattering in, she insisted everyone move to a large round table to sit in a circle, accompanied by some bullshit about how the 'energies flowed better this way.'

If they could see me now, Luke thought, his mind not far from Dave and Nick at the office and the absolute field day they'd have if this ever got out. Not to mention Clare, who was still barely speaking to him. Long, long way to go there, he knew only too well. Amy had at least softened a little towards him, with the firm, unbreakable promise that their zoo day out would 100 per cent happen at the weekend and with a freezer bag full of treats for her and her cousins, which Luke had dropped off at Clare's on his way to the cafe. Clare was a very different story though. She was treating him with an ice-cold fury that was borderline terrifying.

He was lost in thought, wondering how best to fix this, when Stella sat down beside him and seemed to echo what he'd been thinking just a minute ago.

'Whatever happens this evening,' she whispered to him,

pulling in her chair and taking care to switch her phone off, 'whether it's good, bad or indifferent, I strongly suggest we keep this to ourselves. That OK with you? If the parents at the school were ever to find out about this...'

'Not a word.' Luke nodded. Message received loud and clear. It was very definitely in both their interests to keep their mouths shut.

'So how are you doing?' she asked, frowning as she took a good look at him. 'If you don't mind me saying, you look exhausted. Bad day at work?'

'Bad day all around,' he replied, trying to make light of it, even though that wasn't easy. 'Put it this way – I'm getting it from all sides right now.'

'We all get days like that,' she said, nodding wisely.

'I shouldn't even be here, by rights,' he said in a low voice. 'You've no idea the row that went on yesterday. Ugly stuff, let me tell you. I feel guilty just for taking time out to turn up tonight.'

'Hey, none of that now,' Stella said firmly. 'You're here for *you*. This is part of helping you to heal, and that's vitally important too. Unless you're coping with your wife's loss then how can you expect anyone around you to, with Amy top of the list?'

He looked back at her, genuinely touched. Stella was the first person who'd shown him any kind of compassion since the horrible row at Clare's. The only one who hadn't been down on him like a tonne of bricks just because he was trying to keep himself sane and keep the show on the road.

'Thanks for that,' he said simply. Then, dying for a good, fast subject change, he quickly added, 'Anyway, that's enough about me. How have you been? How is your week going?'

'Shh!' she whispered distractedly. 'Plenty of time for that later. Looks like we're about to start. Hold on to your hat – this could be interesting.'

Just then, Lucasta took her seat at the table and began to fumble around in one of the many bags she'd dragged in with her. 'Well, good evening, everyone,' she said in her cut-glass accent, with those bright blue eyes of hers twinkling. 'What a surprisingly good turnout, and may I say you're all terribly welcome. Now, the critical thing to remember about a night like this is that anything can happen – or nothing might happen. I do believe the spirit world are with us here, in the strongest way imaginable, but you must be well warned. Sometimes they can be obtuse and not bother to contact us at all. The key thing to remember is that one never knows.'

There was a loud sniggering at that and when Luke glanced up to see who it was, to his surprise it was Alex, one of the twins. Shock horror, she actually seemed to be joining in this evening, and was sitting at the table looking animatedly all around her. Like a completely different person tonight, Luke thought.

'You're most welcome to join us, dear,' Lucasta said to her, looking for all the world like her batty granny, yanking all those multifarious layers of coloured cardigans around her, even though it was a warm, early summer's day. 'It's Alex, isn't it?'

Alex nodded. 'This is actually kind of cool,' she said in a surprisingly deep, gravelly voice, so different from Lucy's. A twenty-a-day voice that was weirdly at odds with her fresh, youthful face. 'Do you think you might, like, get possessed or something? Be amazing to see that. Mind if I video you, if you do?'

'I think it's probably best if everyone switches their mobile off now, please,' Phoebe interjected, looking horrified at the very suggestion. 'No recording devices are permitted, thank you.'

'Let's just see how the night unfolds, shall we?' said Lucasta kindly.

'I told my English teacher in school that I'd met you,' Alex went on, hugging her knees to her chest. 'She was dead impressed. And normally she's a complete bitch-faced wagon from hell.'

'Miss Jenkins?' Lucy piped up innocently from beside her. 'No, she's not, she's really nice. She's one of the good ones.'

'She's nice to you, you lick-arse,' Alex muttered back darkly. 'Try being in my shoes for a change.'

'That's terribly kind of your teacher,' Lucasta interrupted. 'Please will you thank her on my behalf? And now I really think it's time we got cracking, don't you?'

There was an excited silence around the table, no one having the first clue what to expect. Then Lucasta scooped out about a dozen brand-new notebooks and pens from her bag, and passed them around the table. 'Take a notebook each, please. It's purely in case we need to spell out letters or anything like that. And, Will, dear? Do you mind turning the lights right down for me, please?'

Will nodded and jumped to it as Lucasta bent down to the floor and opened up yet another one of her bags, this time producing all manner of candles – enough to set fire to the whole place, Luke thought. Jesus, what had he let himself in for?

'Phoebe, dear?' Lucasta said, calling over to her assistant who always looked so miserable. 'Help me light the candles, will you? We need them scattered all around the room, please. And will you be gracing us with your presence at the circle?'

Luke looked from one to the other, aware of the undercurrent of tension that was playing out.

'Because if you don't,' Lucasta added sternly, 'then you'll just have to wait outside. No negativity at the table, please. It's strictly prohibited. Don't want any bad vibes scaring off the spirits, now, do we?'

Phoebe lit the candles, said nothing and just stayed tight-lipped and frowning. She strode silently to the table and plonked angrily down onto a free seat. 'Fine,' she answered tightly. 'I'm here.'

Lucasta ignored her and went back to addressing the whole group, now all sitting in a far more atmospheric circle with dozens of candles blazing all around them. 'Now, everyone,' she said, lowering her voice. It was almost dark outside and as the overhead lights had been switched off, the candlelight gave the place an eerie, otherworldly feel. 'I'd like you all to join hands, please. Just touching fingers, that's enough for now. We as a group must present a united connection. That's terribly important, you know.'

Everyone did as she said, Luke suddenly aware that he and Stella were touching on one side. Meanwhile the young woman who thought she was getting calls on a battered old Nokia phone was lightly connecting her thumb to his little finger on the other. For the life of him, he couldn't remember her name. He noticed she'd brought the Nokia here with her this evening though. There it was, sitting on her lap, bulky, heavy and knackered-looking.

'Ever see the movie *Blithe Spirit*?' he hissed to her.

'Ever see the play?' she whispered back with a little half-smile. 'I was in it.'

'No way,' he said, impressed. 'You're an actor?'

She nodded and smiled even wider this time, just as Lucasta caught them at it, like the two messers down the back of the class.

'I'm afraid I really do need to insist on absolute quiet from the table,' she said uber-politely, eyeing them both. 'If you'd be good enough to oblige me, please.'

Silence fell. All you could hear in the background was the gentle rhythmic ticking of a clock. Then a fresh peal of titters from Alex, who, yet again, everyone swivelled to look at.

'Sorry, sorry.' She smirked, looking as though she wasn't in the least sorry at all. As if she thought this was some kind of school field trip where she could act the eejit all she liked. 'I know, I'll shut up now. Seriously, though, am I the only one who thinks this is hilarious?'

'Shh, Alex, stop it!' Lucy, beside her, hissed back. 'Don't ruin it for everyone else.'

'I wasn't ruining it. I was actually enjoying myself. For once.'

'Shut up!'

'Get off my case, will you?'

'Just have a bit of respect, would you?' Lucy pleaded.

Lucasta interrupted and every eye turned back to her to hear what she'd have to say.

'Now, everyone,' she began, speaking slowly and calmly, shaking her long grey hair back over her shoulders, breathing deeply and closing her eyes. 'I must please ask you all to let me concentrate, while we try to see who's out there.'

A silence fell and even the twins piped down. Luke caught Stella's eye as she shrugged her shoulders a tiny bit, as if to say, 'We're here. We've come this far. So let's just go with whatever happens.'

'Our beloved spirits,' Lucasta intoned, as if she were reciting a prayer. 'We're gathered here with you tonight, at the borderline between our world and yours. We come in good faith and we're listening. Is there anyone out there? Can anyone hear me?'

You could have heard a pin drop.

'Anyone out there?' Lucasta said gently again. 'Is there someone here you'd like to leave a message for?'

Again, deep silence. Just the clock ticking and the sound of an ambulance thundering past on the street outside, sirens blaring. Nothing happened for a minute, then a loud banging noise from somewhere within the cafe. Everyone jumped, except, Luke noticed, Lucasta herself, who continued staring out into the middle distance, as if she was in another place.

'Jesus! What was that?' Stella hissed worriedly.

'Outside boiler,' Will whispered back, but Lucasta was quick to silence them.

'Shh, please!' she urged. 'I think there's someone here. I'm definitely picking up something... a male presence I think... he's terribly short in height with glasses... he's wearing an apron with something written on it, but I can't tell what... I get the sense of a very hard-working man... working around the clock, even at weekends...'

There was a sharp intake of breath and everyone turned to see Dee with her mouth dangling open and looking as if she was in the deepest shock.

'Mother,' she said urgently, nudging Mildred beside her, so all you could see were their two identical white heads of hair urgently conferring.

'What is it, love?'

'I think that might be Daddy!'

'What makes you think that, pet?'

'Hard-working man, glasses, wears an apron, and even works on weekends – that's Daddy to a T!'

Actually, Luke thought a bit cynically, *the description is so vague, it could be anyone. It could even be me. I work hard, I work weekends, if I'm reading I wear glasses and if I'm cooking for me and Amy, I'll wear an apron. Big deal.*

'Was your father a chef?' Mia asked from where she sat directly opposite them at the table.

'In a way, yes,' Dee replied. 'He ran his own very successful catering business.'

'What she means is that he drove an ice-cream van,' Mildred explained. 'Worked around the clock, even in the winter months, when he used to do a bit of trade by the beach. Poor old Jim,' she added sadly. 'I'd love a message from him, I really would.'

'Just to let us know that he's OK,' Dee finished the sentence for her.

'Ask him if he's happy where I keep his ashes.'

'Inside one of his pitch and putt trophies on top of the telly.'

'Shh, please,' said Lucasta, 'I really need to tune in!'

They've just spoon-fed her all the information she needs, Luke thought. *If the woman starts hearing the tinkly music from an ice-cream van and seeing 99s and Magnums, I am so out of here.* From the corner of his eye, he could see Stella shooting him a concerned look and he couldn't resist rolling his eyes back at her.

You OK? she mouthed silently.

Pile of shite, he mouthed back and you could see her stifling a subtle little smile.

But then Lucasta surprised them both.

'Oh, please, everyone, do be quiet – there's someone else who's just come in, who I'm sensing and sensing quite strongly too... a much younger person... young, fit, healthy and smiling...'

Luke sat up. *Let this be Helen. Please let this whole evening be worthwhile. Please be Helen.*

'I'm getting the sense of a young man,' Lucasta half muttered, half whispered, so you really had to strain to hear her. 'Oh my goodness, he's handsome too! Wearing sunglasses and so tanned and virile – the very picture of health and fitness – why do I think that he's a mountaineer? I see him very clearly at the top of a snow-capped peak...'

Luke froze and turned to Stella beside him, who'd gone completely white.

'Anything else?' she piped up in a quivering voice. Luke could feel her hand trembling against his and automatically gave it a reassuring squeeze, then back to touching fingers.

'I think he's here for you,' Lucasta replied, turning to her, but not looking like herself at all; her eyes were almost rolling into the back of her head. *Now this is interesting,* Luke thought. *This might be Stella's late fiancé. And if it's him, it might give her a bit of comfort.* Not that Stella seemed to need much comforting; she struck him as one of those self-sufficient people who dealt with grief and all that went with it quietly, privately and, above all, discreetly.

'I'm getting something about a piece of jewellery?' Lucasta persisted. 'Something around your neck?'

Stella's hand flew to her throat, where a silver locket hung. She began to twiddle with it nervously, sitting forward in her seat and anxiously waiting for more.

'Yes,' she said in a very, very quiet voice. 'That makes perfect sense to me. And are you picking up anything else? Maybe some kind of message for me?'

Lucasta inclined her head, as if she was straining to hear something being said that no one else could.

'Oh dear, no,' she muttered crossly to herself. 'Really, there needs to be some sort of queueing system in the spirit world. How am I expected to hear a thing clearly with them all clamouring in on top of me at once?'

'I'm still here, Lucasta,' Stella said to her, sounding more agitated now. 'Anything? Anything at all for me?'

'He's been interrupted, I'm afraid,' Lucasta said, shaking her head. 'Oh dear, such a nuisance when this happens – really, it's impossible to hear anything clearly when they're all battling for airtime.' Then raising her voice, she spoke up far louder this time and to thin air. 'Please, please, one at a time! Now where's that terribly good-looking mountaineering chap got to? There's a lady here who's very eager to connect with you. Name of Stella. Are you still there? Hello?'

But now there was nothing, just silence. All around the table, glances were exchanged but if Stella was deflated, she kept it to herself.

'Oh, who are you now?' Lucasta piped up, completely changing her tone. 'There's someone new here, methinks... Is that a spirit who hasn't contacted us before? Are you there? Who have you come here for?'

'Come on, Mum,' Luke heard Connie whispering under her breath from right beside him. 'One little message? You can do it, Mum! If you can manage a Nokia phone from the far side, you can manage this. Come on!'

'Now, who's here?' Lucasta said, sounding miles away and a bit creepy, if Luke was being honest. 'Woods, irons, putters, hybrids... My goodness, it's all like a foreign language to me...'

'Can I say something?' young Lucy said, timidly venturing her hand upwards.

'Yes, dear?' Lucasta said, still miles away.

'They all sound like golf clubs to me. Different kinds of golf clubs.'

'So, do you think...?' Alex said to her, staring at her twin now.

'Yeah, maybe.' Lucy shrugged. 'Our dad loved golf, you see,' she explained to the table.

'Hold on, please,' said Lucasta, getting visibly excited now, as if she was really latching on to someone or something. 'Yes...' she said, drifting away again. 'Yes, I do see...'

'See what?' Alex asked impatiently.

'The eighteenth hole,' Lucasta said decisively. 'I'm definitely picking up something about the eighteenth hole.'

Nice try, Luke thought, all his old cynicism flooding back to him again. *Maybe that's because Lucy already told you exactly where her dad's ashes were buried.* At his very first meeting; he could remember it vividly. Lucy had told the entire room that they'd scattered him at the eighteenth hole on his favourite golf course. He remembered, so wasn't there a good chance that Lucasta did too?

Not that he thought Lucasta was a bad person, deliberately out to deceive people, far from it. He sat back and looked at her dispassionately. No, he decided. She was just mad as a box of frogs and had it in her head that the spirit world communed through her. So now, she saw it as her life's mission to organise nights like this and fill people's heads with a whole load of crap. Stuff she'd picked up subliminally, forgotten all about, then rehashed under the illusion it was coming from some 'inner voice' prompting her, when it was nothing of the sort.

There's a lot of gullible people sitting around this table, he thought, looking all around him. Grieving people who'd believe any old shite you told them, if it gave them comfort. It was a pity there were no more messages for Stella, but then it was all artifice. It was all a big waste of time. It was all complete bollocks.

'Oh my actual God,' Lucy said, almost bursting out of her skin. 'Did you say the eighteenth hole? Because that's where we put Dad's ashes! Didn't we, Alex?'

Course you did, Luke thought, starting to get angry now. *All she's doing is regurgitating information she's already been fed, that's it. There's about as much spirituality going on around this table as there is in the off-licence across the road. Anyone who thinks otherwise is delusional.*

He sat back against the chair, exhaling deeply, and wondering how soon he could reasonably get out of there. Sure, Lucasta had once come out with the names Helen and Amy, which had freaked him at the time, but now? It was a mystery all right, but, like all wizards once you got to peek behind the curtain, you could be bloody sure there was some perfectly simple, rational explanation for it.

Lucasta was mumbling and moaning again, the full monty.

'Yes, yes, your father really is a very strong presence here this evening,' she said as Lucy looked ready to explode with joy and even Alex looked excited.

Shame on you, Luke thought, firing the woman a filthy look. Leading two vulnerable teenage schoolgirls down the garden path like this, for feck's sake. How low could you go? The only thing he could say in Lucasta's favour was that at least she wasn't charging money for this. If she had been, Luke would have reported her to the fraud squad, then outed her on every shock-jock radio phone-in show out there.

'Shh, please!' she was urging. 'I think your father has got some kind of message for you both...'

'Yes?' said Lucy eagerly.

'What is it?' Alex chimed in.

'He wants you both to be kind to each other,' Lucasta half whispered. 'To work hard in school and to take care of your mum too...'

Oh, good Jesus, Luke thought, unable to take another minute of this drivel. For fuck's sake, the time he was wasting here, he could be spending precious time with Amy. He could be building bridges with Clare or at least trying to. Anything rather than sitting here listening to this load of horse manure.

'I'm so sorry to break up the circle,' he said, the minute his mind was made up. 'But I really do need to leave. Not my thing, I'm afraid. Thanks, Lucasta, thanks, everyone. Apologies once again and enjoy the rest of your evening.'

Every single eye was on him as he stood up, picked up his briefcase and laptop and made for the door. *Let them all stare,* he thought. *I tried this, it didn't work.* Besides, if Helen really was trying to reach out to him, surely she could find another way, rather than through a load of time-wasting nonsense like this?

22

CONNIE

What the hell did Luke think he was doing? Connie wondered, her eyes following after him, along with everyone else's. What kind of an eejit was he? Connie stared after him as he apologised to everyone, said a perfectly polite goodbye, and then was out of the door like a hot snot. You could barely see him for dust. What was going on with him anyway? Why come this far, only to walk out halfway through?

No sooner was he gone than that big, heavy table everyone was gathered around began to wobble. At first, gently. Nothing you'd bat an eye at really. It was no more than a barely perceptible rocking motion, like you'd get at any table if one leg was a tiny bit shorter than the others. But then, to Connie's astonishment, it became stronger, so much stronger. In no time, the rocking from side to side became forceful, noisy, almost powerful.

'Is someone doing this on purpose?' Mia asked, looking seriously scared, as the table kept on rocking from side to side. 'Is someone deliberately messing with the table?'

'Not me.'

'Nor me either.'

'Well, someone has to be making this happen,' Mia insisted. 'Tables don't just move by themselves. So whoever it is, you can stop it right now, you're scaring me.'

One by one, they all lifted their hands up from the table, as if to prove, Look, it's not me! And still the table, a pretty heavy Victorian-looking job, by the way, kept on rocking, except it was almost violent now. Completely by itself, defying every law of physics Connie knew about. She didn't know whether to be fearful or else to start giggling, just as Alex was opposite her.

'Everyone, please,' Lucasta said calmly, taking control of the room again. 'She's here again, and, oh, my dears, she's stronger than ever.'

'Who's here?' Stella, that school principal, asked. 'Who exactly are you referring to, and who is she here for?' Typical teacher, Connie thought wryly. Looking for a full explanation. In the middle of a seance. Jaysus.

'It's you, isn't it?' Lucasta whispered. 'Helen? Yes, yes, I felt it must be you...'

'Helen?' Mildred piped up. 'Who's she?'

'Oh, you remember, Mother,' Dee whispered back to her. 'Luke's late wife. The very first time he was here, she tried to get in touch with him through Lucasta.'

'Should I run after him?' Connie blurted out, concerned that he was missing all the action.

'No, dear, it's very important that you all stay just as you are,' Lucasta said, seemingly locked in her trance. 'She's here though, she's very much present and... Oh, goodness, she's so angry with him now for leaving here when he did.'

'Anything else?' Stella said. 'If it's a message for him, I'll gladly let him know.'

'She says... she says—' Lucasta started to say, but then she broke off abruptly.

'She says what?' Stella insisted.

'She says she knows tomorrow night's winning Lotto numbers?' Alex said, before peeling off into more titters.

'Shh, please!' Lucasta said more firmly. 'She says... Oh, dear. Now I think she's getting upset, desperately upset. She says why did he leave? Before she'd even had the chance to speak to him. She says...'

'Says what?' said Stella, almost on the edge of her seat.

'She says why didn't he trust her? Doesn't he know that she'd never let him down? Ever?'

* * *

The following afternoon was summery: warm, bright and gorgeous. Connie had just been to see a play in Bewley's Cafe Theatre, a cracking little venue that specialised in lunchtime plays by new up-and-coming playwrights and which her pal Mbeki had just written her very first play for. The show was about two pals who join a weight-loss group, one to lose three stone, the other to maintain her perfect body shape and to piss everyone else off. The whole play had been funny, wise and thought-provoking, raising all manner of issues about the strides feminism had made versus the pressures of social media and how it fuelled the modern-day obsession with the perfect body.

'And all for the price of twenty euro!' Connie said afterwards, hugging Mbeki proudly and telling her over and over how brilliant her play was. The two had grabbed a coffee and were now outside the theatre saying their fond goodbyes before each going their separate ways. Mbeki was heading towards where her bike was parked at the bottom of Grafton Street, whereas Connie was zipping up to a handy supermarket that was right at the opposite end of the street, to pick up a few bits and pieces she needed.

'You're a superstar for coming.' Mbeki beamed delightedly, strapping her backpack to her shoulders and putting on her bike helmet. 'Next time I write a play, I'll remember to write one with parts for you and me, babes. That's a promise!'

'I'll hold you to that.' Connie laughed as they peeled off in their separate directions. A few minutes later, she was in the supermarket at the self-service checkout queue with a basket full of the essentials, i.e., wine, popcorn and tampons, when a voice directly behind her made her jump.

'Didn't expect to see you here.'

She turned around to see Will laden down with his own groceries, except, in his case, his basket looked a hell of a lot more nutritious than hers: he had actual vegetables in there, all very organic-looking and still covered in dirt, as well as apples, bananas, a bottle of freshly squeezed orange juice and a head of lettuce. And a large bottle of Pantene conditioner. *Ahh, now I have your secret,* she thought, smiling to herself. *That's how the man-bun always looks in such shiny, glossy, salon-esque condition. You're well and truly sussed, mate.*

'Hey, good to see you.' She smiled as the queue inched forward.

'Still in one piece after last night, then?'

'Absolutely.'

'I have this awful feeling,' he said, keeping up the chat, 'that one or two people might have been scared off.'

'I hear you,' she said, taking care to lower her voice so no one else would. 'Wobbling tables? Messages from the other side? It was all a first for me. And I'm so glad some people got to hear from loved ones.' Just about everyone except me, she could have added, but didn't. You could hardly hold poor old Will to blame because her late mother's spirit hadn't been at the front of the queue to leave her some deep and meaningful message from the other side. Maybe another time. Maybe.

'Not to everyone's taste, I know,' Will said as two self-service scanners close together became free. Side by side, they beeped and scanned their products, keeping the chat going.

'Not at all, it was a great night,' Connie lied stoutly.

'Oh yeah? I'm not too sure that Luke, our architect friend, might agree with you,' Will said dryly as Connie's machine announced, 'Approval needed.'

'It's because of her freakishly youthful looks,' Will joked with the sales assistant who stumped over, looking bored out of her skull, barely even bothering to look at Connie before tapping the screen where it said 'User over 18'.

'Happens to me all the time,' Connie joked back. 'I'm always getting ID'd in bars. It's mortifying. Ruins your night out.'

He helped her to bag her shopping, tampons included, without raising an eyelid, and they made for the escalators to take them back up to the ground floor then out onto the street, still yakking away all the while.

'So why do you think Luke left so abruptly?' Connie asked as they headed back out onto South King Street and naturally fell into step together. 'Fear of the unknown? Or maybe he just got a bit pissed off with the whole set-up?'

'To be honest,' said Luke, 'I was amazed he turned up at all. He always strikes me as a guy who's operating at stress levels that could easily land him inside an A & E one of these fine days. He needs to chill out, badly.'

'He seems to be friendly with Stella, the school principal?'

'I think his kid goes to the school she works in,' Will chatted away as they both automatically started walking in the same direction, towards Stephen's Green and in the direction of Leeson

Street. Connie had a bit of time to spare, so continuing the conversation was an added boost to the day for her and Will was such a talker, it was too hard to pull away.

'And do you really think that was his late wife banging tables and trying to get in touch with him after he left?' she asked.

'I've absolutely no idea who or what it was,' Will said thoughtfully as they weaved their way in and out of the crowds and tourists all out enjoying the city in the warm, early summer sun. 'I've never been to a seance before.'

'Me neither.'

'I just hope we see Luke again soon. He strikes me as a man who doesn't get the chance to talk about what he's going through in any way, shape or form. I'd love to see him back at our meetings, but maybe this time contributing a bit and talking about Helen, his wife. When grief gets bottled up like that...' He just whistled there, and Connie didn't need him to finish the sentence for her.

They kept on walking, this time taking a less crowded shortcut through the Green and past the pond, where hordes of parents with kids fed hungry ducks at the water's edge, everyone seemingly Instagramming as they did.

'You never told me something,' Connie said, figuring this was her only chance so she might as well go for it.

'I never told you what?' Will asked. 'Hey, I've got no boundaries – I'd tell anyone anything.'

'Well... what exactly made you set up a Bereavement Cafe in the first place?' she probed. 'I know it's a fast-growing phenomenon abroad, but I have to know what inspired you to open one in Dublin. How did you know it would catch on here?'

At that Will pulled a face and looked straight ahead of him. 'Not sure that it has really caught on here,' he said ruefully. 'I mean, sure, we have about a dozen or so regulars, and it's always magic to welcome new faces like yourself,' he added with a bit of a half-wink. 'But it's been slow, let me tell you. Other countries have branched out and opened up multiple Bereavement Cafes all over the place in the space of time I've been up for business, which is just over a year now. But here in Dublin? The concept is taking time to sprout the way I'd like it to.'

'You really do want to help people badly, don't you?' Connie said, looking across at him.

'I studied psychology in college,' he replied as they made their way over a little ornamental bridge where a clatter of Asian tourists were almost dangling off the edge of it, all in quest of the perfect selfie. 'And I wrote my thesis on the psychology of grief. But on the side, I was always interested in catering too – I trained as a barista and worked in coffee shops to put myself through college. Then, not long after I managed to land the lease on the Leeson Street premises, I heard about Bereavement Cafes in the UK and the US, and I thought I'd punt it here, just to see if there were any takers. And now one year on...'

'Here you still are,' Connie said, finishing the sentence for him as the path took them to the central fountain slap bang in the middle of the Green, where a gang of teenagers were sitting on the edge of it, dangling their bare feet into the water to cool off and drinking cans of Heineken.

'Here I still am.'

'Do you mind me asking you something else?' she persisted as they strolled on. Feck it, she thought. She was enjoying the chat and it wasn't as though Will hadn't seen her at her most vulnerable, now, was it?

'Ask anything.' He grinned back at her. Big, friendly, warm, open smile too, she thought. Sparkly white teeth. Jesus, casting directors would go absolutely nuts over this fella; he'd be so perfect in an ad for a dating site.

'The minute I walked into your cafe,' she said, 'I knew everyone there would have at least one thing in common: we're all grieving. Some of us have recent losses and some of us are a bit further down the road with it, but still. We're all in this together. Would I be a million miles out,' she went on, 'in thinking you yourself have personal experience with grief?'

Will nodded as they headed for one of the main entrances to the Green, the one closest to Leeson Street.

'My dad,' he said. 'Gone just over a year now.'

'You must have been close.'

'So close that we actually lived together,' he replied. 'With not a single cross word between us. Not once, not ever. It was almost like there was no generation gap at all.'

'That's just like me and Mum!'

'Really?'

'I lived with her for years and it was more like living with my best friend than with a parent. There was absolutely nothing I couldn't tell her. And believe me, I did.'

Often about online dates that had been so disastrous, they were borderline hilarious, but Connie felt there was no need to go into that. Certainly not now, anyway.

'That's good to hear.' Will smiled. 'It was just the same with me and Dad. I was a penniless student working on my thesis, and he was a bit lonely living on his own, so it made perfect sense for the two of us to move in together. Then when he was diagnosed with dementia a few years ago, it was awful, but at least I was there with him, day and night, around the clock to look after him properly, the way he deserved.'

'I'm sorry to hear he had dementia,' Connie said gently. 'That can't have been easy. On either of you.'

'They say with dementia that you actually lose the person twice. First, you lose them mentally and that can drag on for years. Then you lose them bodily when they finally do pass away and, even though that's harrowing, I still think losing Dad mentally was the worst of all.'

'I really am so sorry,' she said uselessly.

'The long, slow farewell, they call it, and I can see why. There were days when Dad didn't even know who I was…' But he broke off there and took a beat before continuing. 'Anyway, put it this way. It's not something I'd wish on my worst enemy.'

'And your mum?' Connie asked tentatively, dying to know.

'I'm happy to say Mum's alive and well and living the high life down in Marbella, if you don't mind,' he replied. 'She and Dad broke up when I was a teenager and I suppose… Well, me and Dad just got on so well, I ended up being far closer to him than I ever was to Mum. Mum's had a new partner for years now, an English guy about Dad's age, and he and I never really had much time for each other, so, in a way, that bonded me and Dad even further.'

'Do you have siblings?'

'Just me.' He shrugged. 'In fact, I wish I had a brother or sister. Someone else I could share all the memories of Dad with.'

'Trust me,' Connie said wryly, with Donald not far from her thoughts, 'you don't.'

'You've got siblings?' he asked, and she nodded.

'And believe me, there have been many long nights when I've lain awake in bed, wishing I was an only child.'

'Ooh, that sounds like a story,' he said, turning to look at her as they stopped at a pedestrian crossing.

'Not a very nice one, I'm afraid. And not one with a happy ending, either.'

'How do you mean?'

'I've got an older brother, Donald.'

'Do you and Donald get on?'

'Yes and no,' she said, really considering her reply. Feck it, Will was just so easy to open up to and it felt good to get this off her chest. 'Except he's insisting the family home be sold now, which he's quite within his rights to do...'

'But you want to keep on living there,' Will said, second-guessing her.

'Exactly. And because I can't afford to buy him out...'

'You've got to sell, then move out of your home? That's rotten for you! Where will you go?'

'The million-dollar question,' Connie said as the lights changed and they strolled the short distance up Leeson Street, past the pubs, past the nightclub and on towards the cafe, where it looked quiet inside and where a young guy of nineteen or twenty tops was sitting behind the counter, reading a novel and looking bored off his head.

'New assistant?' she asked, peering through the window.

'One of my neighbour's kids. He's first year in college and I promised his mum I'd help him out. I'd say he's dying to get out of here, but at least he's making a few quid, so he can go out drinking with his college mates after work.'

'Well, I'd better leave you to it,' Connie said, making to go.

'Why don't you come on in and tell me all about your house being sold?' Will insisted. 'As you can see, the place isn't exactly out the door with customers during the daytime, so I've got time if you do.'

'I wish I could...' Connie said, shrugging her shoulders. 'But I'd really better get going.'

'No,' Will insisted, 'come on in! I'll even throw in a free coffee for you, how's that? Look, I dragged you all this way, it's the very least I can do.'

'You didn't drag me at all.' She smiled. 'I don't live too far from here, as it happens. And while I'd love a good, strong coffee, not this time, I'm afraid.'

'Pressing engagement?' he asked, putting his shopping bags down and shoving his hands into his pockets.

'You said it,' she replied. 'Her name is Karen and she's terrifying. She supposedly is selling my house and finding me somewhere to live that's within my budget. Best of luck with that!'

'Go on, then, off you go. You go and meet the scary estate agent and best of luck with it. I might have to insist on dragging you here another time though,' he added lightly.

'Goodbye, Will. And yes, another time.'

He stood at the door of the cafe, but wouldn't actually go in, instead he kept watching her for a bit, until she'd walked all the way to the top of Leeson Street. She could feel his eyes on her back. Embarrassing, but kind of cute at the same time.

23

LUCASTA

'Goodness, who are all these people, Phoebe? What are they doing here at this ungodly hour of the morning?'

'Climate-change activists. Don't worry, it's not you they're protesting against. You're not that important, so don't kid yourself. They're here for the Minister of the Environment. He's on the same breakfast TV show as you.'

'Oh, really? Is that right?' Lucasta said, genuinely impressed, giving the protestors the equivalent of a royal wave as their car and driver inched their way through the gates of Channel Six.

'Fuck's sake, look!' one of the protestors screamed the minute she spotted who was inside the chauffeur-driven limo. 'That's Lucasta Liversidge!' Then, with a few of his fellow protestors joining in for good measure, they all started banging on the roof of the car to loud yells along the lines of, 'My mum and me have all your books! The two of us bawled crying at your last movie! When's the new one out?'

Lucasta rolled down her window fully as the car gingerly worked its way through them all and waved again.

'It's wonderful to see young people so passionate about the

environment!' she called back to them as the driver inched his way through. 'Do keep up the great work!' At that, she got a very loud cheer and, with one final thumbs up, she slumped back down into her seat again.

'Imagine getting up out of bed at an insane hour of the morning to protest and wave placards about,' she said to Phoebe beside her. 'You'd have to really care, wouldn't you?'

'Hmmm, very worthy cause,' Phoebe said flatly, glued to her iPad and paying no attention to the protestors whatsoever. They'd quickly lost interest in Lucasta's car though, as just then a very official-looking sleek black Mercedes glided up behind them at the entrance to Channel Six studios. This time, the protestors were onto the car like a swarm of angry bees.

'It's him, it's him!' the yelling started. 'Come on, get him, quick!'

'How do you know it's him?' the protestor who was such a fan of Lucasta's shouted back. 'The windows are tinted, you eejit!'

'Yeah!' someone else cried out. 'Could be the fecking weatherman for all you know!'

'Since when do weather reporters come to work in chauffeur-driven limos? It's the minister, you moron... Come on, get going!' With that, like a well-trained unit, the gang of protestors started violently pelting boxes of eggs all over the government car, then chasing it all the way up the driveway that led to TV Reception, as a lone security man ran after them, frantically calling for backup on a walkie-talkie.

'This is what they should be filming, you know,' Lucasta commented as her car glided through unscathed. 'Far more interesting than whatever nonsense they've got on TV at this hour of the morning. Of that, you can be certain.'

'That's as may be,' said Phoebe crisply, 'but for now, we need to run through the order of questions for your interview as pre-agreed with the producer. I really need you to pay attention, please,' she said impatiently as, yet again, Lucasta stuck her head, neck and shoulders halfway out of the window, clapping and cheering on the protestors.

'Please, will you listen to me?' Phoebe insisted. 'The *Good Morning Ireland* show has a massive audience share and it's vital you don't do what you normally do.'

'Which is what, dear?' Lucasta said, rolling her window back up again as the car moved on towards the main entrance.

'Which is segue off on a tangent, then start talking about something utterly unconnected with your new book. Please try to remember, no matter what the question is, the answer is the new *Mercy* paperback, now available online and in all good bookstores nationwide. Got it?'

'Yes, yes, yes, no need to worry, dear, I'll stay "on message", as you're always nagging me to do,' Lucasta replied automatically as the chauffeur sent by the studio leapt out of the driver's seat and came around to open up the car door for her. 'Thank you so much.' She beamed up at him. 'I could get used to this kind of five-star treatment, you know.'

Once inside, they were met at TV Reception by a smiling, friendly and incredibly fresh-faced production assistant who introduced himself as Clive and who couldn't take his eyes off Lucasta.

'Oh my actual Gowd,' he gushed as Phoebe restrained herself from rolling her eyes. 'I can't believe I'm actually meeting you – I almost feel like I should be curtseying!'

'Nonsense, Clive, I'm just delighted to be here,' Lucasta said, graciously allowing him to kiss her hand, like an eighteenth-century duchess out on stately progress.

'If I may interrupt,' Phoebe intruded, 'it's almost 7 a.m.

Shouldn't we get Lucasta directly to Make-Up? She can't possibly go on television looking the way she does.'

'Of course,' Clive said enthusiastically, 'although, if I may say so, you could go on the show just as you are, Lucasta, and be just as beautiful as any of them.'

'Make-Up,' Phoebe said bossily, looking as if she was trying not to vomit. 'Now, please.'

'Follow me, if you please,' Clive said, leading them down a long corridor, through a whole succession of locked and coded security doors, until they finally got to the make-up department, where the equivalent of a SWAT team descended on Lucasta, armed with make-up brushes, bronzers, powders, hair straighteners, you name it.

Twenty minutes later, a transformed Lucasta sat under full lights in the *Good Morning Ireland* studio, perched on a fuchsia-pink sofa as a sound man clipped a mic into one of the many, many voluminous cardigans she was wearing. In bright canary yellow today, so there was certainly no missing her against the hot-pink sofa.

The hosts of the show, Bill and Becky, were a celebrity married couple both onscreen and off, they'd been hosting the morning slot successfully for years, and audiences everywhere seemed to get as much of a kick out of the regular on-air rows they'd have as the actual content of the show. Bill was fifties, portly and greying, with a facial expression that might as well have read, 'why am I wasted on a nonsensical load of fluff like this when I should be presenting prime-time current affairs?' Becky, meanwhile, was exactly the same age as him, but desperately trying to look twenty years younger, with blonde hair extensions, puffed-out lips, a boob job she regularly referred to on air as her 'marriage saver', and facial filler that seemed to have a life of its own and tended to trend on X every time it appeared to move live on air.

'So now for all our lovely early-birdie viewers out there—' Becky was beaming brightly to camera '—we have a very special treat lined up. In the studio right here beside me, we have none other than—'

'Well, actually,' Bill interrupted her with a big hearty grin plastered on his face, 'it's surely more accurate to categorise our next guest as a treat for all our *bookish* viewers out there.'

'Oh, really, Bill?' Becky said, turning to him, but with her megawatt smile unbudging. 'Because I'd have said our next guest is a national treasure, who all of our viewers, whether they're literary types or not, can enjoy. Wouldn't you agree?'

'Well, I'm not sure I would, actually,' Bill replied, with just about the fakest chuckle Lucasta had ever heard, as she sat patiently on the sofa beside them. 'Literary? People who read these kinds of books? I don't think so.'

There was a patronising edge to his fake cackle, but Becky was having none of it.

'Don't tell me you're distinguishing one kind of reader from another, Bill?' she asked sweetly, but with a distinct edge to her tone now.

'I just think there's a world of difference between someone who reads Booker Prize winners,' came the cool reply, 'and the kind of reader who'd pick up something you might grab in an airport for a tenner, on your way to lie on a beach in Tenerife for a fortnight.'

'Books are books and reading is reading, surely,' Becky said acidly, 'and we're incredibly lucky to have our next guest on the show – she has sold over eighty million books, you know, Bill. Or perhaps you were too busy working your way through this year's Booker Prize shortlist to bother reading the researcher's notes?'

Bill gave a condescending little snort. 'Obviously,' he said directly down the camera lens, 'I research every guest who comes on with considerable thoroughness. In this case, though, she is so well known, she really transcends all that and needs no introduction—'

Lucasta could hold her tongue no longer. 'Then, for God's sake, will one of you just introduce me?' she burst out, to snorts and sniggers from the camera crew on the studio floor. 'Goodness me, what a pair of squabblers you are. And you're really married? Seriously? I do wonder about your home life, you know, if this is how you behave in public. And on national television too. Gracious me. My Johnnie and I had our ding-dongs, but we never went public on a tiff – that was our golden rule.'

That seemed to do the trick and shut both Becky and Bill up as they turned to welcome her, almost as if they were only for the first time noticing she was sitting there.

'And here she is.' Becky smiled warmly. 'The one and only Lucasta Liversidge, one of the most beloved writers, not just in this country, but all over the world. You're more than welcome, Lucasta.'

'Thank you, my dear. Although I could do with a stiff drink after witnessing the way you pair carry on.'

'Oh, that's all good-natured fun,' Bill chimed in. 'Pay no attention to us!'

'So we have some wonderful news for all our viewers out there,' Becky went on, really finding her stride now. 'Our beloved Mercy is back by popular demand and there's a new *Mercy* novel about to hit our shelves! I'll bet fans of this wonderful book series are dancing about their kitchens now. I know I certainly was when I first heard the great news.'

'How very kind of you,' Lucasta purred.

'And admittedly, the *Mercy* stories may not be something that the "literary" readers Bill refers to might go for,' she added pointedly, 'but for tens of millions of people worldwide, this is very welcome news. Perhaps you'd like to tell us all about your new book, Lucasta?'

'Just to clarify to all our viewers out there,' Bill interrupted with a sharp edge to his voice, 'I absolutely do not distinguish between readers of a more literary persuasion and anyone who reads books by our next guest. That's absolutely not the case at all, Becky. As you know perfectly well.'

'And yet that's exactly what you *did* do,' Becky fired back, still holding that fixed grin and looking straight to camera.

'Oh, will you stop all this bickering, the pair of you?' said Lucasta, looking disgusted and making a swatting gesture. 'Really, all this nonsense over nothing. Books are books and reading is reading and personal taste is neither here nor there. Now, do you want to chat about my new one or not? I got out of bed at five in the morning for this, you know, and my assistant, Phoebe, would murder me if I didn't at least mention the book.'

'Of course we want to talk about your latest book.' Becky grinned cheesily. 'We're honoured to have you here this morning, Lucasta, to tell us all about the brand-new *Mercy* novel, which is available in all good bookshops now. This one is set on the *Titanic*, I understand, is that right?'

'Yes, indeed, thank you, Becky,' said Lucasta, 'and it was the most wonderful fun researching it.'

'Presumably you watched all of the many *Titanic* documentaries out there as part of your research?' Bill asked her, looking bored.

'Oh, goodness me, no,' said Lucasta. 'I never watch television. I don't even own a telly box. No, I researched the book in a far more interesting way.'

'Which is how exactly?' Becky said, sensing something that would grip viewers was coming.

'I went to visit the Fairview Lawns cemetery all the way over in Halifax,' Lucasta chatted away, 'and spent a huge amount of time there, communing with the dead.'

At that, Bill's ears pricked up. 'Did you just say "communing with the dead"?' he asked, actually starting to look involved in the conversation now.

'Yes, absolutely.' Lucasta nodded, as though this were the most normal thing in the world. 'Why not? And utterly fascinating it was too. Oh, let me tell you, my dears, I was in direct communication with the most wonderful passengers from all walks of life. I was in touch with people from first, second and third class, as well as a few of the seamen whose final resting place is in Halifax. Astonishing stories! So inspirational for me.'

'So, just to get this straight,' said Bill, sitting forward and really engaging now, like a bloodhound who'd just picked up an interesting scent. 'You claim you were in touch with the dead who lost their lives on the *Titanic*?'

'Oh, believe me, that's nothing,' Lucasta said dismissively, with a wave of her wrist. 'Dead people talk to me all the time. To the point where it can be a bit embarrassing. Take my late husband, Johnnie, for instance. I actually think he and I communicate far more now than we ever did when he was alive. Morning, noon and night he's in touch with me. When he was alive, there were times when I'd be doing well to get so much as a grunt out of him.'

'So you really think the dead speak to you from beyond the grave?' Bill persisted, as even the crew went silent in the background.

'Oh, I don't just think it, I know it,' she replied, as if this were all quite sound. 'There's absolutely no doubt about it at all. Why, only last night I was conducting a seance with a terrific group of people I've met through a local Bereavement Cafe.'

'You were *what*?' said Becky, looking as if she could hardly believe her ears at the scoop that was unfolding live on TV.

'What's a Bereavement Cafe?' Bill asked at exactly the same time, like someone who sensed TV gold here, where he'd least expected it.

'It's an absolute godsend of a place.' Lucasta smiled. 'A delightful little old-fashioned coffee shop on Leeson Street where like-minded souls meet and chat and tell stories about their dear departed. All kinds of stories too: funny ones, sad ones—'

'New one on me,' Bill muttered under his breath as Becky anxiously looked down to her notes.

'Do you know, there's a gentleman I met there,' Lucasta went on, completely ignoring the pair of them, almost musing away to herself, 'name of Luke somebody or other. Wright. Yes, I think that's it, Luke Wright. I remember him telling me he was an architect because I distinctly remember thinking what a suitable name it was for one – you know, just like Frank Lloyd Wright. Anyway, he's recently widowed and not coping with it at all well. He's got a little girl by the name of Amy and I think he's finding life a huge struggle since his wife passed away. Of course, his late wife, Helen, hasn't gone anywhere at all. She's with him all the time and has even begun speaking through me, at times. Poor soul, she's dreadfully worried about both of them, and I don't blame her either.'

'And you're saying you held a seance at this Bereavement Cafe place?' Bill asked, shaking his head in disbelief. 'Because you were trying to make contact with a dead woman called Helen?'

'Absolutely.' Lucasta nodded. 'But it didn't end well. Sadly, Luke got up and left just when it began to get interesting. So if you're watching, Luke, dear, do please come to our next meeting – Helen desperately wants to contact you and I'm certain she's been trying her very best to, only perhaps you haven't noticed.'

'So you're appealing for an architect by the name of Luke Wright to get in touch with this Bereavement Cafe?' Becky asked.

'And you really believe that the dead can try to contact the living?' said Bill.

'Absolutely,' Lucasta replied breezily. 'The deceased often do that, you know. Come to you in a dream, or maybe leave coins lying on the ground, or else send lovely white feathers to you. You know, you'll spot a feather as you're walking down a path, and you may well think no more of it. But, trust me, that's your late loved one sending you a little sign, just to say they still love you and are still with you. But with Luke's late wife, Helen, you see, I think the poor lady feels she needs to do something more dramatic to absolutely capture his attention.' Then turning directly to camera, she added, 'Helen is desperate to speak to you, Luke. And it seems I'm her last resort. I know you left disappointed, but you should give me another chance. Unorthodox as it may seem, this really is your best hope.'

Within minutes, the interview was trending on X with the hashtag #lucastaseesdeadpeoplealIthetime, much to the chagrin of the climate-change activists who went on the show directly after Lucasta.

'Wait till you see,' one of them moaned at the top of his voice as they were hurriedly ushered into the TV studio. 'There won't be a breather about us on social media. It'll all be about that mad aul one talking to the dead.'

Within an hour, Lucasta had gone viral. Within two hours, the clip of her interview was on YouTube, with close to seven hundred and fifty thousand views. But her main memory of the interview was of looking behind the cameras only to see a grim-faced Phoebe standing there, completely ashen-faced and holding her head in her hands.

'So how do you think that went, Phoebe, dear?' Lucasta asked her as soon as they were safely back in the car post-interview and on their way home. Normally Phoebe would be busily tapping away on social media now, announcing to the world that Lucasta had a brand-new book out and drawing everyone's attention to her interview. Normally she'd be forwarding clips of the interview to Lucasta's many editors all over the globe, regardless of the time difference.

But instead, she slumped back wearily on the back seat of the car, looking utterly drained, as if all the fight had gone clean out of her.

'Phoebe, dear?' Lucasta tentatively repeated herself. 'I was just asking how you thought it went?'

'Shoot me,' Phoebe said, turning to face her. 'Just get a gun and shoot me now.'

24

LUKE

Luke's morning was going surprisingly well – all things considered. With the complete memory wipeouts that kids miraculously got, Amy seemed to have blanked out the blow-up row they'd had over their postponed zoo visit and now all she could chat about was the coming weekend, and how they were definitely, definitely, *definitely* – her new favourite word – going to see the giraffes, gorillas and monkeys – with as much ice cream as she could handle for the entire day.

It wasn't quite 8.30 a.m. and Luke had her at the school gates nice and early, where a chirpy, happy Amy skipped out of the car clutching her bright pink schoolbag, hugged her dad warmly, then instantly forgot all about him as she spotted her best friend, Emily, arriving at exactly the same time.

'Emily!' Amy cried out as the two of them ran towards each other. 'Guess what? We're *definitely, definitely* going to the zoo on Saturday and my dad says I can have ice cream for the whole day *and* they have a new panda bear there that I'm gonna have my picture taken with!'

'You're so lucky!' Emily said as the two headed for the school door together, deep in happy chat. 'And then will you come on a playdate to my house too? I got a new Wendy house for my birthday and I want to play in it with you – it's brilliant!'

'Yeah! I'd *love* a go in your Wendy house!' Amy squealed with excitement.

'Mum!' Emily called out as her mother got out of her car and came over to join the girls. 'Look, Amy's dad is here now. Will you ask him about the playdate? Please?'

Luke, witnessing all of this, smiled. It did his heart good to see Amy back to her usual chirpy, bouncy self – I've you to thank for that, he said silently, offering up a little prayer to Helen. As he did about a hundred times a day. He waved over at Emily's mum and was just back in his car when he noticed her coming his way, waving at him, as if she needed to speak to him. He rolled down the window, presuming this was about arranging a playdate for the girls. Jean, Emily's mum, was a nice woman, a family GP who worked at a busy surgery in the city centre. Helen had always been very fond of her and he had a vivid memory of Jean at her funeral, calling to his packed house after the service with tray loads of food, then effortlessly putting together a charcuterie board and a chicken casserole before serving it up to guests, as if she were a paid caterer. She came over to him to speak through the rolled-down car window.

'Good morning, Jean, how are you?' He smiled.

She didn't answer though. Instead, she looked at him worriedly.

'So did you see it?' she asked.

'Did I see what?' said Luke, puzzled. Some school notice he'd missed, maybe? Something on the class WhatsApp group?

'On TV this morning? The *Good Morning Ireland* show?' Jean said.

Was I watching breakfast TV? Luke thought wryly. As if. It was quite enough of a struggle getting Amy up, dressed and out of the door in time for school every morning as it was. The idea that he'd have time to linger over an early morning TV show almost made him laugh in her face.

'I'm afraid I didn't see it, Jean,' he said. 'Why, what did I miss?'

'Well, you know that famous writer, Lucasta Liversidge? Course you do, everyone knows her,' Jean replied. Just at the mention of her name, Luke could feel himself reddening, but she kept on talking, oblivious. 'Anyway, she was a guest on the show first thing this morning. I presumed to chat about her new book, but, in actual fact, I think she was speaking about you.'

'About me?' Luke froze.

'Well, yeah, I'm pretty certain it was you. She was all talk about a seance she'd held at a place called – the Bereavement Cafe? Does that make any sense to you?'

Luke felt his bowels wither as he clung to the wheel.

'Anyway, she said there was a man there whose late wife was desperately trying to contact him from beyond the grave.'

'So how did you make the connection to me?' he asked, wondering how much damage limitation he needed to do here. This was private, so bloody private. Had Lucasta Liversidge really gone live on air and talked about his personal business?

'Simple,' said Jean. 'She said she was really anxious about a man who was called Luke Wright.'

This mightn't be too bad, Luke thought doubtfully. *I might just be able to ride this one out.* After all, Luke was a fairly ordinary name. And wasn't Wright a common enough surname?

'An architect,' Jean went on. 'Whose late wife was called Helen. Who passed away just a few months ago. And who has a little daughter called Amy. Well, I thought it had to be you. Too much of a coincidence otherwise, don't you think so?'

* * *

It got worse. Far worse. By the time Luke got to the office, he was running just a few minutes late for a meeting with new clients, a couple who had commissioned the firm to design a new house for them on a two-acre site outside Dublin, with no expense spared and with all the bells and whistles. The Dicksons were a fabulous couple, as it happened, and Luke was deeply fond of them, so he'd taken particular pride in this one, and hoped they'd be pleased with what he'd come up with. Which was effectively a version of the dream home he would have designed for himself and Helen and Amy, had money been no object.

'Good morning, thanks for coming in,' he greeted them warmly, coming into the conference room, with his preliminary designs tucked safely under his arm. To his dismay, though, that insidious little arsehole Nick was there ahead of him, sitting at the table, arms folded, deep in chat with the clients. Even though he'd no right to be there; this was Luke's baby and his alone. So what the feck, he thought, was Nick doing there? Muscling in on his territory? Yet again?

'Hiya, man, great you made it,' Nick said, making no attempt to get up and leave whatsoever.

Luke gave him a curt, 'Good morning,' then came around the other side of the table to shake hands warmly with the Dicksons, who both stood up to greet him. They were his kind of people. Both busy professionals who'd emigrated to San Francisco years ago and made their money working for a global software firm that was headquartered out there. Now they were newly returned to Ireland with three kids, determined to build a state-of-the-art house, with an unlimited budget and a brief that was like music to Luke's ears. 'A palatial home with all mod cons.' This, for any architect, was the dream project. If all the clients were like the

Dicksons, he often thought, his whole life would be about 99.9 per cent easier.

So what in the name of arse was Nick doing there?

'We were just talking about you, actually,' Nick said, with a sly smirk that Luke didn't trust for a second.

'Is that right?' Luke managed to say politely enough, anxious not to let himself down in front of two such nice clients.

'Seems that some famous novelist was on live TV this morning talking all about you,' Nick said gleefully. 'Says she met you at a cafe where everyone goes to talk about bereavement? And that she held an actual seance trying to reach out to your wife? Late wife, I should say, sorry about that.'

He was smiling smugly and you could tell that the little shit was really determined to wring every last drop out of his moment. *You've probably been sitting in here for the last half-hour,* Luke thought furiously, *waiting to land this on me at the most embarrassing time possible.*

'It was on *Good Morning Ireland* this morning,' Nick said, to silence around the room.

'That's as may be,' said Rose Dickson, a perfectly lovely woman in her late forties, who, even at this early stage in the project, knew exactly what it was that she wanted down to the minutest measurement and who only ever called Luke if it was vitally important 'Not that we saw it, did we, darling?' she added, turning to her husband, Terry, who was from Kerry and who was the absolute salt of the earth. The type of fella who called everyone 'lads', proudly wore the Kerry GAA jersey in and out of work and who took absolutely no shite from anyone.

'Sure who'd have time to be watching the telly first thing in the morning, lads?' he said jovially to the room. 'Apparently it was on social media. Not that anyone with a blind bit of sense would pay the slightest bit of attention to what's trending and what isn't. You'd need to have very little else to be doing with your time, isn't that right?'

In that moment, Luke could have hugged him. But Nick was still determined to eke out his pound of flesh.

'You were named and everything, Luke,' he said, his sickening smile widening. 'This novelist really was trying to reach out to you. Says Helen is desperately trying to communicate with you from the other side and that you really should turn up at the next Bereavement Cafe meeting, whenever that is. If you like,' he added poisonously, 'I can show you the clip that's all over X?'

'There's no need, thanks,' Luke said firmly, wishing the little shit would just leave the room.

'Actually, you know what?' said Rose, making it perfectly clear that she'd taken a huge dislike to Nick too. 'We're here for a work meeting. Frankly, we don't have time to waste looking at videos circulating around social media.'

'No problem,' said Nick, making an 'I surrender' gesture as he rose to leave. 'It was only a bit of fun, that's all.'

'My wife's death is a bit of fun to you?' Luke couldn't resist saying to Nick's face, before he sloped out of the room. But the walls of the conference room were made of glass so you could see everything that was going on in the main office outside and, sure enough, moments later, there Nick was, deep in conversation with two other colleagues, showing them whatever image was on his phone. The telltale glances Luke's way told him all he needed to know – confirmation, if it were needed, that he was the source of all office gossip that morning.

Lovely. Just what he needed. His personal business trending on X and the talk of the whole office. Making a big effort to put it out of his mind and focus on work instead, he produced his latest updated drawings for the Dicksons and was just rolling them out on the conference table, when Terry piped up.

'I didn't like that fella one bit,' he said, folding his arms and not even looking at the drawings, just staring out of the glass wall to where Nick was doubtless having a great laugh at Luke's expense. 'I wouldn't like to be working with an eejit like that, I can tell you.'

'I certainly didn't take to him either,' said Rose. 'The cheek of him. I had no idea you lost your wife, Luke. I really am so sorry to hear it. That's awful.'

'Thank you,' said Luke, genuinely touched.

'But from the way that aul gobshite was going on,' said Terry, 'you'd think it was some kind of a joke to him. As if it's any business of his what's going on with you or how you're dealing with the loss of your wife, God be good to the poor woman. Sure aren't you entitled to a private life, same as everyone else?'

'Lucasta Liversidge shouldn't have mentioned you like that on live TV,' said Rose thoughtfully. 'She had no right to do that.'

'It's OK,' said Luke. 'She's a good soul, really. Just a little on the eccentric side, that's all. I'm sure she meant well.'

'And as for that eejit Nick?' said Rose. 'It's like he was deliberately out to humiliate you. Over something as tragic as your wife's passing away? Horrendous thing to do. Cruel.' Then she turned sharply to her husband. 'Terry, love? I don't want that man having anything to do with you or me or with our project. I don't even want him within a mile of our home, do you hear me?'

'Me aul lad had a shotgun back at home in Kerry,' Terry said, half joking, half serious, sitting forwards. 'He never used it, but it came in fierce handy to threaten the likes of a moron like that fella Nick, let me tell you.'

'Now, we're not suggesting that you go out and shoot anyone, just to clarify, love,' said Rose, patting his arm. Then turning back to Luke, she added, 'All I'm saying is this. You're a good architect.

You're a *great* architect. Are these really the kinds of people you want to be working with?'

'Good point,' said Terry. 'If you just left it to me, Luke, I'd have someone like you up to your neck in work in no time. Sure everyone I know from our company who have relocated back here from the States all want huge, big country-house piles built for them. Oh, it's no expense spared with this lot; they all want underfloor heating and kitchens the size of football pitches and wine cellars and floor-to-ceiling windows and gyms and home cinemas and all that malarkey. Wouldn't that be a grand bit of work for you now?'

Luke looked back at him, his head swimming, unable to work out where this was going.

'What Terry is suggesting,' said Rose, 'is that you might just think of going out on your own, with a few recommendations from us to get you started? Be a nice change, wouldn't it? And that way you'd never have to deal with horrible people like Nick ever again. Think about it. If you're really up for it, then you know where to reach us, so please, call either of us any time.'

That evening, when everyone else had left the office, Luke called them. Correctly, Rose Dickson, who answered her number when he called.

'Hey,' he said. 'This is Luke Wright here.'

'Great to hear from you, Luke. So how are you doing?'

'Good, all well here.'

'Ahh, glad to hear it. So why are you calling?'

'Rose, I think I might have news for you. You remember you saying I could go out on my own this morning? Well, I'm interested. Tell me some more.'

'Well, it could be tempting for someone like you...'

On she spoke, and the more she talked, the more keen Luke became.

* * *

Later that evening, when Luke called around to Clare's to collect Amy, he offered to order a takeout for everyone on him and with absolutely no expense spared, as a special treat. Amy and her two cousins squealed delightedly in the background, and all three of them immediately dashed to the family computer in the living room to check out takeout menus from their favourite restaurants, out-shouting each other over what to order.

'Pizza!' Amy kept saying. 'With everything on top – even yeukky old pineapples, if that's what you all want.'

'No, Uncle Luke,' Holly squealed, 'please can we have takeout from Eddie Rocket's – burgers and loads and loads of chips? With the garlic sauce too?'

'Oh yeah!' Amy said. 'I changed my mind, Dad, now that's what I want too!'

'You just set the table for me, girls,' said Clare. 'Uncle Luke and I will decide what we're all going to have.'

'But if you've got any say in it,' said her eldest, Poppy, looking at her worriedly, 'then we'll end up with pukey green vegetables for dinner and fruit for dessert, that you keep saying is good for us, but that tastes *bleaughh*.'

'Boring!' said Holly at the same time. 'Then it won't be a treat at all.'

'Just do what your mum says,' Luke said, backing Clare up, 'and don't worry, I promised you all a special treat, so that's what you're getting.'

'Thanks, Dad,' said Amy, her eyes shining proudly. 'Your treats are always the best.'

His heart swelled, just as it always did whenever Amy was happy. Then Clare led him into the study so they could order online, taking care to close the door behind them so little ears wouldn't overhear.

'You're in much better form today,' she said, sitting at her desk and firing her laptop up. 'That's good to see. Normally you come in here after you've left work for the day and you're like a demon.'

'Work was... unexpectedly good today,' Luke said with a half-smile. 'I think... no, it's more than "think". I got the chance to go out on my own from lovely people, the Dicksons.'

'That's great! So what do you do?'

'Well, I have to think about it, of course, but all being well... Clare, this could turn out to be terrific, with all the bells and whistles.'

Clare focused on him and him alone. 'Maybe this could be the big turning point for you. You do realise that you're due a turning point?'

'I know,' he said. 'And speaking of turning points, I wanted to make it up to you for the awful row we had. I really am so sorry, Clare. You've been on my conscience ever since.'

'Well, that's certainly a first,' she teased. 'When we were kids and you used to eat my selection boxes at Christmas and then blame Rudolph and Santa, you never once said you were sorry. Scarred me for life, you bastard.'

He smiled. He'd never seen Clare so icily furious as she'd been with him, but this definitely felt as though there was a distinct thaw starting. The very last thing Luke would ever want was a falling-out with Clare. She'd been amazing to him and Amy, and not just since Helen passed away either. When Helen had first been diagnosed and had had to start an aggressive course of chemo almost immediately after her surgery, Clare was the one who'd held them all together. Luke had been in total shock at the time and had been flailing around, desperately trying to keep the show on the road and to keep things as near to normal for Amy, all while he'd been eaten up with worry, not knowing what the next scan or consultation with Helen's oncologist would bring. Yet Clare was there for him and Amy, day in and day out. Always cheerful, always smiling, always positive. How blessed was he, he often thought, to have a little sister like this? She'd been a bloody diamond to him and to Amy.

'You do so much for us,' he said to her, a bit more seriously now. 'You know I can never even begin to thank you enough. I'll never be able to make it up to you, Clare. And I hope you know how much Amy loves you and her cousins too, of course. She really loves being here – she loves being part of just a normal, happy family. And that's what you've got here, right under this roof that you're so lucky to have. And that's what I miss so much.'

His voice cracked and Clare turned to face him.

'I know you do,' she said gently. 'I know how much you miss Helen – I miss her too. So much. She was the best sister-in-law anyone could have asked for and the void she's left in all our lives can't ever be filled. But you know I'm here for you, through thick and thin. And as for minding Amy, it's only a pleasure having that child here. We all love her and I'd do anything for her, you know that.'

Luke sniffed and hoped she didn't notice him welling up, then did what he always did whenever things got too emotional for him. Changed the subject and moved on. 'Go on, then,' he said, tapping her playfully on the shoulder, hugely relieved that, after the worst row the two of them had ever had, things finally seemed to be back to normal. 'Order whatever you want, no expense spared. My treat. Go as posh as you like, and I'll even throw in a fancy bottle of wine for you and Tony to have later on, when the kids are asleep.'

Tony, Clare's husband, was well known to be a wine connoisseur and would turn his nose up at any bottle that didn't cost at least €100, so this represented a pretty major extravagance. Worth it though, Luke thought. Worth every bloody penny.

'You might well regret saying that.' Clare smiled, tapping away on her laptop until she finally settled on what to order. Expensive steak for the grown-ups from a local restaurant that provided a terrific children's menu too, along with chicken goujons and fries for the kids, with a dessert aptly called 'death by chocolate'.

'We'll pay the price later on tonight,' she added wryly, tapping in the address for delivery and the Eircode, 'when they're all too high on sugar to sleep.'

'Go on, go for it,' Luke said, gently nudging his way in front of the laptop and keying in his card details. 'Treat nights don't come along that often and you all deserve it. Deserve far more, actually.'

Order placed, Clare closed her laptop, sat back on her swivel chair and took off her glasses, so she could really look at Luke properly.

'It's so good to see you like this,' she said. 'I wish we saw this side of you more often. And I wonder, these great things in your life...'

'What?'

'You know, like those people who made you the job offer, all of that thing.'

'Yeah?' he said.

'Might it be something to do with that Bereavement Cafe? Trying to get in touch with Helen? The number of calls and texts I've had from people saying, "Isn't that your brother they're talking about on telly?"'

Shit. More people who'd seen Lucasta Liversidge on TV that morning. Jeez, was there anyone out there who hadn't seen it? Luke shoved his hands deep into his pockets and rocked back and forth on his heels, hoping she'd just let it drop. Then he thought about it and decided if Lucasta hadn't outed him on TV, he'd never have been slagged off by Nick, and if that hadn't happened, then he'd never have had a chance of going out on his own from the Dicksons.

'Just hear me out,' said Clare. 'I know how hard you work and whatever you choose to do in your own spare time is your concern and no one else's. Now, you know me, I'm probably the least spiritual person out there and generally I think any of that mind body spirit malarkey is a load of horse dung. But for what it's worth—'

'You don't need to say another word,' said Luke firmly. 'I tried it out, it didn't work for me, end of story.'

'You didn't let me finish,' Clare said, rising to her feet to go back to the kitchen, as the squeals and giggles coming from there grew steadily louder. 'Because it was actually Helen I was thinking of.'

'Yeah?' That silenced Luke. But then pretty much any time he heard Helen's name mentioned, it stopped him dead in his tracks.

'Kids?' Clare yelled out at the top of her voice. 'Keep it down in there, will you? Your food is on its way, so just relax!' Then she turned back to Luke, pulling open the study door and facing him. 'You don't need me to remind you, of all people, what Helen was like. She was by far the most spiritual person I ever met. She was the one who insisted that Amy go to a Catholic school, remember?'

Luke nodded, of course he remembered. They'd even had to move house to get closer to St Teresa's, just to make sure they were in the right catchment area.

'And then when you were getting married,' Clare went on, 'it meant so much to her to have the ceremony in a Catholic church. Not that she was a holy Joe, or a God-botherer or anything like it.

But she firmly believed in another dimension, I know she did. She was always giving me books about past lives and the law of attraction and the whole notion of an afterlife to read up on, because I'm so cynical about anything like that.'

'So what are you saying?' Luke said, wondering ahead.

'I'm saying that if someone as spiritual as Helen was genuinely trying to reach out to you, don't you think through a medium at some Bereavement Cafe place is exactly the kind of thing that she'd do?'

25

CONNIE

Connie had just been to a miserable viewing with Karen's assistant and was inconsolable. It had started to rain and rain heavily by the time she was going home and, two buses later, when she was finally trudging up her street, she was beside herself. How much more of this could she take? She was just putting the key in her front door—Ha! she interrupted herself. For how much longer exactly could she keep referring to this as her own front door?

'Connie, love! There you are!' She turned around to see Edith Devlin from next door waving over at her from her own front garden. Even though she was soaking wet, Connie smiled and went over to chat. Edith was in her seventies, fit as a fiddle and with so many grandchildren it was easy to lose count. Edith was one of those active retired folk you wanted to be like when you were that age; every year she set challenges for herself and every day brought her fresh adventures. It was impossible to keep up with her. She stood huddled under an umbrella and was as likely to be coming home after a skydiving lesson as a Latin American salsa class. With Edith, you could never tell.

'Oh, it's great to see you!' Connie smiled at her, glad to see such a friendly face. 'How are you? Did you ever see such a horrendous evening?'

'Oh, don't mind me, love,' said Edith brightly. 'How are you doing? We're all so upset at your house being sold! I was just saying to my judo instructor earlier, our street won't be the same without you. Your mum and I were such great pals – I still miss her every single day.'

Connie nodded, not sure what to answer without bursting into big, ugly tears. Feck it anyway, it had just been one of those days.

'You know you're welcome to stay with me any time,' Edith added, looking as though she really meant it. 'And for as long as you like too. Shameful that Donald won't just sign the place over to you, utterly disgraceful, if you ask me. Him with all the money in the world, living the high life in Paris? Your poor mother would spin in her grave.'

Connie could have hugged her.

'Anyway, you'd better get yourself in out of the rain, love,' Edith said. 'But in the meantime, you know I'm here for you, any time. Your mum was always so good to me, especially after my marriage broke up. She used to come to all my solicitors' meetings with me and, I can tell you, that woman didn't take any crap from anyone!'

'That was Mum all right,' Connie said wistfully. 'Anyway, it's good to see you, Edith. I better let you get out of the rain too, or you'll catch your death.'

'Oh no, love,' said Edith brightly. 'I'm actually going out on a date tonight. Fella I met on one of those silver surfers dating apps. He tells me he's seventy-nine years young and a dead ringer for Jack Nicholson. Although knowing my luck, he'll be closer to ninety and a dead ringer for one of those eejits you see on *World's Most Notorious Criminals*. Wish me luck!'

Connie waved Edith off, marvelling at her energy and her unstoppable *joie de vivre*, and then she finally let herself through her front door, drenched to the bone and wanting nothing more than a big glass of wine and a nice, soothing chat with Kate.

There was the famous Nokia mobile phone, sitting on the hall table where, unusually for her, she'd forgotten to take it with her when she went out earlier. In fact, she'd forgotten to take any phone with her. She picked up the Nokia and pondered for a minute. It was completely silent, no missed calls, no nothing. *Come on, Mum,* she found herself silently praying, even though she didn't for a minute believe her mother could hear her. *I don't know how it happened, or if I was just imagining things all along. All I do know is that you were well able to call this phone at the most inconvenient times imaginable. But now, just as I'm about to be turfed out of the house you and I loved so much, there's nothing but silence from you. Seriously? What the feck is going on with you, Mum?*

She picked up her own mobile then to see three missed calls from Karen and was just about to return the calls, when it rang out, shattering the silence. Her brother, Donald, calling from Paris.

'So hi, sis, yeah, yeah, I'm good, I'm terrific here actually, all is great,' he said, even though she'd never asked him. 'I'm working from home today, you know yourself. Anyway, I'm crazy busy, really run off my feet, so I won't stay on for too long. Where have you been, by the way? Your woman Karen has been trying to reach you. Anyway, she got on to me, and it seems the news is good. Very good, in fact.'

'Oh, really, is that right?' said Connie, standing rooted to the spot, still dripping wet in the hallway and with a rising sense of dread deep down in her gut. Karen's idea of very good news was probably her own idea of Armageddon.

'Anyway,' Donald chatted away breezily, 'it seems that, just in the last hour, we had two offers in on the house, both for the asking price. Which is bloody brilliant if you ask me. Now, I don't particularly care which of them we sell to, money is money, right? It's the same either way. So choose one, and let's get them to sign on the dotted line. Right now, while the market is hot.'

'What?' Connie said. 'But... but—' Her brain scrambled around for a reason to put this off, but she couldn't think of one. *So this is it, then,* she thought. *It's happening. It's actually, finally happening.*

'If you have a preference as to who we sell to, then I suggest you get on to Karen at the agency right now. Otherwise, I'm not particularly bothered. Once the funds are there, who even cares?'

'Well, as a matter of fact, I do care,' said Connie, for once putting her foot down with Donald. 'Do you know who exactly these offers are from?'

'Ehh, yeah,' said Donald vaguely, sounding supremely uninterested. 'Karen mentioned something about one offer being from a single guy who wants to demolish the place and completely redesign it. Which is exactly what I'd do myself, to be honest.'

'Absolutely *not*,' Connie insisted. 'Anyone but him.' She hadn't a clue who this mystery buyer was, but she vividly remembered his architect and engineer calling to her house one evening. They'd let it slip that their brief was to gut the place from the attic down, then turn it into an uber-cool bachelor pad with a design that wouldn't look out of place in a Bond movie.

This, in a humble terraced row of corporation houses? Connie had thought at the time. *Over my dead body.* Aside from anything else, it would be horrendous to inflict all that noise and dirt and disruption on lovely neighbours like Edith. Her mum would turn in her grave and no way in hell was Connie letting that happen.

'Jeez, you're not fussy, are you?' He whistled down the phone. 'OK, then, the only other alternative is to sell to a young couple with two small kids. Apparently they're attracted to the area because of the good schools on their doorstep and blah, blah, blah.'

The decision was a complete no-brainer as far as Connie was concerned. 'This is a family home, and a happy one at that,' she told Donald firmly. 'I'd like it to stay that way and I know that's what Mum would have wanted too. If we're selling to anyone, then we sell to that family and that's all there is to it.'

'Right then,' said Donald, not particularly caring either way. 'Decision made. Can you relay that back to the agency?'

Connie couldn't even answer him though. Instead she just slumped down onto the bottom stair, peeled off her wet jacket and stared blankly ahead of her.

'Better go, then,' Donald added. 'Crazy busy here, you know how it is!'

She'd almost have believed him, only just then she heard a clink of ice in the background and her sister-in-law, Francine, saying quite clearly, 'Donald, darling, here's your aperitif. Come on, then, let's celebrate the house finally being sold. And so fast too!'

He hung up and Connie didn't even care. Instead she shook off her soaking wet trainers as her eye wandered to a photo of herself and her mum, taken during happier times on a holiday in Gran Canaria to celebrate her mum's seventieth birthday. They were in a fancy beach restaurant, the sun was dazzling, they were each holding up a glass of fizz and both of them looked as though they hadn't a single care in the world. And all Connie could think was this.

Where did you go to, Mum? Where are you? Now when I really need you?

26

LUCASTA

'For goodness' sake, Lucasta, it's a Zoom,' Phoebe said. 'It's not brain surgery. You've done dozens of them when we were in lockdown, when we had absolutely no other choice. Remember? It's talking. That's all you're being asked to do here. Talk. Surely not such a big ask for you?'

'All very well for you to say, dear,' said Lucasta, looking distastefully at the computer screen that was being set up in front of her. 'But I'll never come to grips with the whole concept. So utterly exhausting, the whole thing. All those faces peering at me and then there's the way the whole screen is divided up, like the opening credits of *The Brady Bunch*. Goodness, how very trying it all is.'

'I hardly need tell you that the producers are calling you all the way from LA.' Phoebe sighed wearily. 'So which would you prefer? To have this meeting – this vitally important meeting, I might add – via a simple, straightforward Zoom? Or do you need me to spell it out to you what the alternative is? Because the alternative is that someone like you, who despises Los Angeles, has to get on a plane, fly for over eleven hours, then arrive into a production studio tired, cranky, jet-lagged and doubtless moaning at me non-stop. Let me remind you that the LA production team are actually doing you a great favour here, so the least you can do is stop giving out and just get on with it.'

'All right, all right,' Lucasta said a bit grumpily, gingerly putting in the earbuds Phoebe handed her and shifting around in her seat at the top of her kitchen table, with the camera perfectly positioned so that she was in the dead centre of the shot, with nothing but a plain white background behind her. 'It's just, well, you know me, dear. I infinitely prefer meeting people in person. Face-to-face. The old-fashioned way. So much easier and far more fun, don't you think?'

'You've got exactly four minutes before the meeting starts,' said Phoebe, looking at her watch and ignoring her comment. 'So if you need to use the bathroom, I'd ask you to go now and go quickly, please.'

'No, thank you,' said Lucasta primly. 'I'm not a dog that needs to be let out at regular intervals, you know. But if you could see your way to pouring me out a nice strong gin, that would be greatly appreciated.'

'You must be joking.' Phoebe snorted incredulously. 'Are you having a laugh? Most definitely not the time to drink and most definitely not the kind of people you can drink in front of.'

'Oh, don't be such an old puritan, dear, it doesn't suit you. Surely the LA lot are well used to me by now?'

'I already told you, *no*.'

'I could always tell them it's water?'

'No alcohol during a work meeting, especially one as important as this. End of story. Particularly when it's still early morning LA time. It's the height of disrespect.'

'Honestly,' Lucasta muttered darkly. 'My own mother never gave me the kind of grief that you do.'

'And another thing,' Phoebe said, ignoring the jibe as she took her own seat at the opposite end of the kitchen table, well out of shot, but on hand to leap in, if things went skew-ways. Which, with Lucasta, they frequently did.

Lucasta glared back at her, still seriously put out at being denied her evening tipple.

'Now what?'

'Absolutely no segueing off topic. In fact, I've made a list of taboo subjects here, which I'll read out to you. Number one, communing with the dead, that's out. Number two, your conviction that your late husband, Johnnie, still speaks to you and, number three, the Bereavement Cafe or anything at all to do with seances. I would kindly remind you that this is a work meeting to discuss the series FilmCorps propose to make with your latest *Mercy* novel.'

'I'm perfectly aware of all this, dear. You've already told me about three hundred times. Interesting that you mention the seance though,' Lucasta added, momentarily distracted. 'Because I actually do want to host another one, if that nice-looking chap Will would be all right with it, that is. It's as though we were just tapping into the most extraordinary energy, before that poor troubled man Luke left so abruptly. Such a lost soul. My heart really does go out to him, you know. What to do, Phoebe, dear?' she mulled out loud. 'What on earth do I do now?'

'And we're live,' Phoebe said, ignoring her and putting on headphones as, one by one, fresh faces began to pop up on the screen in front of Lucasta, all set for the Zoom conference call.

'Well, hey there, good to see you again, Lucasta,' said one of the senior producers, a portly, middle-aged man by the name of Harry Shapiro, who was sitting in a leather-backed swivel chair and looking for all the world as if he rightfully belonged in one of those gentlemen's clubs in London.

Lucasta had met him before on her last visit to LA and recognised him instantly. Harry Shapiro had been in the movie business ever since he first started out working in the mail room at the tender age of fifteen and had steadily risen up through the ranks, before branching out on his own in the past decade, with stunning success. He was now one of the owners of the FilmCorps studio and was well known for backing clever, witty, well-written independent movies and series starring big-name actors, which subsequently went on to be huge global hits. The kind that swept the boards come awards season. Actors from all over the world were queueing up to work with him and you could clearly see why: Harry Shapiro and the FilmCorps studio had the golden touch when it came to producing smash-hits.

'Oh, Harry, dear, it's you!' Lucasta said, momentarily lighting up. 'How nice to see you again. How have you been? Goodness, you've gained weight. I thought all you LA movie types lived off lettuce and that revolting wheatgrass stuff? And you all spent every spare moment doing yoga?'

Out of shot, Phoebe furiously made a 'slit throat' gesture at Lucasta, which was her cue to shut up, but, instead of taking offence, Harry burst out laughing.

'That's what I've always loved about you, Lucasta,' he chortled, happily patting his impressive girth. 'You sure as hell tell it like it is! Now, let me introduce you to the rest of my team. You remember Meredith?'

'Hi there.' Meredith smiled down the screen, a perfect, dazzling Hollywood smile too. Meredith had honey-blonde, immaculately blow-dried hair, with her face so frozen and unnaturally unlined and lips so puffed you immediately knew she had her plastic surgeon on speed dial.

'I'm so excited at the chance to speak to you. I've been a lifelong fan of yours, so this is a real honour for me.'

'Oh, how very kind of you.' Lucasta smiled warmly as Phoebe kept a close eye from the far side of the kitchen table.

'So to the bottom left and right of your screen,' Harry went on, 'we got Janine, our executive producer and beside Janine is Danny, who's our showrunner. Danny? Janine? You better be real nice to Lucasta now, she's the lady with the golden touch so whatever she says, goes!'

All four of them started yakking over each other to Lucasta about a kaleidoscope of things that meant absolutely nothing to her: projected budget streams, distribution percentages, locations, costumes, design, advance press and publicity. All manner of movie terminology that she was perfectly sure was terribly important but which she hadn't the first clue about.

It wasn't long before Lucasta got bored and started miming at Phoebe that she really could use a stiff G & T *now* when Harry suddenly piped up with something that actually did catch her attention.

'Which brings us to the very minor little matter of casting,' he said, when his voice could finally be heard. 'Always such an easy, straightforward task, as my team here will testify,' he added dryly.

'Oh, pay no attention to him,' Meredith tossed back, flashing that megawatt smile. 'Harry of all people knows that casting is critical. Any show will succeed or fail depending on the names you've got up there on screen.'

'Of course, we're well aware that, over the decades, other actors have taken on the role of Mercy and with great success too,' said Danny the showrunner from the bottom right of the screen. 'But for FilmCorps, this will be a long-running series, so our Mercy is going to be on viewers' laptops, iPads and phones for a very, very long time to come.'

'And let's not forget,' Meredith chimed in, 'that FilmCorps

will be amalgamating these wonderful stories and then presenting them to a fresh new audience of predominantly Gen Z viewers. So we gotta stay current, we gotta stay relevant. We need huge, recognisable names for each of the key roles.'

'But the good news,' said Harry, delighted with himself, 'is that we got a lot of interest from a whole lot of A-listers. Had it from the head of CAA myself over lunch last week. And there's big excitement in the trade papers already. Casting the role of Mercy in itself is going to be like a modern-day search for Scarlett O'Hara.'

'Which of course puts us in the strongest position imaginable,' someone else said, Lucasta couldn't tell who. Dear Lord, Zoom was so exhausting trying to keep up with everyone.

'Once the *Mercy* series airs, we're hoping to attract new subscribers to FilmCorps from Gen Z, the slide-rule boys tell me, possibly up to as much as 37.5 per cent new market share.'

'Montana Jones is apparently interested in playing Mercy. Says she'll make herself available too. Can you imagine the huge audience share she'd bring with her?'

'And Lionel Larabie's agent was on – he wants to be considered for the key role of the duke,' Danny replied. 'He's just off the set from a Marvel movie, which of course means he'd automatically bring an army of fresh new fans to the Mercy stories with him. That's priceless for us.'

'So I calculated that in series one alone,' said Janine, 'we got upwards of seventy-five recurring roles, all speaking parts.'

'But we can get established names in every single one of them,' said Meredith, brightly smiling.

Lucasta looked blankly at the screen in front of her as her head began to swim.

'Hello? Hello, everyone? Might I possibly say a few words, please?'

The Zoom call instantly went silent, every eye on her. 'Thank you, thank you all,' she said, getting a bit flustered, now that all the focus was on her and her alone.

'Hey, you're the boss, Lucasta,' said Harry, steepling his fingers and sitting back. 'You're the reason we're all here and whatever you say, goes. So please, tell us whatever is on your mind. The floor is yours.'

'Thank you.' She nodded back to him, aware that Phoebe was looking worriedly across the kitchen table at her. 'You all seem like such lovely people, so I really am so very sorry to have to say this,' she began. 'But as far as I'm concerned, you may as well be speaking in a foreign language. Who are all these names you're mentioning? I've never heard of a single one of them. Gen Z? Sounds like the name of a boyband from twenty years ago.'

Once again, she looked over to Phoebe, who was now shaking her head in total despair.

'Lucasta?' She heard Harry's voice from LA. 'Are you still with us? No need to worry about the names. We can talk you through who they all are.'

'And Gen Z just refers to a demographic age group, that's all,' Meredith with the perfect teeth was saying.

'But all those actors...' she said slowly. 'Am I right in thinking that they're mostly American?'

'Not entirely,' said Meredith. 'We got some great Canadian actors interested, plus a few well-known actors from the good old UK too...'

'Oh, but, my dears,' Lucasta said, shaking her head, 'I'm afraid I foresee a problem ahead. Not an insignificant one either.'

'Whatever it is, just tell us. I promise we can fix it,' said Danny, but Lucasta had never heard such gobbledegook and that was before they had begun to bombard her with names she'd never heard of. Was this really meant to impress her? Handing over the movie rights to these complete strangers, only to have to see her beloved books, which she'd been working on for decades, popping up on one of those streaming services with a load of actors she didn't know from a bar of soap?

Over her dead body.

'Now, please, just listen up, everyone,' she said, quite bossily for her, just as Johnnie used to when he managed her career all those years ago. 'I'm perfectly sure the actors you mentioned are absolutely wonderful at their jobs and that they're lovely people to work with too. But you're all forgetting one significant thing. A "deal breaker", as my assistant, Phoebe, is so fond of saying.'

Phoebe's face shot up from her iPad to glare warningly over at her. Just then, a loud pinging noise sounded, as an email marked urgent came through to Lucasta, which she completely ignored. 'Firstly, where are all the Irish actors? Mercy is from Ireland. And you know my one firm and fast rule when it comes to casting,' Lucasta said primly.

'Name it,' said Meredith. 'Just name it, we'll take care of it.'

'I like to give nice, big, jammy jobs to some unknown actors,' Lucasta decreed, sitting back in her chair, as Phoebe frantically made 'shut up' gestures across the table at her. 'You say all those actors who are interested are terribly famous established stars,' she went on, undeterred. 'So what use is yet more fame and money to them? Stars of that calibre tend to be a nightmare. So high maintenance, it's dreadful! Back when my first novel was turned into a big-budget Hollywood movie with all the bells and whistles, Johnnie and I found that the movie stars working on it were such desperately unpleasant people in real life. All of this carry-on about the size of their trailers and the exact brand of bottled water they like to drink. Utter nonsense, if you ask me. And some of those big names were rude to the crew too, which I found intolerable. So now, my dears, I like to give work to a local cast who no one has heard of. What could be better than employing fresh talent who might actually be grateful for the gig? We've got it in our power to make someone's whole career here, so why not do it? If you were a struggling actor, wouldn't you kill for a chance to make a name for yourself in an ongoing series like this?'

Silence from the other side of the Zoom call, complete pin-drop silence. Meanwhile Phoebe frantically scribbled on a Post-it note and held it up towards Lucasta.

SHUT UP NOW!

'OK,' said Harry, speaking slowly and noticeably choosing his words with particular care. 'So how do we fix this?'

'Well, there's nothing to fix,' said Meredith, butting in. 'Every name we just pitched to you will attract revenue to the Film-Corps site. It's a complete no-brainer. We need star names attached to this project or else that's the death of it.'

'I get that Lucasta is set on using unknowns,' said Danny, talking over her as if she weren't there, 'and she does have the right to her opinion. But surely there's room for a little compromise here. Lots of room. Say, for instance, by casting unknowns, but in much smaller, cameo roles that maybe get a day's work on the shoot?'

'Hmm,' said Harry, making a 'weighing up' gesture. 'Lucasta? That work for you? You happy enough with that?'

'Oh, my dears.' Lucasta smiled sweetly. 'I don't think you're quite hearing me. When it comes to casting, I don't want unknown actors to be tossed the crumbs from the table. As I said, I want all those lovely, big, fat, jammy leading roles to be played by actors that no one has ever heard of. If it's a no from you, then

I'll thank you for your time, wish you all a very good day and say goodbye.'

Silence. Which was weird on any Zoom call, but on this particular one was bordering on threatening.

'I hate to draw everyone's attention to the obvious,' said Meredith, clearing her throat and speaking low and clear. 'But while Lucasta does have a certain amount of input regarding casting, that's largely just a goodwill gesture on our part. When it comes down to it, you'll find that we do have final say.'

'Do you really?' Lucasta frowned, as if this was news to her.

'Sure we do,' Meredith replied coolly. 'If you don't believe me, then I suggest you read your contract properly.' Then under her breath, she said to Harry and Danny, 'I'll never understand why creatives don't read their contracts. Never. Then they act shocked when they don't like what's actually in them.'

'Read my contracts?' said Lucasta. 'Don't be so ridiculous. I've never read a contract in my life. I pay lawyers to do that. They're just about the only people who can understand all that legal jargon. Honestly, those godawful contracts you people present us with might as well be written in gobbledegook.'

'I'm sorry to tell you that Meredith is quite right,' said Danny, weighing in as 'bad cop'. 'I think you will find you have very little control over this, Lucasta.'

'Oh, really?' she replied, really putting her foot down now. 'Is that right? Well, in that case, it was terribly nice chatting to you all and I'll wish you a good day. It seems there's not much more for either of us to say. Goodbye now!'

'No!' Harry shouted. '*No*, Lucasta? Are you still there? Are you still hearing me?'

For the second time, that pinging noise sounded as another email landed in Lucasta's inbox, but this time, it distracted her. Particularly when she saw who it was from and what it concerned. Seconds later, she was utterly absorbed in something *far* more interesting.

'Lucasta?' a voice in LA said, she hadn't the first clue who. Didn't much care either now that she was busily scanning through what had just been sent to her.

'You still there, Lucasta?'

'Hello? Do we still have the live connection to Dublin?'

'Oh, my dear Phoebe,' Lucasta said, the Zoom call completely banished from her mind as her eye greedily devoured what was on the screen in front of her. 'Are you reading this too? Well, now. Didn't I tell you everything would all work out beautifully?'

27

From: Will_Kempton@leesonstreetcafe.com
To: LucastaLiversidgeBooks@Mercy.com

Hi Lucasta,

Forgive the intrusion. You're a busy lady out conquering the world of fiction and entertainment media, I know that. It's just there's been a lot – and I really do mean a LOT – of follow-on emails from my regulars at the cafe, all effusively singing your praises after the seance and wanting to know whether you might see your way towards hosting another one?

As you know I was initially opposed to the whole idea mainly because I was afraid it would scare off my regulars. But seeing the overwhelmingly positive response has taken me by surprise. It's hard to put into words the effect you had on anyone lucky enough to be there, so I've taken the liberty of forwarding you on the chain of emails I've received. It's you they're all reaching out towards, Lucasta, not me, so it's only right that you should read them.

You moved people, you really did. Even the few who didn't

actually get messages from the other side still said they felt privileged to have been there.

So here's the million-dollar question. Do you think you might feel up to hosting another one soon? No pressure, the decision is yours alone. But if you did, you'd be making so many people very happy.

You have my number and you know where to reach me. The cafe is yours any night that suits you. I'll gladly organise everything. All you need to do is say yes, then turn up.

I await your call. And I won't give up hope.

A BIG ask, I know.

Yours hopefully,

Will x

To: Will_Kempton@leesonstreetcafe.com
From: Lucy_Moynihan@Ireland.com

Hi Will,

It's Lucy here, I'm one of the twins who comes to your cafe regularly on Thursday nights. I thought the seance was brilliant. I was telling Mum and even she got excited. I think she was sorry she wasn't there with us herself, so she could hear the messages we heard that really seemed like they were coming from Dad. Mum works as a midwife, you see, and she's usually on call at the hospital where she works, so she can never make plans to go out at night, in case one of her patients goes into labour. But if she does have a night off soon, please can I bring her to one of our meetings? Please will you tell Lucasta we both really hope she holds another seance soon? The last one was epic!

Thanks once again,

Lucy

PS on behalf of Alex, I really am so sorry she was messing and giddy at the seance. Trust me, that's nothing to the way she normally goes on in school. Nothing.

To: Will_Kempton@leesonstreetcafe.com
From: Alex_zerofucks@gmail.com

Hey Will,

Alex here, 'the other twin', as everyone calls me. Can we have another seance soon? I was telling my mates and we came up with a list of dead people we'd all love to get in touch with. Top of the list are Jim Morrison from The Doors and Elvis, because we all saw the movie. If we're doing another one, can I bring a few pals with me? And are we allowed to take a few cans into the cafe with us?

Let me know if it's a runner. And will you tell Lucasta that, for a really old lady, she's banging. I'm going to get her a T-shirt made that says 'I have zero fucks to give'. She can wear it when she's being interviewed on the TV.

See you Thursday,

Alex

PS sorry about my sap-head of a sister. Lucy is a total embarrassment. In school, I even tried to change my last name and pretend I wasn't related to her, but it didn't work, we look too alike. I asked her what dead celebrities she'd like to get a message from at the seance and she said either Oscar Wilde or Jane Austen. FFS.

Welcome to my world. I despair of her. It's a mystery how I share genetic material with such a toolkit.

To: Will_Kempton@leesonstreetcafe.com
From: Dee_MildredDevine@Ireland.com

Good morning Will,

Well! My mother Mildred and I are still beside ourselves with excitement since the seance! We literally can't stop talking about it. There's no doubt in either of our minds that it was my father trying to get in touch with us, and although poor Mother has been a little bit emotional about it, mostly she's just overjoyed that Father's at peace now and able to reach out to us. And all these wonderful messages given to us by someone like Lucasta Liversidge? We're just astonished. Mother has been up and down the road all morning going in and out of the neighbours' houses boasting about it to anyone who'll listen. We can't get over how accurate Lucasta was, it was like she was staring at a photo of my darling father. She described him to a T, right down to his bald head, the apron he always wore and the fact that he worked around food so much. As Mother says, you couldn't make it up!

We sincerely hope Lucasta will see her way towards hosting another seance? I know that man Luke wasn't very polite – Mother and I thought it very rude of him to walk out in the middle of it. But for those of us who loved it and who want to hear more, please, please, please will you ask her to host another one very soon?

Mother says she'll make her speciality if she does: cherry cake slices with apricot jam. They were once second runner-up in the provincial charity Christmas cake sale, so it should be a nice treat for everyone.

See you very soon, and thank you again from both of us,

Dee x

PS I hope no one is allergic to nuts. Mother's cherry cake is riddled with them.

To: Will_Kempton@leesonstreetcafe.com

From: glamorousgranny@Ireland.com

Hi Will,

Mia here. Forgive my contacting you out of the blue like this, but the fact was I couldn't not get in touch with you after the seance. Will, it was extraordinary! I pitched up, unsure of what lay ahead and, if I'm being perfectly honest with you, a little nervous about the whole thing. But in no time at all, Lucasta brushed all my fears away; the messages she was receiving and communicating to us felt so real, so genuine, so full of love and hope. I was telling all my girlfriends at my yoga class, the 'Namaste Bitches' as we like to call ourselves, and they were all so interested you wouldn't believe it. A few of them who are also coping with bereavement issues just like me asked if they could come along sometime. Admittedly Lucasta didn't have a personal message from the other side for me, at least not this time, but somehow that didn't matter. It was seeing other people's faces light up as she channelled their late, lamented loved ones that did my heart such good. Those two young girls, the twins? Did you see how happy they were when Lucasta managed to get in touch with their dad? Even the silent, problematic one, Alex, cracked a big, wide smile and that's so much more and so much better than you ever see in grief therapy.

In short, what you and Lucasta are doing is helping people, Will. It's healing and that's beyond price. Take it from me, as someone who's tried just about everything going to get over the death of my folks, so close to each other. You name it; I've tried it, from laughter yoga (and yes, there really is such a thing) to visiting therapy alpacas, which I don't recommend unless you wear wellies and you don't mind the smell of dung. I even went on a 'grief cruise' a few months ago with some like-minded pals, to see if that might help. Which it didn't. All we did was skull back the vino every night, then wake up at a different port the next morning, still grieving, but this time with a throbbing hangover. Not to be recommended.

All of which is a very long-winded way of saying if by any miracle you could forward this on to Lucasta, please will you tell her that she has to host another seance at the cafe? Soon. Please. I know she's a big superstar author but this is something she absolutely has to do. This is like a public service.

With love and light,

Namaste,

Mia

To: Will_Kempton@leesonstreetcafe.com
From: Connie_theatrescene@Ireland.com

Hi Will,

Connie here. Great to bump into you and I hope all is good with you. Quick one: I know Lucasta Liversidge is a celebrity and that she's got far better things to be doing than hosting seances but, by any miracle, do you think she might be amenable to hosting another one? Like, really soon?

I'm cheeky for even asking, I know, but I have a personal reason; remember I was bolting off to meet an estate agent when we met? The good news and the bad news is that she's actually gone and sold my house. Long story short, but if ever there was a time when I needed to hear a message from Mum, it's now, right now. That phone I was hauling around everywhere with me has gone strangely silent on me – ever since I first started going to the Bereavement Cafe meetings, actually.

It's a huge ask and I know I've a right cheek approaching

you about this. But if by any miracle Lucasta was to host one more seance, just one more, you would let me know, wouldn't you?

I'll shut up now and leave you in peace to run your cafe. But thanks, Will. What you do means so much to an awful lot of people stuck in deep, horrible, godawful grief. And I should know, I'm one of them.

See you very soon, hopefully,

Connie

From: Stellamackeyprincipal@primary.com
To: Luke_Wright@gmail.com

Hi Luke,

It's Stella here. I hope you're having a good day and indeed a good week. I've seen you fleetingly at the school gates, but naturally, it's impossible for us to really talk properly there. Hence my email, which is just to say I really do hope to see you this week at the cafe. You may perhaps want to read the email I'm attaching below from Will, he of the man-bun hair you've always been so intrigued by. The quote from Henry V, I thought, was a particularly nice touch. It certainly makes for an interesting read.

Of course, it's not for me to tell you what to say or do, but as you're mentioned in dispatches, it might be worth your while. Just this one last time.

Stella.

PS I've been keeping a close and watchful eye on Amy and am delighted to say she's having a particularly good week this week. But then, you're a wonderful dad and you already knew that, didn't you?

From: Will_Kempton@leesonstreetcafe.com
Subject: Once more unto the breach, dear friends.

Dear Stella,

I've just heard from Lucasta Liversidge who says she'd very much like to host another seance at the cafe, if people were willing and up for it? She mentioned Luke in particular and asked if you might pass this email on to him. (He never gave me his email, so I figured you two are in touch through the school his daughter goes to.)

Lucasta also says to tell you that she felt your late fiancé's presence very distinctly and she really hopes to have more news for you this time. You know what she's like though; adorable, but difficult to keep on one topic for very long. Suffice to say she feels there are far more considerable energies at the cafe which she hopes to tap into further. So what do you say? One more shot at it?

No pressure, but it would be terrific to see you there – and of course Luke, if you'd be good enough to forward this email on to him. Till we meet again, hopefully, Will.

28

LUCASTA

'You heard me. Loud and clear. Might not be what you expected to hear, but still. You most definitely heard me.'

'Goodness, Phoebe, have you taken leave of your senses?' Lucasta replied, completely and utterly bewildered at what was unfolding before her eyes. 'There's really no need for all the theatrics. Just come back into the house and you and I shall talk. Calmly. Over a nice, soothing gin.'

'No need for the theatrics?' Phoebe snorted ironically. 'This? From *you*? There's more drama around you than in an entire season at the RSC.'

Phoebe was standing at the boot of her car, a good, sensible Volvo, loading it up with her laptop, briefcase, notes and copious amounts of stuffed cardboard boxes. 'That's just the start of everything I need to clear out of here,' she muttered, 'but it'll do for now. I'll be back in time for the rest of my stuff.'

'Phoebe, dear,' Lucasta said, with a rising sense of alarm, 'is it possible that you're actually being serious?'

'I've never been more serious in my life,' came the crisp reply. 'I've had it, Lucasta. I've had enough. I'm out, over and out. You're making my job impossible to do and, not only that, it's a complete nightmare too. There's only so much that I can take and I've officially reached breaking point.'

Lucasta felt as though she'd been slapped across the face. She looked back at her one-time assistant with a dawning sense of horror – and this didn't appear to be a joke either. Clearly, the woman was hell-bent on leaving. This was it, this was absolutely for real.

'I'm fifty-five years of age,' Phoebe went on, still busily loading up the boot. 'I first came to work for you when I had just left school, when I was still a teenager. You probably don't even remember, Lucasta, but I do. I was in awe of you. Your first book had just come out and you were, quite simply, the best and most exciting writing talent we had in this country.'

'Of course I remember when you first came to me...' Lucasta tried to say, nice and placatingly. Anything to avoid this. Whatever it took.

'You interviewed me,' said Phoebe, 'but you never even bothered asking me about typing skills or whether I knew my way around what passed for a home computer back in those days.'

'Oh? Didn't I?'

'Not at all. Instead, all you wanted to know was what my favourite books were. Who did I love to read. And what were my guilty reading pleasures.'

'Do you know...' Lucasta nodded as it all came back to her so vividly '...I can even recall your answer. You said you were a huge fan of Victorian three-volume novels, and that *The Woman in White* by Wilkie Collins was your absolute favourite. You'd just come back from holidays in Tenerife, I remember, and you told me you were attracting strange looks on the beach for reading it there, when everyone else seemed to have their nose stuck into either a Jackie Collins or a Jilly Cooper. No sooner were you out of the door than I said to Johnnie, "That's her. That's the assistant for me." I even chased down the drive after you, to lure you into staying, didn't I?'

Phoebe said nothing, just kept on trying to squish large cardboard boxes into the finite space in her car boot. 'Yes,' she eventually said. 'Yes, you did. So I came back into this house and from that day on, I've never left. And the reason why? Because I loved working for you. I loved the fact that no two days were ever the same. I took such pride in nurturing your career and seeing it grow from strength to strength. I loved travelling the world with you and seeing the *Mercy* novels become bestsellers. One country and one continent at a time. You opened up the whole world to me and I loved it. Well, I used to love it.'

She just needs a little bit of soothing, that's all, Lucasta thought. *Poor thing has had a long and emotional time of it and now she just needs to know how loved and valued she is in this house.*

She went in gently. 'So here I am for the second time in our lives together, Phoebe, dear. Standing in the driveway and not just asking you – *begging* you to come back inside and to work for me again. I know I can be trying. I know I can drive you potty. It seems I drive everyone a bit mad at some point – Johnnie used to tease me and ask if pissing people off was something I did on purpose. So forgive me, Phoebe, for whatever I've done that's brought all this on. Please. You're worrying me now. All this is so unlike you. Let me take you out to dinner wherever you like and let's talk about it and let's put it to bed and just get back to normal.'

'I wish that were possible, but I'm afraid it's not,' said Phoebe, finally clunking down the lid of the car boot and coming around to the driver's door.

'Nothing is impossible,' said Lucasta, reaching out and taking a gentle grip of her arm. 'Just come inside the house and let's work it all out. Whatever is bothering you, we can get to the bottom of it over a nice gin. Come on, dear, what do you say?'

'It's pointless,' said Phoebe, looking her employer straight in the eye and speaking calmly. So calmly it was almost scary; it made this whole drama seem so premeditated, almost as though she'd been planning it out for a long, long time.

'Pointless how?' Lucasta asked, bewildered.

'Look,' Phoebe sighed, as if she were talking to a small child. 'I accepted long ago that working for someone like you was never going to be straightforward. But today really was the straw that broke the camel's back.'

'Are you speaking about that dreadful Zoom call?' Lucasta asked, desperately trying to keep up. 'Who even cares about that? You're far more important to me, you know that.'

'Do you realise the days and months and years of work and preparation that went on behind the scenes just to get this project this far with those people? Do you even realise the long hours I've slaved over it? Yet today, you threw it all back in our faces and, as is your wont, just suddenly lost all interest.'

'Oh, now, is that quite fair? I may have been a little distracted...'

'You and I had signed legal agreements with those people,' Phoebe said, standing by the driver's door, poised to get into her seat, 'and FilmCorps isn't a company I'd relish coming up against in court. Look what you've just unleashed on us! They'll go for the jugular, they'll really go to town on you and these people don't take prisoners. Which of course now means months, if not years, of lawsuits ahead of you. Water off a duck's back to someone like you, Lucasta, I know, but it's not to me. Because it's me that has to clean up your mess, isn't it? Yet again. For about the thousandth time. So this is it. This is me, over and out. Find someone else to put up with you and your lack of professionalism and your mad obsession with contacting the dead and seances and all sorts of nonsense. And good luck with it.'

Lucasta's head began to swim. This couldn't be happening. Phoebe was her right hand, her consigliere, her bulwark against the world. At all costs, this couldn't happen.

'Just tell me what it'll take to make you come back inside the house,' she offered in a very, very small voice. 'Whatever it takes, I'll do it. If you want me to change, then I will. Because I simply can't manage without you, Phoebe. What on earth would I do?'

'To quote from one of your favourite films,' said Phoebe, stepping into her car, slamming the door shut and rolling down the window as she started up the engine, '"Frankly, my dear, I don't give a damn".'

29

LUKE

'Oh, Dad, that was the best day *ever*! That was better than my birthday *and* Christmas all in one! I even preferred today to last time when Santa brought me a bike *and* roller blades!' Amy giggled happily from the back seat of Luke's car as he drove them away from the zoo and on to their next port of call.

'I'm so glad you enjoyed it, pet.' He smiled into the rear-view mirror from the driver's seat, happy just to see her so happy. 'So what was your favourite animal?'

Amy's brow furrowed as she really gave it thought. Unbelievable. Luke snatched a quick look at her face as the traffic lights turned red. How exactly like Helen she looked when she was concentrating. *There is nothing of me in this child,* he often thought. *She is completely 100 per cent Helen.*

'Well,' she said after a pause, 'I think the monkeys and the baby chimps were my very favourite, because they're just so cute and cuddly and swingy and friendly. But remember the orang-utan, Dad? Remember how funny he was? Remember when he bent down and showed his bum and all the people laughed?'

'Course I do, pet. That was hilarious, wasn't it?'

'There were some scary animals there too though, Dad,' Amy said, suddenly very serious. 'Like the snakes. I didn't like them a single bit. My friend Molly in school says that when she went to the zoo, one got out of the glass box they keep them in and bit her little brother and that he nearly died. That's what she told me, Dad.'

'I'm sure she was only pulling your leg. The zoo is very careful to keep dangerous animals like the snakes and the lions locked up.'

'I wish I had a pet chimp, Dad!' Amy chatted away, ripping open a pack of Jelly Babies he'd bought her earlier and sticking two into her mouth a second later. 'Can I get one for my next birthday? I'd play with him every single day and I promise I'd clean up all his poos. I even know what I'd call him – Chuckles. Isn't that a great name, Dad? Just the very same as the monkey in the zoo! And Chuckles could sleep beside me in my bed and all my friends could come and play with him and I'd take him for sleepovers at Auntie Clare's, so Holly and Poppy could have a go of him too.'

Last thing Luke wanted was a marsupial pet, but he wisely said nothing, knowing she'd have forgotten all about it by bedtime. Sure enough, Amy instantly changed the subject.

'Dad, where are we driving to now?' came her little voice from the back.

'Well, how about we pay Mum a visit? I'm sure she'd like to hear all about what a great day you had. What do you say?'

Not long before she passed away, Helen had expressly asked to be cremated, but then buried on consecrated ground with a headstone so that Luke and Amy would have somewhere to visit at Christmas, Easter, Mother's Day and birthdays. Luke had promised her that was what they'd do and he'd kept to his word. In fact, ever since the funeral, he'd been doing his best to normalise the notion of going to visit the grave for Amy, so that it never became creepy for her, or something that she'd come to dread in years to come. More like a fun day out where she got to chat to her mum and tell her all the news, exactly as they used to do as a family.

By her own choice, Helen had taken complete control of her own funeral a few weeks before she'd passed away and, like everything else she'd turned her hand to, it had been organised seamlessly and to utter perfection. She'd even chosen her final resting place: a cemetery on the outskirts of Dublin close to the mountains, with a panoramic view of the city that stretched all the way out to the sea. It was peaceful and serene and the perfect resting place. Helen had thought of absolutely everything down to the finest detail; it was even close to a park bench, so Amy and Luke could sit and chat to Helen and remember her in just about the most tranquil place imaginable.

But at the suggestion that they go there now, suddenly Amy's whole mood changed.

'Please can we not, Dad?' she asked him in a tiny voice, her happy, bouncy spirits from barely a moment ago completely evaporated. 'I don't want to go there. I don't like that place. Please, Dad? Don't take me there.'

Luke pulled the car over at the side of the road, switched the engine off, then turned around, so he could really focus on Amy.

'Why, darling?' he asked gently. 'You always used to like going to visit Mummy. Don't you want to tell her all about the great day you just had?'

But she just shook her head and now looked as if she was on the verge of tears.

'I don't want to go there. Really, *please*, Dad. Please don't make me.'

'Amy,' he said, looking at her, deeply concerned. 'Of course I won't make you do anything you don't want to, you know that, sweetheart.'

At that, she looked a bit mollified, so Luke persisted.

'So will you tell me why you don't want to go?' he asked her softly. 'I promise, I don't mind a bit. Today is your treat day, like I promised. Today we do whatever you want. Today, you're the boss.'

'Then don't take me there,' she said. 'I don't like it there any more.'

'Why not, pet?'

Amy wrinkled up her nose and had to think about this very seriously for a moment.

'Because... because it makes you sad. And then I'm even sadder because you're sad. Mummy is dead and she's not coming back to us ever and that makes me sad but sometimes I forget and then I'm happy. Like on a nice day like today or when I'm having fun with my friends in school or when I'm playing with Holly and Poppy in Auntie Clare's house. But, Dad, you're sad all the time and visiting Mum makes you even sadder so I don't ever want to go there again. Promise me, Dad? Pinkie promise?'

Luke got Amy home. He got her back to her laughing, playful self again. OK, so it might have taken pizza with the toppings of her choice for her dinner, but, somehow, he managed to get Amy back to her factory-default setting, which was happy and full of chat. Somehow.

Now she was dozing in front of an iPad with cartoons on it, so Luke tiptoed out to the back garden, for a sneaky glass of wine and a chance to clear his own head. What the hell had brought that on earlier? The last thing he'd ever want was Amy getting upset at the mere mention of Helen so how was he supposed to cope with this?

He could take her back to the child psychologist, but the last one he'd taken Amy to, kicking and screaming he might add, had been about as much use as a chocolate teapot. If anything, the poor kid had come out of there even more upset than she had been going in.

He could gloss over the grief Amy was going through as much as anyone possibly could by taking her out on treat days like this one, but that would just be papering over the cracks. He was no psychologist, but Amy seemed to be moving into a new stage of grief – so how to dig their way out of it?

OK, so here goes, he found himself praying to Helen. *If you can hear me at all, then help me, Helen. It's a tough one. Amy is struggling with grief and I don't know what to do or where to go from here. If you can hear me, send a sign. Send something. Send anything you can.*

Just then, Amy appeared in the garden doorway. 'Dad, can I have a KitKat from the fridge?' she asked.

'Well, honey, it's still your treat day, so why not?' he said, hauling himself up to the fridge in the kitchen and handing it down to her. Not two minutes later, his phone pinged as a text message came through. Stella.

'What are you reading?' Amy asked, already halfway through the KitKat.

'It's Miss Mackey from the school,' he said, distractedly reading it.

> Hi there. Another seance at the cafe has just been confirmed for next Wednesday night. Back by popular demand, apparently. Hope to see you there. What harm?

Amy's face lit up. 'I like Miss Mackey. She's always so nice to me. She told me I was very good in class, and that I didn't have to do my homework if I didn't want to. Zoe Gibbons was mad jealous, 'cos she hates doing her homework!'

'Amy, love,' Luke asked her, thinking aloud, 'how would you like to spend this Wednesday evening in Auntie Clare's with Poppy and Holly? Daddy has to be somewhere, but what do you think? Would you like that?'

'Yes please!' she squealed with joy, clambering down from the kitchen table and racing back up to her bedroom.

'Hey, missy,' Luke called down the hallway after her. 'Where do you think you're off to?'

'I'm just telling my teddies we bought at the zoo I'm going to see Holly and Poppy next week!' she yelled back to him, sounding as though she were on top of the world.

Luke made himself a pot of coffee, sat down and reread the message on his phone, then he tossed it aside.

Was this a sign? No. Had his prayers been heard? Not a chance. So why, he wondered, did he even bother?

30

CONNIE

Connie was having a rare phone call with her agent. Really rare. To give an indication of just how much of a blue-moon-type event this was, the last time they had spoken, her mum had been alive and well, hale and hearty. His name was Sean Mussolides, the name Sean coming from his Irish mother, whereas Mussolides came from his dad, who was Greek. Which was where his nickname among the acting community came from: 'Sean Must One Of These Days'.

'Yeah, so there's absolutely nothing doing at the moment, Connie,' he was telling her, sounding like the voice of doom and gloom. 'Not a single sausage. There's a few plays in all right, but you're way too old for the ingénues and you're still too young to play the old hags sitting in corners.'

'You're saying that's what's ahead of me career-wise?' Connie said. 'That's what I have to look forward to? Old hags sitting in corners?'

'Hey, don't blame me. That's showbiz.'

'Any movies or TV that you could put me forward for?' she persisted. 'I wouldn't ask you, Sean, but I have done a fair amount of telly and bit parts on movies over the past few years. Anything? Anything at all that you think I might be suitable for?'

Connie was trying hard to keep the desperation out of her voice, but the fact was she needed work badly and she needed it now. The house sale was agreed and, although official contracts had yet to be signed, the deal was more or less done. It was only a matter of weeks before removal trucks would start rolling up outside to load up every single stick of furniture in the place, and Connie would effectively be out on her ear.

Kate had been an absolute stalwart pal and had insisted Connie crash out on her sofa till she had somewhere more permanent sorted out. For all that she was touched though, Connie knew that wasn't a runner. Not in a house with a husband, three small boys and a very finite amount of space. She needed somewhere to rent as a matter of urgency, but had yet to find anywhere within her budget that was halfway habitable – or even safe. Her only solution was to get an acting job fast, and hope that the extra few quid coming in might at least enable her to live somewhere she wouldn't have to witness drug deals going on right under her nose, in broad daylight, with no one batting an eyelid.

'Movies or TV?' Sean almost snorted. 'Nah, 'fraid not. There's precious little being shot here right now. Sorry about that, but you know how it is.'

'But what about the sequel to *Thrones to Kill For*?' Connie persisted. 'I know loads of actors who've been asked to self-tape for that.'

Thrones to Kill For was a huge, sprawling, epic fantasy series that was all sex and wars and violent, muddy battles, and which was being shot in Northern Ireland.

At that, Sean Must One Of These Days almost choked himself laughing. 'Only someone who has never actually *seen* the show could possibly come out with something like that,' he said as Connie tried not to bristle at the condescending tone. 'You are aware of the casting ratio in that show? If not, let me enlighten you. Because it's a staggering fifty to one.'

'Fifty to one?' she repeated, confused. Show ratios? What the hell was he on about now?

'Sure, fifty to one. Which means for every fifty guys cast, there's one female role. And that's it.'

'So you're telling me I've got a fifty to one chance of getting a part in it? Even just a tiny part?'

'Well...' Sean said, making that irritating 'sucking through his teeth' sound. 'Not really. Because the only female part that was up for grabs went to a previous Oscar winner for Best Supporting Actress. Who was aged nineteen, by the way.'

Connie stayed silent. No fecking answer to that one. *Give up,* seemed to be the clear subtext of this call. *Give up and go and work on the tills in Tesco. It's never gonna happen for you on stage or screen.*

'Course, there were rumours circulating for a long time about a brand-new adaptation of the Mercy stories that FilmCorps were supposedly going into production on.'

At that, Connie's ears pricked up. 'The Mercy stories – by Lucasta Liversidge?'

'Yeah. Have you read them?'

Not only that, but I actually know the author through a Bereavement Cafe didn't seem like the appropriate thing to say here, so instead Connie just trailed off with a weak, 'I have met her, yes. She's a fabulous lady, and one of the kindest people I think I've ever met.'

'It was only ever rumoured,' Sean went on, 'but the word on the grapevine is that it's not happening now. No idea why – they couldn't get it green-lit, I suppose. If they'd filmed it here in Ireland, there definitely would have been a few one- or two-day roles in it for an Irish cast. Not to be, though. Sorry I don't have better news for you, Connie, but, as your agent, I have to be honest and upfront with you. And as of now, that's just how it is. If ever there was a time where I'd advise you to consider other career options, then now really is that time.'

* * *

Connie rarely felt sorry for herself. Grief was one thing, but whingeing just because there was no work seemed self-indulgent compared with what so many other people were trying to deal with.

So it was no one single thing; it was the combination that was killing her. The sale of a much-loved home. Missing her mum so much she could still be reduced to a sobbing, snotty, bawling mess at the most unexpected times and for the most unexpected reasons. And now? The one thing that sustained her and kept her going, when everything else was falling apart; the career that she'd never not loved, even on the worst, shittiest days and at the shittiest of times... and now she was more or less being told – give up.

It was too much, Connie thought, leaving the house later that evening and pounding her way back into town and back to the cafe on Leeson Street, heartsore, weary and crushed. *Why am I even bothering to do this?* she wailed inwardly, brushing past scores of delighted-with-life mid-week revellers, all out for the craic. *What exactly do I think I'm going to get out of this? Signs from Mum? A message to tell me everything is going to be OK? A reason to get out of bed in the morning? What's the fucking point?* The phone she could have sworn she was hearing her mum's voice on had gone completely stone-cold silent on her. Even that tiny morsel of hope and comfort had been snatched away from her and now here she was, at rock bottom.

She arrived on Leeson Street just as it started to pelt rain and, yet again, the heavy, glass-paned door pinged obediently as she made her way back into the cafe, back for what was most likely another wasted night. Fat chance of it being anything else.

31

LUKE

Just as Luke dropped Amy off at Clare's for the evening, a summer deluge started to bucket down, one of those rainstorms so heavy it was almost a tropical storm.

He'd said his goodbyes to hysterical squeals from the girls, as if they hadn't seen each other in years, instead of just last week, as Holly and Poppy leapt on Amy, instantly pleading with Luke to let her stay the night.

'Oh, go on, Uncle Luke,' Poppy tried her best to cajole him, with big, innocent, saucer eyes. 'Please, please, *pleeeeeeeeeeease*... just this one time?'

'It's not like we want to have midnight feasts with her or anything,' Holly chimed in, always the more guileless of the two and therefore the one most likely to accidentally let slip if there was any mischief afoot.

'Oh yes, Dad, *pleeeeease* can I stay?' Amy begged. 'I'll be no trouble for Auntie Clare, and I'll go to bed when I'm told... I pinkie promise!'

'Hmmm... I don't know about this,' said Luke doubtfully, as three hopeful little faces looked up at him. 'It's a school night,

Amy, sweetheart. You don't want to be all cranky for school in the morning, now, do you?'

'Go on, let her,' said Clare, appearing from the kitchen as the most delicious smell hit Luke and instantly set his tummy rumbling. 'It's not like she's studying honours maths or quantum physics in school tomorrow, now, is it?'

'Go on, then,' said Luke, caving in to them, to a chorus of deafening whoops. 'But tomorrow morning, I'll collect all three of you to take you all to school – that's a deal, ladies?'

'Yay!' Amy squealed, leaping up and down on the spot with excitement, before throwing herself headlong into a huge hug with her dad as Luke scooped her up in his arms and kissed her goodbye. 'I love you so much, Dad!' Her face beamed at him. 'You're the *best*!'

Luke's heart melted, and with faithful promises to Clare that he'd do the school run the following day, he left them giggling and messing and full of high jinks.

'You sure you know what you've let yourself in for?' he said to Clare with a wry smile as she showed him out.

'You need a break,' she replied wisely. 'You look like you could do with a bit of time out for *you*. So here's your chance, take it. Enjoy. Just tell me you're going somewhere nice? Not heading off to a building site with those gobshites you still work with?'

'As a matter of fact,' Luke said, shifting on his feet and hoping she wouldn't grill him any further, 'I'm taking a piece of advice you gave me not so long ago. Don't ask me any more, just... Well, watch this space.'

'Those people you needed to talk to about your potential job?'

'The Dicksons. Kind of. Sort of... Yes.'

At that, Clare took a huge breath. 'Luke, do you mean that...?'

'I think so.' He smiled and nodded. 'Today I called both of them, and we spoke for ages and… let's just not tell anyone.'

'I won't! I'm only telling Tony. And Brian, his workmate. And Adi, who's my best pal. That's it, honestly.'

'Clare, it's too soon! Wait a bit, will you?'

Clare looked up at him, nodded, but said nothing. Just smiled a tiny half-smile at her big brother as she showed him out of the hall door and back into the rain.

* * *

The downpour was even heavier now so, on impulse, just before Luke set off for the cafe, he whipped out his phone and texted Stella.

> Given this weather, how about I pick you up on the way to the cafe? Save you a soaking on that bike of yours.

She was back to him in a flash.

> So kind. Will text you the address and see you shortly.

Then he did a strange thing while he was still outside Clare's house. There was no one watching, so he went ahead.

'Helen?' he said out loud, the word sounding gorgeous and familiar. 'Can you hear me?'

There was just the sound of other cars passing, so he really listened. Nothing.

Feeling like an eejit, he tried a second time. 'Helen, love? Are you out there?'

'Look,' he said, 'I'll go ahead and ask anyway. I'm on my way to a seance tonight, and I know you'd laugh, but I'm doing it for you, Helen. Will you… come to me? Will you leave me some kind of message?'

He listened acutely. There were traffic and ambulances and police cars and all sorts, but no Helen. 'Helen?'

Damn. He could tell that there was definitely nothing there. Nada.

* * *

Twenty minutes later, Google Maps had brought Luke to a neat little terraced row of former railway cottages in Phibsboro, not too far from the city centre. The houses on Primrose Street were all red-bricked and two-up, two-down, Edwardian, he guessed, eyeing them up, but remarkably sturdy and bearing their age incredibly well. It was an up-and-coming, rapidly gentrified area and he had no problem finding the right house – it was the one with immaculately maintained window boxes, and a hall door painted in what he could tell immediately was Farrow & Ball's Elephant's Breath. Very popular with a lot of his clients. So neat, so pristine, so very Stella.

She answered the door, still wearing her work 'uniform' of a beige-coloured trouser suit and a tidy white blouse, but with a pair of trainers as if this was her one and only concession to being off duty.

'Come in.' She smiled when she saw him huddled under an umbrella on her doorstep. 'Get out of that rain before you catch your death! This is so kind of you. I was dreading heading out tonight on the bike.'

'It's the very least I could do,' said Luke, following her down a narrow, dark corridor to the kitchen, then doing what he automatically did whenever he came into any new space – instantly sizing it up, his quick, professional brain ticking over with all the improvements he could make to it, if money were no object. It was spotlessly tidy, but still – there was no hiding the fact that this was a dark, poky kitchen, with just a tiny window overlooking an outdoor space that barely held two wheelie bins.

'You're giving my kitchen the once-over.' Stella smiled at him. 'I know that professional look in your eyes. Happens every time I drag a builder in here to take a look at the place. Go easy on me!'

'No, no, not at all,' Luke said politely. 'It's a terrific space – a south-westerly orientation, I'm guessing?'

'Wow, you could tell that just by looking?' Stella half whistled, impressed.

'Kind of my job to know,' said Luke. 'These houses are great, so well built. I've worked on a lot of them and it's amazing what you can do to really open out a space like this. How long have you been here?'

At that, Stella bent down to fumble with keys in her handbag, so Luke couldn't see her face.

'Tom and I bought it together,' she said, after a tiny giveaway pause. 'Just over two years ago now. We had big plans to completely renovate the house – Tom was even going to tackle a lot of the building work himself. But then... Well, that all went by the wayside, didn't it?' she said factually, without a single scrap of self-pity.

'You don't need to say another word.' Luke nodded understandingly. 'I know. I get it.' Then his eye fell on a cork noticeboard tucked in beside the fridge. It was covered with all the usual things you saw on any kitchen noticeboard: fliers from local takeaways, timetables and business cards with all sorts of appointments scribbled on them. As well, though, there were photos of Stella's fiancé, young, fit-looking, dressed in black tie, with his arms wrapped around a younger version of Stella, who was laughing back up at him and looking as if she hadn't a single care in the world. *Wow,* Luke thought. *When she laughs, she looks like a completely different person.*

'That's Tom?' he asked, pointing at one of the photos.

'That's us on our way to a do at the Intercontinental,' Stella said, coming over to the noticeboard. 'Taken five years ago now. Five years and another lifetime ago.'

'You look so happy together.'

'We were like any other couple,' Stella said practically as she pulled on a raincoat with a big, thick, fleece-lined hood and gathered up her bag to go. 'We had our ups and downs, of course. But when I look at photos of us together, all I can remember are the good times. And there really were some terrific times – Tom was adventurous, a real risk-taker in a way that I'm not. He made me do things and go places I never would have dreamt of and I suppose, for my part, I tempered that slightly reckless side of him.'

'It's important to keep talking about him,' Luke said as Stella led him down the tiny hallway, having to duck his head because the ceiling was so low. Stella punched the code into her alarm as the two of them made to leave. 'It's the only way to really keep their memory alive. I try to do it with Amy all the time. Talk about Helen every chance I get, so she doesn't forget what a fabulous person her mum was.'

Helen. Again, Helen, Luke thought. *Why won't you answer me?* A natural silence continued as they rolled up wet umbrellas and strapped themselves into their seats.

'If you ever did decide to do something with your house though,' Luke said, changing the subject as he checked the rear-view mirror before driving off, 'you know, modernise it and upgrade it, I'd be delighted to help out.'

'Budget constraints are holding me back a bit, I'm afraid,' Stella replied, shaking the rain off her hood. 'Even on a primary school principal's salary like mine. Builders are a fortune now and that's if you're lucky enough to get one in the first place. Employing an architect is out of my league.'

'Oh, now, come on,' said Luke, pulling out onto the road and picking up speed. 'After everything you do for Amy, don't you know that this particular architect's services would be on the house?'

32

LUCASTA

Lucasta arrived at the Bereavement Cafe distinctly out of sorts and feeling such a great weight of expectation on her shoulders for the evening ahead, it was almost unbearable. Instead of bursting through the cafe door as she normally did, then breezing about the place, full of banter and chat, this time, she practically had to heave herself through the door feeling utterly exhausted and drained before the whole evening had even started.

There was no Phoebe at home, so of course that meant no car or driver, so for someone like Lucasta, who'd never driven, that had meant having to organise a taxi. Which might have sounded perfectly straightforward, but was something she hadn't actually done in decades. Which in turn had meant having to come to grips with one of those app thingies to order the cab but, like royalty, Lucasta never carried cash, and hadn't the first clue where all her cards were even kept, so at least a dozen times before she'd left the house she'd been on the verge of ringing Phoebe and flat out begging her to come back.

She'd held strong though. If Phoebe wanted to quit, then the best of good luck to her. Lucasta had never seen such disloyalty and the more she thought about it, the more disgusted she grew. Honestly, what had possessed the woman? After Lucasta had been so kind and generous to her? Over nothing more trivial than an argument with a producer on one of those horrendous Zoom calls? Nonsensical carry-on. If that was how little Lucasta meant to her, after all these years together, then, fine. Let her go.

Half of Lucasta was quietly hoping and praying that Phoebe would reconsider and turn up at work one morning, as though nothing had happened, while the other half of her was resolute. After all, there were plenty more assistants out there who she could hire in a heartbeat, weren't there? Someone younger, someone from Gen Z, as all those movie people referred to them, who were all over social media and who wouldn't give her grief every time she fancied a little G & T. And, hopefully, who knew how to order cabs online.

Unlike Lucasta, who, with the clock against her, had had to give up in despair, then run out onto her road and hail a passing bus, the first time she'd been on one since approximately 1970, the conversation on which had run thusly:

Driver: 'Fucking hell, you're what's her name... Lucasta Liversidge, that's who!'

Lucasta: 'I'm terribly sorry, but... oh... emmm... do I have to pay? With actual money?'

Driver: 'Nah... you don't have to. Come on and sit up at the top of the bus, and regale me with some of your stories, will you?' Then, picking up the microphone, he announced, 'Everyone? Look who's just come aboard! Only the actual Lucasta Liversidge! In the flesh!'

A cheer had broken out, which had temporarily heartened Lucasta, but the bus had left her a fair bit from where she'd wanted to be, of course. On top of that the heavens had opened, so when she finally did arrive at the Leeson Street cafe, she was late, soaked to the skin and frankly not in the right frame of mind to make contact with the other side.

The regulars had arrived ahead of her and were already milling around the same circular table, just as they'd done the last time. Every face turned to greet her and the hope in their eyes broke Lucasta's heart. Luke was here, with his hands shoved deep into his pockets, looking as though he was trying desperately hard not to be embarrassed at having crawled back again with his tail between his legs, but not fooling anyone. He was deep in conversation with Stella, the school principal with the warm eyes and the silver locket she always seemed to wear around her neck. Two broken souls right there, Lucasta thought, looking over at them and trying her best to smile and act as if everything were perfectly all right with her.

'There you are, Lucasta!' said Dee as she and her mother ambushed her with a freshly made tray of cherry slices. 'Look what we made – especially for you, isn't that right, Mother?'

'Oh yes,' Mildred twittered back at her. 'Last time, we noticed that you have a very sweet tooth, didn't we, Dee, love? So we thought we'd spoil you rotten with these cherry treats.'

'And we made some doggie biscuits too,' said her daughter. 'Because we read in *Woman's Way* that you have a little dog that you adore...'

'Called Sausage,' Mildred finished the sentence for her.

'So kind,' Lucasta said wanly, 'very thoughtful of you...'

The young twins were here too, at opposite ends of the table, as if they couldn't bear to be a single degree closer to each other. The gentler one, Lucy, smiled at Lucasta and came over to say a warm hello while the other one, Alex, waved, but stayed sitting at the table, with that wretched phone of hers glued to her hands.

'Last week was so amazing,' Lucy said shyly, twirling the ends of her hair, which was tied back in a long braid tonight. 'Wouldn't it be great if you could channel my dad again? Like you did before?'

Oh dear, Lucasta thought, reading the hope in those enormous, lost eyes and praying she wouldn't be disappointed. 'Well, of course, I'll try my best, but that's the thing about evenings like this, you just never know what's going to transpire.'

'Yeah, but that's the really cool part too,' Alex said from across the table. 'Because you could end up tuning into anyone – like *anyone* at all. Me and my pals think it would be, like, seriously cool if you could channel one of The Beatles, this *ancient* rock band. Do you think you could?'

'Well, generally it doesn't work like that,' Lucasta said, starting to get flustered now.

'OK... Well, in that case, then I suppose Jim Morrison would be cool too. Or even Kurt Cobain from Nirvana?'

'Don't mind her,' Lucy said, looking embarrassed now.

'The one you shouldn't pay any attention to,' said Alex cattily, 'is my dork of a sister there. On the way here, she said she was hoping you might channel Ruth Bader Ginsburg, because she thinks they'd have a load in common. Honestly. I despair, I really do.'

'Let's just see what unfolds, shall we?' said Lucasta as, one by one, everyone else took their seats around the table, eagerly waiting for her to kick things off. Connie was already seated. She so clearly missed her mother dreadfully and was clinging to anything at all that might lift her spirits. Lucasta looked into her pale, worried face and badly hoped that she might somehow be able to help tonight. She simply had to. Far too many people were depending on her – letting them all down was out of the question.

Will took over. 'That's it, everyone, grab a seat, you all know the drill, and should I turn the lights down a bit, Lucasta? Make the place a bit more atmospheric?'

'Oh yes, yes, please do,' she replied, rummaging in her battered, oversized handbag, then realising she'd completely forgotten to bring candles. To bring anything, in fact, including money so she could get home again. She resisted the temptation to think that none of this would have happened if Phoebe had been there and instead just smiled at the room as she welcomed them.

'You're all completely wonderful for coming out on a horrible evening like this,' she said, trying to sound like her usual confident self. Particularly when she was so out of sorts. 'We've come together again to speak to our dear departed in a spirit of love and peace...'

'Oh yeah,' Alex piped up, as everyone sitting around the table pivoted to look at her. 'That's another thing, Lucasta. Do you ever conjure up, like, *evil* spirits? You know... who possess you and make you want to do all kinds of insane things? Like set fire to buildings, or stuff like that?'

'Shh, will you?' Lucy hissed across the table at her. 'You're ruining the atmosphere for everyone else.'

Truth to tell, though, there was precious little atmosphere without incense or candles or any of the things Lucasta had with her last time. But on she ploughed, undeterred.

'All right, everyone, that's it,' she said gently. 'Just place your palms on the table lightly in contact with whoever is beside you. That's it. Now, let's just have a little moment or two of silence, so I can tune in to whoever may be here...'

Titters from Alex as Stella, with her best 'school principal' face on, glared across the table at her. It did the job and stopped the giggling, for the moment at least.

'If anyone is here, we're listening...' said Lucasta, trying to dig deep and summon up someone. 'Anyone there? At all?'

Silence. Around the table, various looks were being exchanged, and still no one spoke. Unconsciously, Lucasta glanced over to Luke, who looked slightly less cynical and slightly more invested in the whole process tonight. More than anything else, that poor man needed to leave here with something concrete, some kind of sign that his late wife hadn't forgotten all about him and his little girl. That she'd never really left.

Come on, Helen, Lucasta silently willed her. *Come through for me. Here we all are, waiting for you. Tonight the floor is yours – so come on now, away you go.*

Nothing. Not a thing. Then suddenly, shattering the silence, there was a deafeningly loud banging noise, followed by the crystal-clear tinging of a bell.

Everyone around the table, Lucasta included, jumped.

'Holy Jesus,' said Mildred, clutching her heart, 'what's that noise?'

'Sorry I'm late, everyone. My yoga class ran over time and then I couldn't get parking—'

All eyes swivelled over to the door, where Mia had just burst in, dripping wet, shaking out an umbrella and weighed down by a heavy-looking gym bag.

'Sweet Jesus, you nearly put the heart crossways in me!' Dee blurted out as everyone else burst into nervous laughter.

'Oops, sorry,' Mia said, instantly dropping her voice to a whisper when she saw that people were already seated around the table, hands touching. 'I hope I haven't interrupted anything?'

'Not to worry, my dear,' said Lucasta. 'We were just getting started. Take a seat whenever you're ready and let's start afresh.'

'Come on in, ghost of Elvis,' Alex chanted, doing a pretty accurate impression of Lucasta. 'Do you read me? You might even sing a number for us?'

'Shh! Let Lucasta concentrate!' Lucy whispered back at her crossly. 'Have a bit of respect, would you?'

'Such a sweet girl, that Lucy,' Stella whispered under her breath to Connie, who was on her right. 'It's refreshing to see a teenager with such impeccable manners. Her twin could learn from her example.'

'Oh, now, come on,' Connie whispered back. 'You've got to give Alex a break. Such a young age to lose your dad. Tough at any age, I know, but those girls are only teenagers. I'm finding it hard to handle Mum's death and I'm twice their age.'

'Oh, dear me,' Lucasta pleaded, having totally lost control of the room. 'Might I ask you all to keep it down a little? I'm really trying so hard to tune in here and it's not easy...'

More silence. Then Mildred blurted out, 'Oh, Mia, dear, just to say we made some nice cherry slices. They're right over on the counter, so please help yourself. You must be hungry after your workout.'

'The skinny size of you, you need a bit of beefing up!' Dee tittered beside her.

'Please, everyone,' said Will, clocking the exasperated look on Lucasta's face. 'Can we save the chat for later? Lucasta really needs to concentrate.'

More silence as Lucasta tried to pick up on anything at all, or rather anyone at all who might be out there. But all her subconscious mind threw back at her was that the final copy-edited draft of her newest book was well past her deadline.

Oh dear, she sighed worriedly, utterly distracted. Normally Phoebe dealt with diplomatic phone calls with her editors about extending deadlines so what on earth to do now? Her concentration broke yet again as her phone, which she'd tossed deep into the bowels of her handbag, pinged loudly with yet more emails. There were so many of the ghastly unread things last time she looked, it gave her a stress headache.

Once again, she tried her very best to focus. Once again, her eyes wandered around the table, taking in all those faces looking at her – for what exactly? A sign? A message? Then she realised exactly what it was they'd all come for. Hope.

Spirits came to her all the time and often at the most embarrassing moments. Yet now, when she really needed them – nothing.

'Is anyone out there?' she asked again softly. 'Anyone at all? Connie's mum, perhaps? Luke's wife, Helen? Stella's fiancé who loved mountaineering so much? Alex and Lucy would love to hear from their father, I know, and Mia suffered the loss of both her parents just last year. Surely there must be someone out there who can hear me?'

'Don't forget Father!' Dee prompted her. 'We'd love to tell him how his petunias are coming on.'

But there was absolute silence. Hopeless, Lucasta thought.

'I really do have to apologise to you all,' she eventually said to the still-silent, still-hopeful room. 'I can't do it tonight. I simply can't do it. I can't fathom it – this has never happened to me before.'

'If you don't mind me saying, Lucasta,' said Stella, reading her face slowly, 'I think you've tried your best and that's the most that anyone can ask for. Maybe it's best to leave it there for tonight? We can always try again another time?'

'Quite right too,' Mildred said, backing her up. 'The spirit world isn't one we can just expect poor Lucasta to tap in and out of, because it happens to suit the rest of us.'

There were more than a few disappointed groans from

around the table, but then Will spoke up. 'You know, there's a great pub just down the road here,' he offered. 'In case anyone fancies a drink?'

'Oh, my dear,' Lucasta said, looking back at him with such gratitude in her eyes, she could have burst into tears. 'That's just about the single best idea I've heard all evening.'

The others, one by one, all burst out of the door, except Luke.

Helen, love, can you hear me? Any message for me? Anything you'd like to say? Doesn't matter at all how little, send me a sign.

But again, nothing. Nada. Sweet damn all.

33

'You're such a fucking dork!' Alex was saying to Lucy, loud enough so everyone could hear, as if she was beyond caring.

'Why? What's your problem?' Lucy said, genuinely bewildered. 'Or should I say, what's your problem *now*? Seeing as how you're permanently annoyed with me over something.'

'We had the chance to go out on the piss with this gang,' Alex griped back at her. 'We could have had a laugh – we could have had a few rum and Cokes and a bit of fun.' Then, clocking the look on Lucy's face, she added, 'OK, so maybe *I* could have had a rum and Coke and you could have stuck to fizzy water or whatever nerds like you drink whenever they're in a boozer. But then you had to go and piss all over it, didn't you?'

'I don't get it,' said Lucy, sounding as if she was starting to get upset now. 'What did I do now? All I did was ring Mum to say we're finished early and to ask her to come and collect us. What's so wrong with that? We can't go to a pub, she'd kill us. Besides, did it occur to you that neither of us has any money?'

'I'm not even dignifying that with an answer.' Alex sighed,

folding her arms. 'There's just no hope for you. You'll never be... like... normal. No wonder no one in school likes you.'

If that stung Lucy, she didn't let it show. 'If no one likes me,' she retorted, 'then how come Miss Hodgkins said that I was a shoo-in for head girl when we get to sixth year?'

'Exactly. That's my whole point in one. Head girl?' Alex sneered. 'Only a complete arse like you could possibly think that's a good thing.'

'Girls, girls, please!' Lucasta said, having to raise her voice to be heard over the rain, as she and Stella walked past them, sharing a huge golf umbrella. 'No more fighting, for goodness' sake. Don't you realise how awful it is for the rest of us to see and hear?'

That shut the twins up for a minute.

'Remember, you only have each other,' Lucasta said. 'You might not think it now, but trust me. In years to come, you'll both be so glad to have one another. Just like it says in that song, we should all be nice to our siblings. They're our best link to the past, and the people most likely to stick with us in the future.'

'Sorry you had to hear that, Lucasta,' Lucy said, red-faced.

Even Alex managed to mutter something that did sound very like, 'Sorry.'

At that, Lucy turned away and burst into big, wet tears.

Alex looked at her for a moment. 'So what's this?' she said.

Lucy just sobbed in the rain. 'It's all right,' she said. 'I'm fine.'

'You're not fine, you dork. What's going on?'

'Nothing.' Lucy sniffed.

'It's not nothing, it's something. It's me, isn't it?'

Lucy nodded. 'It's like every time I say something, you're straight on to it, putting it down and being mean.'

'Ahh, for fuck's sake! The one night I try to get offside and have a bit of fun? And now... it's all gone pear-shaped.'

Lucy just shrugged her away, but had at least stopped crying by then.

'OK, OK,' said Alex. 'Look, I'm sorry, all right? But sometimes you're mean to me too.'

'I am?'

'Yeah, like this week in maths class. The teacher was being an arse and you outed me in front of the whole class for never doing my homework. It was horrible.'

'Did not!'

'Did too!'

'Well, sorry about that,' said Lucy.

'OK, well, quits.'

'No, not quits!'

'Jeez, all right!' said Alex. 'Look, here's Mum with the car. Let's get in, OK? But I swear if you say one more word to me, I'll kill you.'

'All right,' Lucy sighed as the car pulled up and they clambered inside. But Alex put her arm around her while she said it.

'Nicely done,' Stella whispered to Lucasta as the two moved on. 'I particularly loved your bossy voice. That's an old teachers' trick too, you know. Adopt a loud, sharp tone of voice and you can terrify the most unruly classroom into a stunned silence.'

'Is that right, my dear?' Lucasta said, with a sly little wink. 'Because that's also exactly how I speak to my little dog, whenever he's acting the maggot. Works a treat, every single time.'

'Thanks so much for at least trying with the seance this evening,' Mia said to Lucasta, catching up with her and Stella as they all walked towards the pub. 'It's not like these things are an exact science, now, are they? Not your fault that there was nothing doing this evening.'

'That's very understanding of you, dear,' said Lucasta as a taxi pulled up, which Dee and Mildred immediately started to clamber into. 'And you know, all the more reason why we could all do with a good stiff drink.'

'Not joining us, ladies?' Stella said to Mildred and Dee as they gave the taxi driver their address.

'I think this is a night for all you young ones to go out and have a bit of fun,' Mildred replied, gingerly climbing up into the back seat. 'I might just head home nice and early, if no one thinks it rude of me.'

'And just think, Mother,' Dee added, waving goodbye to everyone as she helped her mum safely into the taxi. 'This way, we'll get to see *New Tricks* before bedtime. Your very favourite!'

The taxi zoomed off, before Mia clicked off the car alarm of a huge Range Rover and bid her fond goodbyes too. 'I'm doing the school run with my grandkids early tomorrow,' she said. 'So no harm in calling it a night. Besides, I'm so boring in bars – I'm one of those teetotallers who drive everyone else mad, drinking fizzy water for the night!'

'Actually,' Connie piped up quietly, trailing at the very back of the remaining group and huddled under a battered-looking umbrella, 'I might just bow out here too.'

'You sure?' Will, who was walking beside her, asked.

'Yeah,' she said wanly, glad that she could slip away unobtrusively and that no one would overhear. 'I'm just... not on form tonight. You know how it is.'

'Bad day?' he asked her gently.

'Shite. Really, really shite. No other word for it.'

'Then let me get you a taxi.'

'No!' she said, the cost of it freaking her out. 'I'm happy to walk. Honestly.'

'In a deluge like this? Are you mad?'

'Really,' she said, pulling away from him. 'I'm happy to. I want to.'

'In that case,' he said, tagging alongside her as they turned in the opposite direction to the way everyone else was headed, 'I'm walking you home.'

'Don't be ridiculous, Will. Then you'll get soaked too!'

'Not taking no for an answer,' he said and, even through the rain, she could tell that he was smiling. A lovely crinkly-eyed smile too. 'You can get thrown out of the gentlemen's club for a lot less, you know.'

34

LUCASTA

'You seemed so stressed out this evening,' Stella said to Lucasta as they sat side by side in a cosy, private snug right at the back of the pub, while Luke went up to get in a round of drinks. 'Not like your usual self at all, if you don't mind me saying it. Rough day, I'm guessing?'

'Oh, my dear, you have absolutely no idea.' Lucasta sighed, sitting back on a cushioned bench against a wooden wall and exhaling deeply, as if this was the first time all evening she could think straight.

'Work?' Stella asked, keenly interested. 'If so, feel free to run it by me. I work in a primary school – I deal with stressful work situations for a living.'

'My assistant walked out on me,' Lucasta told her truthfully.

'That tall, thin lady who was always with you? Phoebe, wasn't that her name?' Stella asked.

'You have a wonderful memory. Yes, that's her.' Lucasta sighed deeply. 'I really don't know what came over her. One minute everything was fine. Well, maybe not fine, per se, but at least everything was normal between us. Next thing, she just blew up in my face. I've never seen her like that before, not in all the decades she's worked for me. She accused me of being unprofessional and said she'd had enough.'

'Unprofessional, how exactly? You're a global bestseller. Surely you don't achieve that without being professional?'

'Well, you know,' Lucasta said, squirming in her chair a bit and wishing Luke would hurry back with the drinks. At that moment, she'd never needed one more. 'Perhaps, just maybe, I mean... obviously I'm not aware of anything at all that might have brought on her meltdown... but just maybe... there were one or two occasions when Phoebe may have been cross with me for... you know... being late with all sorts of deeply boring things like deadlines.'

'Missing deadlines?' Stella probed, as expertly as a barrister in the High Court. 'Sounds like something more to me.'

'That's exactly it,' Lucasta said, deeply relieved that Stella seemed to 'get it'. 'Honestly, it was just the tiniest little thing and Phoebe exploded, then walked out on me. Left me completely high and dry, I can tell you.'

'Mind me asking what this tiny thing was?' Stella went on.

'Oh, nothing much. I may perhaps have broken a contract with some movie producers. Nothing important at all.'

'Movie producers?'

'FilmCorps? Ever heard of them?'

Stella looked across the table at her as her jaw fell to her collarbone. 'I think there must be very few people in the world who haven't heard of FilmCorps. They're huge. And they're not people I'd care to get into a legal tussle with.'

'That's exactly what Phoebe said,' Lucasta said, staring disconsolately ahead of her into space. 'Before she walked out the door.' Then snapping out of it, she added, 'Oh, such a lot of nonsense over nothing. Yes, she blew off steam a bit, but, with any luck, she'll come to her senses in a few days and turn up for work as normal.'

Finally, finally, finally, Luke made his way back into the snug, with the drinks.

'Here you go, ladies.' He smiled, handing them over. 'Sorry it took so long. There's a lot of big boozers in and, for such a stormy night, it's packed. Got you a double G & T, Lucasta, you looked like you could use one. Sauvignon Blanc for you, Stella, and just a coffee for me. I'm driving.'

'Oh, you are wonderful, thank you,' said Lucasta, taking a huge gulp and, for the first time all day, feeling vaguely relaxed. 'I'm just so terribly sorry that I was no use to either of you tonight. Poor Helen. She wants to reach out to you so badly, you know, Luke. She must have loved you and your daughter so much.'

* * *

Luke

Luke nodded politely, then went silent.

'You're grieving now,' Lucasta went on. 'And it's hell. Dear Lord, don't talk to me about it. When my Johnnie passed away, I could barely get out of bed. But in time that will pass. Till then, you just love and look after that little girl of yours.'

'He's doing a wonderful job there,' Stella chipped in. 'I should know, I see them both every day at school. Amy is a terrific kid. She's happy, she's well adjusted, she's bright as a button and she's a joy to be around. You need to give yourself credit for the great job you're doing,' she said pointedly to Luke.

Luke could have said plenty here, but chose not to. Lucasta

was bonkers, but then there was Stella. She was normal and nice and sane.

'And as for you, my dear,' Lucasta said, turning to Stella now. 'You've been stuck in grief for quite long enough. Don't you feel it's time to move on? Isn't that what your fiancé would want you to do? An attractive, successful woman like you?'

Stella brushed the compliment aside. 'Seeing as how we're all bent on fixing each other's problems,' she replied, 'I have a suggestion for you too, Lucasta. First thing tomorrow, you need to find Phoebe, wherever she's got to. Talk to her. Build bridges. It sounds like you two have worked together forever – isn't that something that's worth salvaging?'

They didn't stay out too late, but it was still bucketing down rain when they came back out onto Leeson Street. Luke insisted on driving Lucasta and Stella home to no arguments from either of them.

'Why would either of you want to take a taxi,' he asked, gallantly holding the car door open, 'when my car is right here?'

'Just as well,' said Lucasta, climbing into the passenger seat as Stella hopped in behind her. 'I haven't got a single bean on me to get home. Phoebe looks after boring things like money and cards and all that jazz. Or rather, she used to.'

'Just remember what I said,' said Stella. 'Trust me. I know what I'm talking about.'

'Hmm,' said Lucasta reluctantly. 'Well, we'll just see what transpires, shall we?'

A silence fell, so all they could hear was the rain pounding off the roof of the car, before Stella piped up again.

'Such a pity the others didn't join us this evening,' she said. 'They really seem like a great bunch. Did you notice how quiet and withdrawn Connie was tonight?'

'I certainly did notice,' Luke said. 'She didn't seem like her usual happy giggly self at all tonight.'

'I know so little about that girl,' Lucasta mused. 'Except that she was very close to her mother and misses her dreadfully now.'

'I know she's an actor,' Luke said as the car ground to a halt at traffic lights. 'Although from what I gather, jobs in her game are few and far between.'

Lucasta's ears pricked up.

'Oh, really? An actor? Well, now, that *is* interesting.'

* * *

Luke had already made the call to the Dicksons, but now was so fired up and, as it was still only about 9 p.m., he went ahead and made another call to Dave, his boss. Then he remembered, Dave was probably out on the razz, knowing him. Feck him, he could take the call if he wanted to and if not, they'd talk in the morning.

'Hey, Dave,' said Luke. Blaring music in the background, loud chatter, yup, it was most definitely a bar of some description, on his way somewhere. Make no mistake, this guy was pulling a serious all-nighter.

'Ehh... yeah. Hey, man, how's it going?'

'Good, and you?' said Luke.

'Ah, just with the lads for a few bevvies, you know yourself,' he said. 'So what can I do for you?'

Feck him. Luke didn't really owe him anything, so in for a penny, in for a pound. He didn't even need to take a deep breath, or anything that you'd normally do.

'Dave, it's bad news,' he began.

'You daughter's not sick again, is she? Jeez, she's forever ill...' The second part of this sentence was muffled as if to some companion, but sounded like, 'This guy is always pulling daughter sickies.' He could still be heard, the roaring eejit.

'She's as healthy as a horse, but that's not why I'm calling.'

'Yeah?'

'I'm quitting. Not my career, my job with you. And it's not negotiable, sorry.'

'*What* did you say?'

'I'll work through my notice,' Luke said, 'then I'm gone. Sorry to call you at night with this, but it's been on my mind, so there you have it.'

'I see.' Dave sighed deeply. 'Look, I'm in the middle of a night out, so can we talk about this in the morning?'

'Sorry, Dave. I'll work through your notice period for the next few weeks, but then I'm gone.'

35

CONNIE

'So he walked you home?' Kate probed from the other end of the phone call. 'Nothing more?'

'What do you mean, nothing more? I thought that was a nice thing, a kind thing. Particularly after it had been such a washout of a day. Literally and figuratively, that is.'

'Didn't make a move on you? You didn't ask him in for coffee? Nothing doing at all? Jesus, I give up on you.'

'Come on, Kate.' Connie sighed. 'It had been a particularly shitty day for me – the last thing I was in the humour for was some random fella making moves on me. I think I'd have shoved him off me and run a mile. All I'm saying is that it was sweet of Will to walk me home.'

'Hmm,' said Kate, sounding unconvinced. 'The guy clearly likes you and a bit of romance in your life right now would take your mind off everything else that's going on, wouldn't it?'

'I'm not much company just at the moment,' Connie said, working her way through the crowds of other shoppers on a packed Grafton Street. 'Last thing I'd want to do is start seeing someone new. Not that I even think Will is interested in me that way, not for two seconds. We're just... mates, that's all. We've a lot in common, loss of a parent, for one thing. We talk and that's it. Nothing more.'

'Hmmm. Famous last words,' said Kate, to the sound of the baby waking in the background, always her cue to go. 'Anyway, hon, you can say you're not much company at the minute, but I beg to differ. And I expect to see you at my kitchen table tonight for dinner – chicken casserole. Boring as arse, I know, but at least this way, I have some small hope of getting a few vitamins into the boys.'

'I'd love nothing more.' Connie smiled, finding the phone shop she'd been looking for, before stepping inside and tagging onto the end of a long, snaking queue. 'Chat to you later, then, hon. I'll even bring the wine!'

'Well, now you're speaking my language.' Kate laughed, before clicking off the call.

Eventually, when Connie had worked her way to the top of the queue, she came face-to-face with a very bored-looking customer sales rep. 'Howaya, yeah, what's up?' He practically yawned into her face.

'It's a bit of a weird one actually,' Connie began to say apologetically, fishing the famous ancient Nokia phone out of her bag and placing it on the counter between them. 'This,' she said, pointing down at it, 'in a nutshell, is my problem. I used to get calls on it and now I don't, and I just wondered if you could maybe take a look at it for me and see if we can repair it?'

Bored customer service rep gazed at her in shock, before picking up the phone and looking at it in deep disgust.

'Wha'?' he said incredulously. '*Wha'* did you just say?'

'I said I'd like to get this phone repaired, please,' Connie replied firmly.

'This?' he said, unable to believe what he was hearing. '*This* is the phone you're still using? Seriously? These yokes went out with the ark!'

'No, it's not the phone I'm using,' Connie rushed to say, 'of course it's not. It's... well, it's kind of my mum's phone. It's the one she calls me on...' She trailed off lamely, reluctant to divulge any more.

'Then tell your ma we can definitely get her a better handset,' said bored sales guy. 'The state of it! I'd say this phone is even older than I am. This is a relic. Should be in some kinda museum for ancient technology, along with fax machines and video recorders. Jaysus, now I've seen it all.'

'I'm not looking for a better handset,' Connie said calmly. 'All I want is to be able to receive calls on this phone. Like I said, I used to be able to and now, for some reason, I can't. So can you help me out, please?'

'So this isn't your own phone, then?'

'No, I have an iPhone, thanks.'

'So why can't your ma call you on your iPhone? Why does it have to be this aul yoke?'

'It's... a long story,' was all Connie could say, hoping he'd stop with all the bloody questions and just say whether he could help her out, yes or no.

'Michelle!' Bored sales guy called out to his pal, over at the till beside him. 'Come here till you get a load of this phone. Look at the state of it! Nearly pulled a muscle just trying to lift it up – the weight of it!'

Another sales rep, a girl with bright pink hair and braces, who looked not much older than Toby, Kate's eldest. 'Wow!' she said, picking it up and scoping out the weight of it. 'I think that's a first-generation Nokia 230... You don't see too many of them around now.'

'And up until recently, it was working,' Connie said. 'But now

– well, the phone won't ring any more. So can you maybe send it off for repairs?'

'Repair this?' said pink-haired sales rep. 'Are you having a laugh? The only place this is fit for is a skip. I can feck it in the dumpster out the back for you, if you like?'

'*No!*' said Connie, horrified. She muttered her apologies and slunk out of the shop, aware that the staff – and probably anyone in the queue who had happened to overhear – now all thought she was a nutjob.

There's only one person who might be able to help me, she thought, clinging tightly to the famous phone and winding her way down the thronged street. *She's a gazillionaire novelist and probably the only person in the whole world who won't write me off as certifiable.*

Come on, Mum, she thought. *If ever I needed a sign from you – it's now. Right now. You came through for me before, surely you can do it again?*

She clung to the phone the whole way home, hoping, praying that it might ring again.

But nothing. Absolutely sweet feck all.

36

LUKE

The following Friday, Amy's class were due to go on a school field trip to the Airfield Estate and the excitement levels were sky-high. Airfield was a working farm in the suburbs of Dublin, where kids got to see working livestock and a dairy farm up close and personal, followed by a tour around Airfield House, the late-Georgian house from which the estate took its name. Parents had been issued with the day's schedule and told to be at the school at 4 p.m. sharp to collect the kids.

So by 4 p.m., like every other parent, Luke had slipped out of work and was waiting patiently at the school gate as the bus drew up, the excited squeals of the children clearly audible from the street. Luke smiled as the kids bolted out, still high as kites from all the fun and excitement of the day, and dying to tell their parents all about it. Luke spotted Amy's little blonde head immediately, surrounded by a gang of her pals, giggling and chatting, but the minute she saw him waving, she was over to him like a shot, beaming from ear to ear and full of chat.

'Oh, Dad, it was *magic*!' she said breathlessly. 'And you'll never guess what – we got to see the hen coop and there were red ones and black ones and white ones and we saw their eggs and the lady in charge told us the white eggs were lucky and you'll never believe it, but we saw two!'

'That's wonderful.' Luke smiled, waving at one of the dads he recognised. Stella, he noticed out of the corner of his eye, was by the school bus with Amy's form teacher and was chatting away to the parents, remembering all their names, and with warm goodbyes for the children. Stella really was something else: so cool, so calm, so unflappable, so bloody good at her job. The school – and the parents – were lucky to have someone like her. One by one, kids were bundled into cars, while Amy chattered away.

'And then we ate our lunch and we had loads of time to play *and* we saw the cows being milked and everyone else said it was a bit stinky, but I didn't mind. And we even got inside the house too and the lady said it was over one hundred years old and we saw an old doll's house and pictures of horses and dogs everywhere and—'

'That's amazing, pet,' Luke said. 'So how about we say goodbye to Miss Mackey before we go? You can thank her for organising such a great day.'

The crowd had thinned out as Luke and Amy approached Stella.

'Thank you, Miss Mackey. I had a really brilliant day.' Amy smiled as Stella bent down to chat to her face-to-face.

'I'm so glad you had fun,' she said. 'You'll have so much to tell your dad. Tell him what a great girl you were! Now have a lovely weekend, both of you.'

She stood up tall and automatically fell into step with Luke as he strolled over to where his jeep was parked.

'You know, I have fresh admiration for you after today.' He smiled as Amy skipped ahead of them. 'I know the form teacher brought the kids, but you organised them.'

'Days like today? Best part of the job,' Stella replied, modestly batting away the compliment. 'Now, if only a few more of the children were as polite and well behaved as Amy, believe me, my job would be 99 per cent easier.'

'So, any plans for the weekend?' Luke asked her, suddenly aware as soon as the words came out that it sounded as if he were fishing. Which he most definitely, categorically was not. *We're just two friends having a normal conversation,* he told himself. *Nothing more.*

Stella sucked her cheeks before answering.

'Actually, I'm kind of dreading this weekend,' she said.

'Why's that?'

'The Irish Mountaineering Society have organised a family day out on the Sugar Loaf mountain this Sunday,' she went on, her whole tone shifting.

'But you don't like to do it without Tom?' Luke said, stopping to face her full-on.

'That's it exactly.' She nodded. 'It'll be my first time even getting back into my North Face gear since he died. Half of me is this close to bailing, but then, it's to raise funds for the society, which Tom was very involved with, so I think I should probably toughen up a bit and get it over with. He'd have wanted me to do this, I'm certain of that.'

'You said it was a family day?' Luke asked, and Stella nodded.

'It's actually one of the easiest climbs you can do. It's open to anyone and kids are welcome too, as long as they have a parent with them. The idea is to try and foster a love of mountain climbing in anyone who's up for it. And it can be wonderful fun – the sense of exhilaration when you make it to the summit is like nothing on earth.'

'Then here's a thought. How about Amy and I come with you? For a bit of moral support? If you'd like company, that is?'

37

CONNIE

Signs. There were signs everywhere, till it got to the point where Connie felt overwhelmed by it all. Firstly – a call from Karen, Estate Agent From Hell.

'This has literally never happened to me before,' she said haughtily down the phone, 'and I sincerely hope it never happens again. Here's the thing though: remember that family who had put a firm offer on your house?'

'Yes, of course I do,' said Connie. Course she remembered. They were called the Farrells and the reason she'd even accepted their offer was because they had a young family. They had apparently fallen in love with the house because it was a great place for their kids to grow up. It was a happy house for me, had been Connie's reasoning, and now it'd be a happy house for a younger generation too. What was not to like about that? She hated having to move, but here at least was one good thing to come out of it.

'Well, it's a disaster,' Karen said down the phone. 'Apparently the Farrells' mortgage offer has fallen through, so, for the moment at least, they're not in any position to finalise the sale or even to move. Not to worry though! I'm already in touch with our other bidder to tell him the great news that the house is his if he wants it.'

'*What* did you say?'

'Your brother said that—'

'Absolutely out of the question!' said Connie, for once putting her foot down with Karen. Truth was she remembered the bidder Karen was talking about too: he was a complete and utter eejit whose plan was to demolish the house with total disregard for their lovely neighbours, who'd not only have to live with the noise but who'd then have to look at a carbuncle of a house in the middle of a humble row of corporation houses. Not very tempting.

So Connie stood firm. Asked Karen for the Farrells' number, thanked her very politely, then told her in no uncertain terms that her services were no longer required, which felt so bloody good, she wondered why she hadn't done it ages ago. Next, she immediately rang up the Farrell family and spoke to Marie Farrell directly.

'So here's my suggestion for you,' Connie said to her, trembling with nerves and hope. 'I hear you've got a bit of a delay at your end. And I still haven't found a place to move into. So how about we just leave things as they are? For the moment, anyway? A bit of breathing space for both of us. Then when you do finalise your mortgage and with absolutely no time pressure on you at all, you and I will talk. How about that?'

The loud squeals from down the other end of the phone told her that she was doing the right thing. She even put in a courtesy call to Donald in Paris, just to fill him in. 'Yeah, whatever,' was his exasperated response. 'Delays are part of any house sale, I get it. As long as this is just a minor delay and nothing more.'

Connie was in the hall and her eye fell on a framed photo of her mum, taken over thirty years ago now and with Connie as a baby perched happily on her knee. Her thoughts began to wander. This was just a bit of time out from the whole selling process and nothing more. But maybe... maybe loads of things would happen in the interim. Maybe she'd get a job, a proper one with an actual wage. Maybe her pal Mbeki, who was looking to rent a place, might move in for a bit and help her out with the mortgage?

This is just a stay of execution and nothing more, she said to her mum in her head. *But it buys me space. And my God, even that much feels so bloody wonderful. So, if this is your doing, just... thank you, thank you, thank you. You may not be calling me on that ridiculous mobile any more, but you know what?*

I think you can hear me.

38

LUKE

Ever since he'd first told her, Amy had been so excited about spending Sunday climbing up a mountain with her dad and Miss Mackey – something that made Luke inordinately pleased. The last thing he ever would do would be to inflict any new friendship of his on Amy, with someone she didn't like. She liked Stella though, of that he was certain. Which made Luke smile, without him quite being able to put his finger on why that was.

On Saturday, Amy was happily deciding what outfit to wear, forcing Luke to choose between two pink glittery backpacks that looked identical to him. But overnight something changed. Holly and Poppy had spent the night with them and as Luke drove his nieces home with Amy wedged in between them in the back seat, he noticed how silent his little girl was. Not a bit like her usual chatty self at all. Initially, he put it down to tiredness; the three girls had all bunked in Amy's room together so that Luke could give Clare and Tony the rare luxury of a date night. It was the very least he could do for them, he'd figured, after everything they did for him.

'Something up, pet?' he asked her as soon as he'd dropped Holly and Poppy off.

'No,' she said sulkily, but he could tell. Something was most definitely, *definitely* up.

'Come on, pet, tell me what's wrong. If you don't tell me, then how can I make it better?'

'I don't want to.'

So that was the way it was going to be. He tried changing tack.

'Tell you what, love. How about we go home, get organised for the mountain climb, then go and meet Miss Mackey at the Sugar Loaf? Look! It's a beautiful sunny day and we are going to have such fun!'

'I'm not going, Dad. I know I said I wanted to, but now I don't.'

Luke had just pulled up at home, so he switched off the engine and turned around to give her his full attention.

'But I thought you were looking forward to today?' he said gently. 'You were so excited about it only yesterday.'

'But then I told Poppy about it and she says it's stupid,' Amy parroted. 'She says going out with your school principal on the weekend is really lame and sad. So I don't want to go now.'

Right, Luke thought. So Poppy, who at the tender age of eleven was already turning into a teenager, had got to her. Lame and stupid were definitely Poppy words and not something Amy would ever say. In a flash, he knew exactly what to do. As Amy clambered out of the jeep ahead of him, he picked up the phone and rang Clare.

'So it's just a fun family day of hillwalking really,' he explained to her. 'But I wondered if Holly and Poppy would like to join us?'

'Yeah, they mentioned that's what you were up to today.'

Clare yawned sleepily down the phone. 'Something to do with Amy's school principal? That right? You've never mentioned her before.'

'She's a pal,' he answered firmly. 'A good pal. And I just think it might be more fun if the kids are together, that's all.' He left out what he was really thinking, which was that Amy, as the younger cousin, would always take her lead from Holly and Poppy. So what better way to nip this nonsense about it being 'sad' and 'lame' to spend a day with a kind person who happened to be a school principal?

Half an hour later, he and Amy were back at Clare's as the girls bundled into the back of the jeep, this time dressed for the great outdoors, in warm puffa jackets, trainers and with backpacks full of juice and nuts to snack on for the climb.

'I don't know what's going on,' Clare said, still in her nightie as she waved them all goodbye, 'between dropping them here, then picking them up again, but you're doing me a huge favour. I've got such a hangover from last night and you'd want to see the state of Tony. It's the world's greatest lie, but I really mean it. Never drinking again. Ever.'

Luke waved goodbye, promised he'd have them back before dark and they were on their way.

'So this is *weird*,' he heard Poppy decreeing from the back seat. 'Can't we go shopping in Dundrum instead?'

Oh, no, you don't, missy, Luke thought.

'Today will be a proper adventure, girls,' he replied. 'How many times do we all get to have a proper adventure together? You can go to Dundrum any time. Just think of the great stories you'll have to tell all your pals in school on Monday.'

Amy, he noticed, seemed a lot happier about the day ahead now that she had her cousins with her, and the mood in the back of the car picked up considerably as soon as they arrived at the car park at the Sugar Loaf, in County Wicklow. It was jam-packed with cars and takeout vans selling teas, coffees, drinks and all kinds of tempting snacks for the day ahead. In the far distance, they could just make out some intrepid families who'd already made it to the summit, while piles of others had started the climb. Luke spotted Stella, wearing a high-vis vest and handing out complimentary bottles of water to all the new arrivals.

He waved, steered the girls over to say hi and made the introductions.

'Great to meet you, Poppy, and you too, Holly.' Stella smiled warmly at the girls. 'Amy has told me so much about you both. So how about a hot chocolate and a warm cookie before we set off? It's a gorgeous day and I think you're going to enjoy yourselves.'

Even Poppy brightened at the suggestion and in no time all five of them had begun ascending the gentle climb to the top.

'As you can see, it's suitable for kids of all ages and all the Mountaineering Society want is for everyone to have a laugh,' Stella said to Luke as they began the climb.

'So far, so good.' Luke smiled as the reassuring sounds of laughter and giggles from the girls a few feet ahead wafted back to them.

'It looks so high up there, Dad,' Amy turned to say. 'Do you really think we'll make it?'

'You're brilliant at sports in school, Amy.' Stella smiled encouragingly. 'I bet you'll be well able. Do you like sports too?' she asked Poppy and Holly, taking care to include them both.

'I like gym class when it's indoors and when we can play with the beam and the trampoline,' said Holly. 'And Poppy is brilliant at hockey. She's on the school's Junior team, you know.'

'Wow, is that right?' Stella asked.

'Hockey is fun.' Poppy shrugged, slowly beginning to open up a little to Stella. 'You get to go on loads of school trips for matches

– this year, we even went to Prague. That's in the Czech Republic,' she added helpfully.

'I'm very impressed,' said Stella. 'Sounds to me like you're going to be the star of the school hockey team some day. Today should be no bother to any of you. Just remember, take it nice and slow, drink lots of water – and going down is always the tricky part!'

The path in front of them was rocky and well worn, and even though Luke offered to give Amy a piggyback if she got tired, she point-blank refused, and in no time they'd all made it safely to the summit.

'Wow, look at the view!' Poppy enthused, now back to herself as Luke took photos, with Stella in the centre of the girls and the sun blazing behind them.

'Doesn't it feel wonderful?' Stella said as they reluctantly began the climb down. 'That sense of achievement you get when you summit?'

'Imagine what Mount Everest must be like,' Holly thought aloud, her eyes like saucers.

'Take more photos, Uncle Luke!' Poppy ordered him. 'And will you share them with me on WhatsApp? So I can show them to all my pals in school tomorrow.'

Poppy, he was glad to see, was back to her restored role as babysitter-in-chief to her younger sister and cousin, all the nonsense of 'it's lame' and 'it's stupid' totally forgotten about.

'It's brilliant, Dad,' Amy said, with a big, happy smile. 'I feel like I could touch the clouds from here!'

The climb down took a little longer, but no one's spirits flagged, and when they got to the bottom Luke spotted a pizza truck with some empty benches beside it and a mercifully short-looking queue.

'You must all be starving,' he said. 'How about pizzas?'

'Oh, yes, please!' came three voices as Stella nodded her approval and walked over to the truck to order with Luke while the girls nabbed a free bench, tired, but still giddy and messing and full of chat.

'I always knew you were a very good dad,' Stella said quietly, 'but now it turns out you're a wonderful uncle too.'

'So... your very first climb since you lost Tom?' Luke asked her as the short queue inched forward. 'Can't have been easy. I was proud of you up there, you know. What you did today really took courage.'

She thought a bit before answering.

'Strange thing,' she said. 'Whenever he and I were on a climb together, and if ever I lagged behind, he'd always say to me, "Just keep putting one foot in front of another and you'll eventually get there." Could have sworn I heard his voice in my head saying the very same thing today. That ever happen to you?'

* * *

As twilight came, the three girls in the back of the car showed no sign of flagging.

'Stella's so cool,' Holly kept saying. 'If she was my school head, I'd love going into school and I'd never complain.'

'And I love the way she dresses too.' Poppy nodded enthusiastically. 'I'm going to save like mad to get a pair of those hiking boots she had. The exact same ones.'

Luke, who'd been avidly eavesdropping, looked in the rear-view mirror at Amy, who sat in between the other two, looking delighted with herself.

'Didn't I tell you?' She beamed from ear to ear. 'Didn't I tell you that Stella is the nicest school headteacher in the whole world?'

'Is she your girlfriend, Uncle Luke? Are you going to marry her?'

'Don't be silly.' Luke smiled. 'We're friends. Good friends. That's all.'

'Because she'll never be your mummy, Amy. Your mummy is gone and she's never coming back.'

At that stinging comment from Poppy, Luke was ready to pull the jeep over, at the slightest hint of tears from Amy or any sign at all that she was upset. But to his surprise, she went completely silent, as if she was really deep in thought.

'I know it's sad,' she said after a thoughtful little pause. 'But I want my dad to be all happy and smiley and I want more days like today. Stella's nice and I like her. She makes my dad smile and she makes me smile and that makes me happy.'

39

Connie loved summer and this one was green and luscious and gorgeous too. All along the streets, the flowers and trees were in full bloom, and bright evenings meant later to bed. It was a gloriously sunny afternoon and she was out and about with Kate and the boys: they'd just been to see the new Marvel movie and were all gathered in a booth in a fifties diner, staring at menus, while the boys bickered over whether to order chicken nuggets or burgers with 'enough room for chocolate milkshakes *and* ice-cream sundaes afterwards', as Toby decreed, still high on a hit movie.

When Connie's phone rang, loud and clear.

'That's your phone?' Kate asked as she tried to referee the row that had broken out at the table between the boys. 'Not... you know... *the* phone?'

'No, just my phone, sadly,' Connie said as she went to answer it. '*That* phone has been stone-cold silent for ages now. Ages! I've completely given up.'

But then she looked down to see who was calling her, and a tingle of shock went down her spine. It was Sean Mussolides. Her agent. Her actual agent, who never called her for any reason, ever.

'Feck's sake,' she muttered under her breath, but the boys, of course, picked up on it and immediately started chanting, 'feck's sake, feck, feck, feck, feck sake!' till they were the focus of the entire restaurant.

'Hello? Sean?' Connie said, getting up from the table with the phone clamped to her ear and stepping away so she could hear him properly. What the hell was this about? Then her heart sank. Was he calling to fire her?

'Hi there,' came his reply, sounding as distracted as ever. 'Have you got a minute? There's been a development and I really need to speak to you about it.'

'Ehh, yeah, of course,' Connie replied, thinking, *Yup. No two ways about it. My arse is so fired.* Bracing herself, she asked him, 'So what's up?'

'Well,' he answered. 'Are you familiar with the first *Mercy* book? You know the one I mean, huge bestseller... author is that lunatic who's always on TV...'

'Yes,' Connie said. 'Lucasta Liversidge is the author. And yeah, I know the book you mean. My mum was a huge fan, and now I am too.'

Where the hell is this going? she wondered as the boys continued yelling 'feck's sake!' in the background, not unlike Father Jack out of *Father Ted.*

'Well, here's the thing,' Sean explained. 'FilmCorps have had a brand-new TV adaptation of it slated for years now, but there were so many rumours going around about this particular project, no one really knew what was going on. Firstly it was full steam ahead, then apparently there was a big falling out between the author and the producers – "artistic differences", I've been told, which can pretty much mean anything. But now, seemingly they've all made up, so the project is in a go mode again.'

'That's wonderful,' Connie said, delighted for Lucasta, but at the same time wondering... *what the hell has this got to do with me?*

Then came the clincher.

'So there's a small part in it...'

'Yeah?' Connie found herself holding her breath.

'A tiny part, really. A nursemaid, a character called Rosie...'

'Yes,' Connie said, 'I remember from the book.'

'It's probably a week's work, maybe two at most,' Sean went on as Connie's heart hammered in double time. 'But Rosie is a featured presence. The exteriors will be filmed here, in Ireland, and the interiors in the FilmCorps studios in Burbank, California.'

'Sean,' Connie said, her head swimming, 'what are you trying to tell me?'

'Long story short, but just now,' he replied, sounding, truth to tell, a bit shocked himself, 'I had a call from one of their casting people, who'd seen online that I represent you.'

'Go on,' said Connie, slumping down in shock into an empty booth as Kate looked over at her worriedly.

'And they want you for the part,' said Sean. 'Straight up fee, worldwide rights: there's some serious money there. So what do you think?'

'What do you mean?' Connie asked, utterly confused. Was this some kind of joke at her expense? Pretty elaborate one, if it was, she thought. 'Do they want me to self-tape or audition for them?'

'Oh no, nothing like that,' said Sean. 'It seems there's no audition process at all. This is a straight offer for you and you alone. Came from the very top, apparently. So, Connie, what do I tell them? Is it a yes, or is it a no?'

40

LUCASTA

Gran Canaria was hot, sticky, sweaty and deeply uncomfortable at this time of year. The elderly English-speaking lady who was wandering about the outdoor sun terrace in the five-star Maspalomas hotel was certainly attracting a great deal of attention. Even holidaymakers splashing about in the pool stopped to have a good gawp at her.

'Please you come this way,' a kindly staff member was saying to her in broken English, clearly having taken pity on her as she meandered around looking lost and bewildered.

'Oh, thank you, thank you, most kind,' the elderly lady replied, before stumbling over a football that two kids were messing with. She yelped out loud and instantly dropped not only her wheelie bag, but also a sizable bag of duty-free, the contents of which smashed into smithereens, leaving a strong smell of gin.

'Oh, please forgive me, I really am so terribly sorry,' she said, flustered. 'Em... here,' she added, taking a fistful of notes out of one of her bulging pockets and handing him over the cash. 'Have some money. Least I can do after causing such a fuss.'

'It's no problem, lady, happens all the time,' the staff member who was by her side replied, clicking his fingers as a team of servers descended on the spillage and broken glass and immediately began to clean up the mess.

'And you're quite sure she's here? On the terrace, I mean?' the lady insisted, as yet more people close by turned to stare at her, some photographing her as she swished past.

'It *is* her,' someone hissed as she walked past them. 'Definitely!'

'No, it's not, it's just a lookalike,' someone else hissed. 'Just because that woman has long grey hair and dresses in mad colours, doesn't mean that it's *her,* does it? I mean to say, what would Lucasta Liversidge be doing here?'

'Irish lady you look for is right over there,' said the waiter who was helping. 'Always she sit in the shade at this time of day. Never sunshine, not for her.'

Lucasta thanked him profusely, taking care to stuff an even bigger wad of notes into his hand before he left her in peace.

Sure enough, just a few feet away from her, there was a woman in black reclining on a sun lounger, clad in a giant bucket-shaped sunhat and Jackie O-style dark glasses, who was looking on in amazement, peering over her glasses so she could really drink in the scene.

'Well, well, well,' she said, speaking slowly and distinctly. 'So you're even tipping now, I see. I thought you didn't carry cash? Wonders will never cease.'

'It's good to see you, my friend,' Lucasta said, wavering by an empty seat and dithering over whether she should sit down or not. On the one hand, it had been a hellish journey, but on the other, this little 'surprise' she'd just staged could well blow up in her face. Particularly given the way she and Phoebe had parted.

In the end, she went for the penance of discomfort and stayed standing.

'I came a very long way,' Lucasta said simply and truthfully, 'to tell you that I'm sorry.'

There was silence as Phoebe pulled an impressed face. 'Now, there's a first,' she said, sounding shocked. 'You've never apologised to me. Not once, not ever.'

'Well, I'm sorry now,' Lucasta replied, anxiously fingering an oversized bead necklace she was wearing. 'So terribly sorry, my dear. Oh, you have no idea how much I've missed you!'

Phoebe sat up, still shaking her head in disbelief, as if she was only now coming to terms with what she was seeing. 'For starters,' she asked, 'how on earth did you manage to find me?'

At this, Lucasta puffed up a bit, looking justifiably proud of herself. 'Well,' she said delightedly. 'You know how you never speak about your family? Well, I racked my brains and distinctly remembered you once saying you had a sister who lived in Cork and who worked as a psychotherapist – Sophie. I'm afraid I did have to wade through an awful lot of psychotherapy practices before I finally found this particular Sophie, but heigh ho, I did! She told me you'd escaped here for a little break – and so here I am.'

Then Lucasta trailed off weakly, still unsure what kind of a welcome she'd get.

'Of course, you're perfectly entitled to toss a drink over me and order me out of here,' she added nervously, 'particularly after that dreadful conversation we had when we last spoke. All I came to do was to tell you in person how miserable I feel about how you and I parted and how greatly you're missed.'

Phoebe weighed this up for a moment.

'Oh, for goodness' sake, will you please sit down?' she eventually said. 'You're driving me mad shuffling about. And I can tell you're gagging for a gin and tonic, so go ahead and order one if you like. I won't bite.'

'Does that mean,' Lucasta offered hopefully, 'that I might be forgiven? Even just a tiny bit?'

'I did wonder how long you'd last without me,' Phoebe said dryly.

'But there's something else I need to say, my dear,' Lucasta said, gratefully plonking down into a comfy-looking rattan armchair beside Phoebe and peeling off some of her layers and layers of wool cardis in the baking heat. 'Something terribly important.'

'I'm all ears,' said Phoebe, folding her arms across her tummy.

'Well... the thing is... Please don't think I'm here to try and coax you to come back to work for me, or anything like that,' Lucasta went on. 'Although, of course, I'd dearly love you to and it goes without saying that the door is always open, you know that. But I respect how you feel about... well, let's just say, the vagaries of working with someone like me. Oh, my dear, what an absolute nightmare I must have been! How richly you deserve to lie here in this gorgeous resort and forget all about me.'

Phoebe looked at her, long and hard, as if she was trying to work something out for herself.

'So I came to say thank you,' Lucasta went on, speaking simply and humbly. 'I've realised such a lot since you left, and one of the biggies is that in all the decades we've worked side by side, I don't think I ever once thanked you. Not one single time. So I'm doing it now. Without you, Lucasta Liversidge simply wouldn't exist. Yes, I wrote the books, but you, Phoebe, you did absolutely everything else for me – all those years, you've kept the show on the road and I want you to know how grateful I am. Always. And for absolutely everything.'

There was a long, long pause as Phoebe digested this, only the sound of children splashing about in the water breaking the silence.

'That's... that's very... nice... to hear,' Phoebe eventually said. 'It feels good to be... appreciated properly. And now, I suppose it's my turn to thank you too, Lucasta. You showed me the whole world and... and... well, now that I've had a bit of distance from you, I've given this a lot of thought. We did have some good times together, didn't we?'

'Oh, we certainly did, my dear! Course, we had our moments too, but then who doesn't? Particularly after working so closely together for so long.'

Just then, a wine waiter bustled over to them, ready to take their order.

'Oh, you kind man,' Lucasta said to him. 'Please will you send over a bottle of the most expensive champagne you have? Not for me, though. It's a gift for my friend. Just a tiny gift, but one I hope you'll enjoy, Phoebe, dear.'

'Please,' Phoebe tried to override her, 'there really is no need.'

'There's every need,' Lucasta insisted, putting her foot down. 'And not only that, but I've also told that very handsome manager at Reception that your hotel bill is to be charged to me. It's the very least I can do.'

'You don't have to do this...' Phoebe tried to say, but Lucasta was having none of it.

'No, my dear,' she said, taking charge. 'I'm treating you and, as you so often say to me, that's not negotiable. Because, my friend, this is a celebration we should have had a long time ago. We're celebrating *you*.'

41

These days, it was almost impossible to get into Will's cafe on Leeson Street on a Thursday night. You had to be there a full hour early, just to make sure you got a seat for the regular Bereavement Cafe meetings, and it wasn't unusual to see a long, snaking queue down the street patiently waiting to get inside. These days, Will would often speculate privately to Connie that he might consider branching out a bit, possibly even opening up a second cafe on the other side of town, an idea she actively encouraged.

It seemed this was mainly down to good old-fashioned word of mouth, coupled with the fact that Lucasta Liversidge raved enthusiastically about these Bereavement Cafe meetings every time the media gave her a chance – which was pretty often, considering. Subsequently, journalists and the wider media wrote widely about the meetings and it had spread from there. It was all very positive feedback and it was all very, very welcome, as Will would gratefully point out.

Lucy was there with Alex, getting on, shock horror, and this particular Thursday night, Connie was bursting to tell Will her news; the two had formed a regular habit of going for a drink with the rest of the gang after their meetings, when they'd inevitably end up spending the rest of the night chatting and gossiping away in a corner, just the pair of them. But there was one person she really, really needed to talk to first. When she eventually worked her way through the queue to get inside, there she was, standing in the dead centre of the room, surrounded by Mildred, Dee and Mia, all of whom were having a heated discussion about Mildred's gluten-free brownies, and the fact that this time they were really worthy of mass-production, they were that mouth-watering.

'Give me half a chance, Mildred,' Mia was saying enthusiastically, 'and I could sell them in a pop-up shop at my gym. Health-conscious brownies? They'd fly out the door. It could make you a fortune!'

Mildred tittered delightedly and even Phoebe was tasting one of the brownies and nodding approvingly – Connie could have sworn she saw the woman crack a smile. The cafe was packed and, almost timidly, Connie approached Lucasta.

'I'm so sorry to interrupt,' she said, 'but could I possibly have a quick word?'

'Perhaps you have some news for me, my dear?' Lucasta asked, with a twinkle in her bright blue eyes.

Phoebe, who had been listening, drifted over to join them, with a knowing smile on her face. 'News that came from your agent, I'd hazard a guess?'

'Since I last saw you...' Connie started to say, until all of a sudden she began choking on her words, she was that close to tears. 'It's like... it's like a kind of miracle has happened. And you are the guardian angel behind it all, Lucasta. I know that – I knew that the minute I got the call.'

'You did say yes, I hope?' Lucasta asked, taking both of Connie's thin, bony hands into her own. 'Because you'll make a wonderful Rosie, I know you will. And Phoebe agrees with me too, don't you, dear?'

'You fit the character description in the book down to a T.' Phoebe smiled. First time Connie had ever heard her say something positive, as it happened. 'Now it's only a small part, of course...'

'But then, there's no such thing as a small part,' Lucasta tactfully finished the sentence for her, 'only small actors. And you, my dear, are most definitely *not* a small actor.'

'How can I thank you enough?' Connie said to both of them, her eyes welling up. 'I mean... if you could only know what this means to me – to my life. This means... that I'm actually going to be on a film set earning money again. This means that casting directors are looking at me with renewed interest. A gig in something as high profile as this might even mean that more work might start to come my way... and it's all because of you. Both of you,' she said, taking care to include Phoebe too.

'Shine, my dear,' was all Lucasta said, smiling proudly. 'This is your time to shine. And you know something else? Do you remember when you first started to come here, to the cafe? And you were so worried about your dear mother, because she'd been contacting you on that terribly old telephone, but then she went completely silent on you?'

'Yes.' Connie laughed through tears. The happy kind, though. The good kind. 'Will I ever forget? I barely went out the door without that useless old phone, and now I hardly even bother to look at it.'

'Do you know, I think there's a reason your mother stopped contacting you that way,' Lucasta said thoughtfully as the cafe grew more and more packed and Will rushed around in the background, trying to make room for everyone and get them all seated.

'You do?'

'Oh, absolutely, my dear. It's because *this* is how she's communicating with you now. By sending you all these blessings. Because it's your mother who's making these wondrous miracles happen in your life. No question about it. So much more effective too, don't you think? What a wonderful lady she must have been.'

Connie had been battling tears, but at that, she full-on broke down.

'Hey, hey, now, none of this,' Stella said, coming over to her with a fat wad of tissues.

'It's OK, I'm fine, honestly,' Connie said to her, noticing that Luke trailed not too far behind Stella. The pair of them seemed inseparable these days. They always seemed to arrive together on Thursday nights and, after every single cafe meeting, you could be guaranteed they were the ones who led the way across the road for a drink in the local bar.

'Come on, now, there's a good girl,' Stella said soothingly, giving Connie a big hug. 'This isn't a day for tears. This is a day for you to celebrate – isn't that what your lovely mum would have wanted?'

Now Connie looked up at her, puzzled.

'Lucasta told us all before you got here,' Luke explained, guiding Connie over to a seat that was free. 'She said it was meant to be confidential news, but that meant she still told everyone, one by one. Amazing news, Connie! Imagine? I'll get to say that I actually know someone in a FilmCorps series – how cool is that?'

'It's a miracle,' Connie said, gratefully sitting down in between him and Stella, just as Will looked over at her from behind the counter, catching her eye and waving that he'd join her just as soon as he could. Lucasta was still hovering close by, though, in the meantime she'd been besieged by newcomers, all wanting selfies. Still, though, she caught the little exchange between Connie and Will and drank it in, nodding sagely.

'Hmm,' she said, almost to herself. 'And do you know? I think perhaps there's one more miracle on its way to Connie, before her mother is quite done.'

'What's that?' Phoebe asked her.

'It's almost as though I can hear Connie's mother's voice in my head right now,' Lucasta replied distractedly. 'Just you wait and see. At least, I could absolutely swear that's what she's saying. Oh, wait... there's another voice...' At that, she gasped. 'It's Helen.' Listening intently, she could be overheard saying, 'Very, very interesting.'

Then something strange happened to Luke. He spoke to Helen, in his head, as he did about a hundred times a day, just checking in that all was well with her.

Hi, pet, is everything good with you? he said to no one.

There was silence for a moment, then suddenly it came to him in a blinding flash, clear as crystal. Helen's voice, Helen's words. He could hear her for the very first time, he could hear absolutely everything.

Hi, love, can you hear me?

Like a lunatic, Luke nodded vigorously.

Oh, Luke, wait until you get here, you're going to love it! It's so beautiful and peaceful and gorgeous. It's heaven, that's what it is.

Silently, Luke said, Helen? Are you still there?

Yes, love. And I've a bit of news for you.

Yes?

About Amy, she's doing great! I should know, I watch over her every day. She can't hear me yet, but she will when she's older. And something else...

Luke was riveted.

You asked me for other signs and I heard you.

You did?

Yes! Look to your left.

Luke turned to his left, but there was no one there, only Stella.

What? he said. What am I seeing?

Look and see.

Stella was there, close to where he sat, but no one else.

Helen? What do you mean?

You have to figure it out for yourself.

Then he thought of all the signs he'd asked for and realised there was one thing they all pointed to, clear as crystal. Stella. That night in the garden, he'd talked to Helen about Amy, but it was Stella who'd messaged him about the seance. And the night he'd talked to her in the car, he was on his way to Stella's. Every day, he'd ask for messages, and every day, she'd sent a little sign about Stella. It was still early days yet, but maybe he had a shot.

Helen?

Silence. She'd gone. Correction, she'd gone for now, but she'd be back.

He looked over at Stella and went bright red. Jeez, what was with him?

'Hey, Stella? Do you fancy going to that pub down the road for a drink with me tonight?'

'Sure,' she whispered. At that, Will began to make 'quiet and calm down' noises.

'Except that... it might be nice?' he offered pathetically.

'It might be *nice*?' said Stella. 'We go there every week, we go with the gang after this evening. What is with you?' But she was smiling as she said it.

At that, Will called a jam-packed, standing-room-only coffee house to order, as he had done so many times in the past, and like so many other times, they began to talk.

EPILOGUE

ALMOST TWO YEARS LATER…

'It's been decided,' Luke's niece Poppy said to him, with all the bossiness and authority of thirteen years of age.

'By *us*,' said her sister, Holly, backing her up. 'And Amy agrees with us too, so you've no choice, Uncle Luke, you *have* to do as we say. Doesn't he, Amy?'

'Oh yes, Dad, because this is the best idea ever!' Amy said, happy and excited because her two cousins were staying with her and Luke for a few weeks. Clare and her husband were having a new extension built, the work was filthy and seemed to have taken over the entire house, so Luke had suggested they all move in with him for the duration. Which, of course, had led to nothing but high jinks and messing and fun and hysterical giggling from the three girls, around the clock.

'What's been decided, then, ladies?' Luke smiled, pulling on the jacket of his good suit in the hall as he got ready to go out for the evening.

'Girls! Leave Uncle Luke alone and come on in for dinner,' Clare called out from the kitchen, but they were having none of it.

'We think,' Poppy announced to more gusts of giggles from the other two, 'that it's about time you get a girlfriend.'

'Is that right, now?' said Luke, pausing for a minute to really give the three of them his full attention. 'And do you think this is a good idea too, Amy?'

'Oh, Dad, it's the best idea ever!' Amy said, in such a happy place right now, it did Luke's heart good to see. 'I'd love it! Could you imagine? She could take me shopping for clothes and—'

'And you could get your nails and hair done together,' Holly chipped in. Holly was obsessed with beauty salons and, at the age of almost eleven, had already announced to her parents that she wanted to open her very own salon when she was grown up, but that they weren't to worry, she'd be sure to give them family discounts. Luke smiled, but didn't say anything.

'And do you want to know what would be the best thing of all about you getting a girlfriend?' Amy said, more seriously now, as Luke bent down to really listen to her.

'What's that, sweetheart?'

'The best thing is that you'd be happy all the time. Like you're happy now. You wouldn't be on your own any more. Because she'd be there for you, you see.'

'And we have the perfect person in mind too,' said Poppy bossily.

'Girls?' said Clare, bustling out of the kitchen with an apron tied around her waist and joining in with this impromptu gathering in the hall. 'Now that's enough. Uncle Luke is getting ready to go out, so just let him get on with it, will you?'

'The ladies are just telling me that I need to get a girlfriend,' Luke said to Clare, with an enigmatic smile. Clare grinned back at him.

'I see,' was all she said.

'And you really think it's a good idea?' he said to the three of them.

'It's the best!' said Amy, who had just turned eight years old. 'The super best!' 'Super' was her new favourite word. 'Isn't it, girls?'

'Absolutely,' said Holly.

'I wish you could take us with you,' said Poppy enviously, changing the subject. 'I'd love to be going to a FilmCorps screening. It would be so cool!'

Luke had been invited to a cast and crew screening of the very first episode of the new *Mercy* series, featuring none other than his friend Connie in a supporting role. It was to be held in a gorgeous cinema, the Stella, an old-fashioned cinema that had been completely refurbished and was now fitted out with luxurious armchair seats with footrests, cushions and a fully serviced bar and restaurant so you could have a drink and even a hamburger served right to your seat. Lucasta and Phoebe had made sure to invite all the gang from the Leeson Street cafe and, of course, Luke was delighted to have been included. As had Stella. Who was in a taxi on her way to the house to collect him now.

'You're going to see all the stars, Uncle Luke, so you better get millions of selfies to show us later, OK?'

'I'll try my best.' Luke laughed, still intrigued by what the girls – and Amy in particular – had said to him. Just then, a taxi pulled up into the front driveway.

'She's here!' Amy squealed, already halfway out of the front door with her cousins hot on her heels. 'Stella's here!'

'Here's the person we were talking about actually,' Poppy said to her Uncle Luke as she ran for the door.

'Stella!' Holly was calling out to her. 'You have to come in and let us do your hair and make-up! We've got really good at it – everyone says!'

'Oh, Stella, you already look fabulous!' said Poppy, nodding her approval, as Stella clambered out of her taxi, dressed in a hot-pink dress with a matching cardigan, a crossover bag and a comfy-looking, strappy pair of summery sandals.

'Thanks, girls, I made an effort just for you! And here's Amy...'

Amy hugged her tight. Stella was a regular visitor these days, especially since Luke and a team of builders had started renovating her house, and she was a great favourite with the girls.

Clare walked with Luke to the front door, waving fondly at Stella. 'Well, well, well,' she said to him. 'They seem OK with the whole idea – Amy particularly. My two have been saying for a while now how well suited you are. How good you both could be for each other.'

Luke grinned, but didn't say anything. Then he was interrupted by Helen, as he was about a hundred times a day.

Hello, love! How are you doing today? Pretty good day working for those people who know the Dicksons?

Helen, hi! Yes, I know, it was a great day.

I was so happy for you! Every step you took along the way, I was bursting with pride. Listen, love, there's something I want to say to you...

What's that? What are you saying?

Stella... I really think you should do as Amy and the girls are telling you to do today. You're lovely together, so why not go for it?

You think?

Just remember, I love you...

Helen? Are you there?

There was a little pause. Then a phrase that was hard to forget.

I'll always love you...

Helen? But she was gone, till tomorrow. Much to think about... but, what the hell? He thought about it and decided there and then.

Clare interrupted, saying, 'You went all quiet for a bit. Helen again?'

'Helen again.' He smiled. 'You know what? Stella's great,' he said admiringly, looking across at her hugging the bejaysus out of the kids: a happy scene unfolding. 'I'm so lucky to have someone like her. She's been there for me, through thick and thin. And if Amy is up for it, then you know what? I think that I am too.'

'And you've been good for her too,' said Clare thoughtfully as Luke scooped up his wallet and double-checked he had his phone, 'so do you think maybe you could do what Amy's saying?'

He was already out of the door as she said it, but at that, he stopped, thought for a moment or two, then turned back.

'I'm not saying yes and I'm not saying no,' he called back to his sister. 'But all I will say is this. When you asked me that – I smiled.'

ACKNOWLEDGMENTS

Thank you, Marianne Gunn O'Connor, always and for everything.

Thank to Pat Lynch. I love our catch-up lunches so much!

Thank you to my new editor, Sarah Ritherdon, for everything. I'm so looking forward to meeting you and working with you.

Thank you to Amanda Ridout, till we meet again!

Thank you to all at Boldwood Books, especially Jenna Houston, Gary Jukes, Claire Fenby, Wendy Neale, Isabelle Flynn, Grace Cooper, Megan Townsend and Ben Wilson. You're the 'A Team' and I can't wait to meet you all.

On a personal level, thank you to my family, Mum, Richard and Maria and Patrick and Sam. Thanks hugely to Clelia Murphy, Pat Kinevane, Frank Mackey, Marion O'Dwyer, Fionnuala Murphy, Karen Nolan, Caroline Finnegan, Isabelle Finnegan, Mary Grennan, Susan McHugh, Sean Murphy, Luke and Oscar Murphy, Pat Moylan, Brian and Miriam Rogers, Sharon Hogan, Lee Kerrigan and finally Fiona Lalor. As my friends, you've all surpassed yourselves in the last year.

Better times ahead, for sure!

ABOUT THE AUTHOR

Claudia Carroll is a Dublin-based bestselling author, actor and broadcaster. She has previously published contemporary romances but has now turned her hand to multi-generational women's fiction.

Sign up to Claudia Carroll's mailing list for news, competitions and updates on future books.

Follow Claudia on social media here:

x.com/carrollclaudia
instagram.com/carrollclaudia

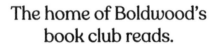

Printed in Great Britain
by Amazon

58329735R00185